A Handful of Pebbles

by

J. Dalrymple

A Handful of Pebbles
Copyright © John Sadler 2007

First published in Australia by Mono Unlimited, Victoria
Email: info@monounlimited.com
Website: www.monounlimited.com
Order securely online at www.monounlimited.com/shoppingcart

Cover design concept by J. Dalrymple
Text and cover layout and design by Monique Lisbon,
Mono Unlimited: Computer & Printing Support

The right of John Dalrymple Sadler to be identified as the author of this work has been asserted by him in accordance with the Copyright Act 1968 (Australia). No part of this publication may be reproduced, stored in a retrieval system, or transmitted, in any form or by any means, electronic, mechanic, photocopying, recording or otherwise, without the prior written permission of the publisher.

National Library of Australia Cataloguing-in-Publication Data:
   Dalrymple, J., 1946– .
   A handful of pebbles.

   ISBN 978-0-9775518-2-8 (pbk.).

   I. Title.

   A823.4

Acknowledgments:
To John Wood for his help with the cover; to family and friends for the encouragement to keep writing; and to Lily Jade Powell for her "Handful of Pebbles".

*Dedicated to my granddaughter
Lily Jade Powell*

Also by J. Dalrymple:

What Time Is Noon?

Order both books by J. Dalrymple
securely online at www.underthesun.net.au

A Handful of Pebbles

by

J. Dalrymple

Prologue

Broken water hissed as it swirled down the port side of *Lapwing*, her bow cutting through the oily swell at twelve knots. On the bridge of the corvette I peered into the fog hanging low over the North Sea on that May morning in 1944, but saw nothing.

The night patrol had been uneventful, except for the brief sound of distant gunfire to the north and soon we would alter course to the west, towards the coast of East Anglia. Above, when the mist thinned, there was an occasional glimpse of clear blue sky and the promise of a fine day.

The black speck above the mast, when I first saw it through my binoculars, could have been a piece of dirt on the lens until I saw three such specks before the visibility closed in again.

'Hard-A-Starboard!' I screamed at the helmsman, as I pushed the red alarm button and gave a double full-ahead ring on the telegraph for maximum revolutions on the main engine. Even as the first peal of the alarm bells faded, the shriek of the dive-bombers reached my ears as they hurtled down above the fog.

So slowly, it seemed, *Lapwing* responded to the helm and began her turn, rolling twenty degrees to port in the process. Commander Elliot arrived on the bridge, his white roll-neck jumper immediately covered in beads of moisture from the fog.

'To your position, number-one!'

As I acknowledged his order, the first bomb exploded in the water close to the port bow, and a second only thirty yards further away. I was half-way down the companionway leading to the main deck when the third bomb hit the superstructure just below the bridge, the blast throwing me to the bottom of the stairs, where I hit my head on the deck before blacking out momentarily.

The flames were close. I could feel the heat and there was the sickly smell of burnt flesh. Lying on the deck ten feet away was seaman Turnbull. I knew it was him by the eagle tattooed on his forearm. I tried to get up to warn him about the fire that I could feel starting to engulf me, but all I did was cry-out in pain as I put weight on my right leg. In the instant before I passed out again I knew Turnbull hadn't heard me. Above the neck there was no head; only his torso lay there.

The cold water from the hose as they extinguished my burning clothes made me think I was drowning and I tried to thrash my arms and legs around in panic before clutching my right leg. The pain was almost as bad when several hands picked me up off the cold, wet deck and carried me, I knew not where.

I must've been drugged, for when I came to the first sounds I heard were the ring of the telegraph, voices and running feet all jumbled up together. As my head cleared, the lack of movement by *Lapwing,* together with little noise from her engine, told me we were in sheltered waters. The honk of a truck horn suggested we were approaching our berth.

On the stretcher I winced when my leg was jarred as they carried me across the brow onto the wharf, and as we turned towards the waiting ambulance I could see the charred remains of the superstructure below the bridge. The blackened, twisted metal with gaping holes and jagged plates gave *Lapwing* the look of some mortally wounded animal as she lay against the wharf with a ten degree list to port. I realised we were lucky to make it home, as I was to be alive. I didn't know it at the time, but three other men, apart from Turnbull, who were part of the gun crew, had also perished in the explosion.

I spent the next eight weeks, all through the D-Day landings, in the hospital at Lowestoft where surgeons did what they could for my mangled leg and the third degree burns on the back of my neck. The skin grafts took well and the multiple fractures healed remarkably quickly, but the metal that had lodged in my thigh had severed several nerves, meaning it was touch and go for a while as to whether I would lose the leg or not.

My parents came up from London the second weekend I was there and then later on mum came up and stayed for a few days while dad stayed behind to look after the business. Before the war he'd made furniture at his mill near Twickenham.

'He's got a huge contract making wooden frames for the Royal Air Force. Of course we don't know what it's for; yer dad just gets the specifications of what he 'as to make.'

'Sounds like he's pretty busy?'

'Hardly see him. Works late every night *and* weekends.'

I patted her hand. 'Never mind mum, it'll all be over soon, the way we're marching through France.'

'Then, maybe, he can get back to making furniture and a normal life.' She looked up at me. 'One day the mill and everything else will be yours to carry on the tradition of making fine furniture.'

I sighed. 'Mum, I've told you many times, I don't want to make furniture. I'd be bloody hopeless at it! Ships and the Navy, they're my life, you know that, and as soon as this leg is right I'll be back at sea.'

'We'll see, Christopher, we'll see.'

She wasn't convinced.

Neither was I, but for different reasons.

By mid-August I was given a pair of crutches and sent to a convalescent home outside Colchester that was full of Navy personnel, who like me, were anxious to get back to sea. Commander Elliot came in to see me at the beginning of September.

'Nearly fit are you Bowden?'

'Coming along sir.'

'Good. I need an experienced number-one for the new frigate they're giving me. The *Cobra*. Much bigger than *Lapwing* and twice as fast with four times the fire-power. She's being fitted-out in Barrow.'

'I'll be there as soon as I can sir,' I said, convinced my leg felt almost ready for a hundred-yard dash.

'Good man. See you soon.'

As he left, he spoke to one of the nurses, nodding slowly at her reply and, although I didn't know it at the time, the conversation was about me. For the next few weeks I put an extra effort into my walking exercises, to try and speed up my discharge from Colchester with the thought of serving under Commander Elliot on *Cobra*.

One Sunday, early in October, the weather was fine, but the first chill of winter was in the air as I waited for my parents, who were coming down to see me after lunch. I was sitting at a small table on the lawn reading through the Admiralty Manual of instructions to refresh my memory so I would be ready to join *Cobra*. I'd already done the afternoon quarter-mile walk, which today I'd expected to do in the company of my parents, but now it was almost 3 p.m. and they still hadn't arrived. It surprised me, even though we were still at war and I knew travel arrangements could be upset at a moment's notice.

I saw, but took no notice, as the padre walked across the grass, engrossed as I was in my reading and I was surprised when he sat down beside me.

'Good afternoon, Bowden. How's the leg coming on?'

'Doing fine, thank you padre. Hopefully it won't be too long before I can go back to active service.'

'I hope so too, Christopher; however today is not a day for good news.'

'I beg your pardon?'

'You were expecting visitors today?'

'Yes, my parents, but why do you ask?'

He looked at me, but said nothing.

Instinctively I looked at my watch, and then suddenly I knew.

I stared back at him but was unable to speak. I was thinking of my sister. Working as a nurse she'd been killed in the blitz four years ago. It seemed unfair our family should suffer twice.

He realised I knew why he had come to see me and nodded. 'They were asleep. They felt no pain; you can take comfort in that.'

Silently, tears rolled down my cheeks. Getting fit to join *Cobra* seemed insignificant compared to the loss of the two people who had loved and guided me through childhood and helped me achieve my position in the Royal Navy. It was several minutes before I composed myself to ask the question. 'How…?'

'The new rocket bomb, the V2. Not a direct hit, just enough of a blast for the roof to collapse. They were in bed asleep when the chimney fell on top of them.'

I stared at the trees, seeing only the faces of my parents and my sister, Susan, remembering our early years: the love and laughter of a family. Now I was the only one left.

'If there's anything I can do?'

I shook my head. He realised I needed time on my own and left me, returning across the grass to the hall after promising to see me again soon.

At the end of November I was discharged from Colchester and sent home on leave for two weeks before taking up a post in the Naval Operations Centre in London. *Cobra* had already sailed to the Far East. Our home had been given temporary repairs, enough to keep out the weather, and was still the comfortable house I'd grown up in, apart from mum and dad's bedroom.

The furniture business had continued under the management of the foreman, Jack Farnshaw who seemed to be handling the job easily when I went to see him.

'Well, it's yours now, Chris.'

He was twenty years my senior and had watched me grow up.

'Do you have any plans for the mill after the war?'

'I haven't thought about it, Jack. I've been trying to get fit to go back to sea. You know I don't know much about the business, you may have to teach me.'

He looked a little doubtful as he replied. 'That shouldn't be a problem, Chris. We'll turn you into a craftsman like your father in no time; I'm sure you've inherited his skills.'

The war came to an end and I continued to work in the operations centre as the Royal Navy assessed its position for Britain in peacetime. It was a busy period co-ordinating the requirements for bases both at home and abroad. By 1948, I realised my leg would never make a full recovery and although I could get around pretty well I wasn't exactly a candidate for the Olympics being held in London that year. During my spare time away from the Admiralty I tried to take an interest in the family business and learn the art of fine furniture construction. However, by early 1951, I knew it was a craft I would never master. Then in August that year I was summoned by my commanding officer to receive the news that would provide the catalyst to my future.

'Commander Bowden, please sit down.'

I had been promoted, even though I'd only sat behind a desk since the accident.

'Thank you for coming in at such short notice.'

The man with a white beard and wearing the gold braid of a Rear Admiral seemed slightly ill-at-ease.

'Now we are no longer at war the Navy has had to re-assess the number of personnel it requires for its peace-time operations. Unfortunately, your injury prevents you from returning to full duties and, I'm sorry Commander, but we are forced to retire you on a full invalid pension.'

There it was. I could no longer pursue the one ambition I'd dreamed of for years; being captain of my own ship. It should have spurred me on to learn the furniture business, but instead I decided it was time for a complete change. Migration was being advertised in all the papers and I started to think about Australia, New Zealand and Canada, even South Africa.

I rang Jack Farnshaw and asked to see him. He was surprised, but delighted by my proposal and said he'd get back to me as soon as he'd spoken to a few people. By the end of October *"Bowden's Fine Furniture est. 1824"* became *"Farnshaw's Furniture for the Fifties."* I now had the funds to establish my future; whatever, and wherever, that might be.

Chapter One

The ring of the phone blended with the pouring rain rattling the windows on that bleak, Sunday afternoon in March 1952.

'Hello, Christopher Bowden speaking.'

The line was faint, but I recognised the voice immediately. 'Malcolm! Great to hear from you. Easter? No, I've nothing planned. I'd love to come down. I haven't seen you for almost two years.'

The weather had improved and spring was in the air when I arrived at his house near Shoreham-by-Sea on the Sussex coast a few weeks later.

'So what are you doing with yourself, now you're out of the Navy?' asked the lean man with curly, black hair.

'Not a lot. I'm not sure what I want to do, except the thought of an office job scares the hell out of me. I wouldn't last five minutes.'

'But with the leg …'

'It's not that bad.' I patted my right thigh. 'Doesn't hurt most of the time, and it's only a slight limp.'

'Still, it'd be almost impossible to go back to sea.'

We had been best friends since junior school, but I hated to admit he might be right and my mind refused to agree with him. 'If I can get up and down the stairs at home, I can get onto the bridge of a ship!'

'*I* know you could,' he said, being kind, 'but would a shipping company be prepared to take you on?'

'I don't know, Malcolm.' I had a horrible vision of being cast aside as a broken-down seafarer, fit only to sit in a deck-chair on the beach with a blanket over my knees.

'If you do go back to sea, what would you do with your house in London?'

'That's something else I must consider. It's where I grew up, but I hate living there. I find it claustrophobic after the Navy.'

'I'm sure something'll turn up. Meanwhile it's lunchtime and I think you'll enjoy where we're going, it overlooks the water!'

As we drove past the harbour I saw her for the first time. It wasn't the appearance that attracted my attention; it was the large "For Sale" sign that hung on the side of her bridge.

The pub was magnificent, but as we sat in the sunshine watching the white-caps in the English Channel, the desire to return to sea intensified and my thoughts strayed back to the little coaster.

'Can we drive round the other side of the harbour on the way home?'

'What do you want to see?'

'I'm just curious about a ship.'

We pulled up alongside the small vessel. She was dirty with grime that had accumulated while she'd been lying idle, and although the paintwork was peeling on the accommodation and rust streaks were starting to appear on the green hull, she gave a first impression of a well-found vessel. I estimated she was about 70 feet long. Her vertical stem-post suggested she may have been a little older than I'd first imagined, a thought confirmed by the shape of the small anchor protruding from the narrow hawse pipe.

The focs'le was tiny, most of its space occupied by the windlass, which had large drums seemingly out of proportion to the anchor cable. Blocks shackled to the deck revealed they were used to heave on the guy ropes to swing the derrick attached to the tall wooden mast stepped in the forward end of the well deck.

'Is there anything special about this boat?' Malcolm asked, obviously bored, 'it looks like a dirty old coaster to me.'

The sun had gone behind grey clouds, the breeze was cool and he pulled the collar of his coat up around his neck. 'I can see beyond the dirt, but if you're cold why don't you wait in the car? I'd like to have a few more minutes here. By the way, it's a ship.'

'No, I'm fine,' he said. 'I just can't see the fascination in an old *ship*, but then, I haven't been to sea.'

He followed me along the wharf as I studied the single hatch. The long derrick that ran the full length of the well-deck had its head resting in a crutch just in front of the accommodation with its peeling, buff paint. Behind the bridge was the small green funnel with a black top and right aft a hand-operated stores crane sat above the mooring lines. Below the bridge and the funnel were a couple of portholes, but it was impossible to tell if they belonged to accommodation or storerooms.

I walked beyond the ropes holding her alongside and looked at the stern. On the green hull in black paint that matched the gunwales, the name *Caillou* was written above her port of registry – Zeebrugge, in Belgium. As the first drops of rain hit my face, the little ship was bathed in sunlight through a break in the dark clouds. Her paint almost shone in the surreal light as she lay there like an orphan waiting to be adopted.

Driving back to Malcolm's house I kept that image in my mind, and by the time we walked inside I think I had made my decision.

He put a cup of tea in front of me. 'What's that silly grin on your face?'

'I think I have the answer to your question.'

'What question?'

'The one you asked me before lunch.'

He looked at me strangely.

'About what I'm going to do with my life. May I use the phone?'

'Of course you can.'

I took a scrap of paper from my pocket and went to dial the number I'd scribbled down. A man called Brian answered. When I enquired about the *Caillou* he told me he was just a friend of the owner and gave me a number to ring in Belgium.

'Did you get through?'

'I need to ring Belgium.'

'Belgium? It's that ship isn't it?'

I nodded. 'I think I'll buy it.'

'Are you serious?'

'I'll pay for the call.'

He waved his hand. 'Go ahead and ring. The least I can contribute to your future is a phone call.'

It took the operator several minutes before a long tone indicated a telephone was ringing on the continent. The female voice that answered didn't understand me and put the phone down. For a moment I thought I'd been cut off.

The man who picked up the receiver and introduced himself as Jacques Kessel spoke excellent English, compared with my non-existent Flemish, or schoolboy French.

'I am interested in buying your coaster,' I said.

'Would you mind telling me if you are a man of the sea?'

'I was a navigator in the Royal Navy.'

'That is good. You can see she is a fine ship.'

For a moment I thought he was trying to push the price up.

'May I ask why you want to buy my little ship?'

It was a question I should've considered. 'I suppose…' I began, before being honest with myself. 'No, that's not right. I *know* it's for a selfish reason. I want to command my own ship, but after an injury to my leg in 1944 the Royal Navy doesn't want me any longer.'

'It seems we share a passion for the sea.'

'A passion I want to sustain.' It seemed easy to be open with Jacques Kessel – maybe because he was a seafarer. 'I need a new direction in life; especially after losing my family during the war.'

'But the *Caillou* isn't a warship – she's a merchant vessel.'

True to my nature I'd gone headlong into the idea of buying a ship in a couple of hours without considering what I would do with it. 'I suppose I'd look for a trading route somewhere.'

'It's not that easy. I'd think about it carefully if I were you.'

As he continued I realised this was good advice.

'I have to tell you I love that ship. For the last few years she has been my life, but recent events mean I must part with her. Although I shall be sad at losing the *Caillou*, it would please me if someone who has an empathy with ships took her; someone who would look after her.'

'I understand, and if I buy the *Caillou* I shall treat her like a daughter.'

'Thank you. You've made an old man very…' there was a choking sound, '…very happy.'

'I haven't said I'll buy her yet,' I reminded him. 'It depends on the price.'

'Please Mr…'

'Bowden, Christopher Bowden.'

'Mr Bowden, when did you first see the *Caillou*?'

'This afternoon.'

'Then let's not talk of money yet. Go and have a good look at her and call me in a few days when you've had time to think it over. I'll get Brian to bring the keys around for you.'

When I returned to the lounge-room Malcolm had poured two glasses of red wine. I glanced at the clock. It was just after four. 'Bit early for this isn't it?'

'To celebrate, or drown your sorrows.' He picked up a glass. 'Which is it?'

I picked up the other glass. 'I'm not sure yet. Here's to a maybe.'

I told Malcolm about the call and then rang Jacques' contact again, who said he'd be round about mid-morning. Easter Sunday dawned with the roads wet from overnight rain, but by ten o'clock the sun was out, matching my mood as I waited impatiently for Brian to arrive.

Malcolm moved out of the way as I returned from the window once more. 'For heavens sake, sit down and finish *that* cup of tea before *it* goes cold!'

The tea was hot. Malcolm must've made a fresh pot, and when the doorbell rang I almost choked as I tried to swallow too quickly. Brian entered and I was still coughing as he and Malcolm stood by the front door staring at me. 'I'll be alright in a minute.'

'I hope so. I don't want it to have been a waste of time bringing these around,' Brian said, holding up a bunch of keys. 'When you're ready.'

Malcolm laughed. 'He's been ready for hours,'

Brian had a brand-new Triumph Renown. Its body was angular; in contrast with the rounded look of most cars. I'd opened one of the rear doors before I remembered. 'Just a minute, I forgot my camera.'

Malcolm shook his head at Brian. 'This ship is definitely getting to him.'

At the wharf I took some photographs before Brian unlocked the bridge, which although small, with only basic equipment, had a homely feel emanating from its varnished woodwork. The brass-work was dull, but not tarnished. On the bulkhead behind the large wooden wheel was a print of an old P&O liner in a discoloured frame with a cracked glass. Everything else, the charts and other navigational equipment, was in good order, neatly stowed away, and immediately I felt an affinity with the seafarer I'd spoken to in Zeebrugge.

'Is it what you expected?' Brian asked.

I'd almost forgotten the other two were there. 'Yes,' I said. 'From what I've seen, it's all of that and more.' Immediately I could have bitten my tongue for saying such a thing to a friend of the owner when I didn't know how much Jacques Kessel wanted for the ship, and I tried to qualify my statement. 'Mind you I've only seen the bridge so far. Who knows what I'll find when I have a look in the engine-room, or down the hold.'

Malcolm turned to Brian. 'I have the feeling this inspection could take some time. I don't know about you, but ships really aren't my scene?'

'Nor mine. I'm only looking after this one because Jacques and my grandfather have been best friends since the First World War.'

'Why don't we go and have a cup of coffee, I know a small café just out of town.' Brian nodded and they both looked at me.

'Go on, I'll be fine. No need to hurry back,' I said, knowing I could happily spend all day aboard. Laughter echoed from the wharf as the pair returned to the car discussing last week's Goon Show on the radio.

In the silence I drank in the atmosphere of the little vessel. Taking notes, I started my inspection, trying to remain rational about the whole idea of running a shipping line with one, somewhat-ageing, coaster.

Behind the bridge was a small cabin for the Captain with a bunk, a small desk and a green armchair beside a door that opened onto the deck in front of the funnel. Stairs led down to the main deck where, facing the hatch, there were three more cabins. The one on the starboard side had the tiny galley behind it. Amidships was a second cabin like the first, both small and basic with only a bunk, a chair, and a very small table. The cabin on the port side was the same, except instead of the galley it had a door to the engine-room at the end of the alleyway.

I opened it and gazed down at the small diesel engine. It seemed like a toy after what I'd sailed with in the Royal Navy. As I took a second look at it, I began to wonder if it would have enough power to keep the ship out of trouble in any sort of a rough sea. I wasn't an engineer.

I descended the steel steps to the bottom of the engine-room. The whole area was so basic that, even with my limited engineering knowledge, I could recognise a small generator and some pumps. I didn't examine the engine-room any further; I would leave that to Scotty. However, the spotless appearance of the area led me to expect that even the dour man from Fife might have a good word to say about this little ship I already felt I must buy.

Back on deck, I peeled back the tarpaulin covering the hold and removed a hatch-board to give me some light when I went below. The access was from a ladder in the darkness of the focs'le and as I went down the rungs some light rust crumbed under my feet. However, when I reached the tank-top at the bottom of the hold, the rust seemed thick. Not that I could see it, but it crunched under my feet as I walked aft towards the daylight entering the hold from the open tarpaulin, the sound making me wonder if there was any deck plating left between the hold and the fuel tank below it.

Suddenly I knew I had to take a deep breath and really think about what I was planning to do. Daydreams would not be supported in this competitive world after the war if you didn't have efficient and well-run equipment.

It seemed only minutes before the other two returned. 'That was a quick cup of coffee.'

They looked at each other and laughed. 'We had lunch as well,' Malcolm said.

I looked at my watch. It was one-thirty.

'We brought you a sandwich in case you were hungry.'

'Jacques will be away until Thursday or Friday,' Brian remarked, as I took a few more photos before we left. 'So don't rush into any decision.'

Back at his house Malcolm made a cup of tea. 'What will you do now?'

'I can't do anything for the next few days, as Brian said, Jacques is away.'

'Will you buy that ship?'

'I want to. I've never wanted to do anything so much in all my life.'

'But what would you do with it?'

'I'm not sure; it's something I have to think about.'

Behind him I noticed a picture of the *Queen Mary* leaving Southampton, the Isle of Wight behind her as she sailed down Spithead. I smiled. 'That's what I'll do,' I said pointing to the picture.

'What?' he asked, looking at the wall behind him.

'The Isle of Wight. I'll go down there for a few days, to where my parents used to rent a cottage at Colwell Bay during the summer holidays. It'll give me a chance to think it over.'

Those few days to "think it over" became almost two weeks on the Isle of Wight and along the coast to Cornwall as I discovered a possible trading route for the *Caillou*. People on the island, it seemed, needed more than a car ferry for commerce in these prosperous days after the war.

I was still uncertain about the venture until I went to see the Harbour-Master in Yarmouth. From the notes I'd made in Shoreham I gave him the details of the coaster – her length and draft – and asked about the availability of a berth.

Jim Middleton smiled as his left hand tugged at the grey beard covering most of his face. 'I wondered when someone would come along with such a proposal. Lord knows, we need something more than the ferry.'

'That's what some men in the pub said; that they needed building materials and transport for livestock and dairy products. Do *you* think it would work?'

'I didn't say that. I said we needed more than the ferry. Whether there's enough cargo to keep a vessel, even a small one, employed full-time… well, I have my doubts. But don't give up yet,' he said, seeing the expression on my face. 'However, I'd do my homework before making any big commitment if I were you.'

It was then I knew I had made up my mind to buy the little ship, even if I had to take it abroad to run. 'What about the berth?' I asked.

He looked at the figures. 'There's no problem at all. At least that part is fine; she's a perfect-sized vessel for here. What's she called?'

'The *Caillou*. She's Belgian, registered in Zeebrugge,' I said, 'but I'd change that.'

'You'd change the port of registration?'

'Yes, to here at Yarmouth, if that's possible?'

'I can help you with that if you decide to go ahead. What would you call her?'

I'd deliberately not thought about a name before making my decision about buying the vessel. Now, somehow, it seemed important and urgent. My mother's name had been Lily, but I felt there should be more. In my mind I saw the green hull in the sunlight that first afternoon in Shoreham.

'The *Lily Jade*,' I said, instinctively.

He nodded. 'I like it: it's different.'

I left his office floating on air. The *Lily Jade*. I was going to buy a ship and the name seemed so right. The *Lily Jade*. She'd need a fresh coat of green paint on the hull and some varnish on the wheelhouse.

I stopped chuckling. The *Lily Jade* was going to need far more maintenance than just a coat of paint if she was to be an operational vessel making a profit. I went back to my little bedroom in the stone cottage I'd rented at Colwell Bay and started to write a list of all the items to check when I returned to Shoreham. All the cargo gear: shackles, wires and ropes. The anchor and cable, navigation equipment – the list was endless and I hadn't even considered the engine-room.

I'd leave that to Scotty.

As I assessed the information from the past two weeks I realised it was now May, and I had promised to ring Jacques Kessel in Belgium a few days after leaving Shoreham. The terrible thought the *Lily Jade* might have been sold sent me into a panic.

It was Saturday morning, 9th May, when I went to the newsagent by the roundabout in Totland and changed pound notes into one-shilling pieces, emptying the till of half the change from their week's takings to use in the phone box across the road.

I needn't have worried.

'Yes, I've had two offers,' Jacques told me.

He sounded older, and tired.

'But somehow, I knew you'd ring.'

'I took your advice. I thought about it and went to investigate the possibilities of running a profitable business – it just took longer than I imagined.'

'What conclusion did you come to?'

'I want to buy the *Caillou;* if she's still for sale?'

He didn't reply; instead, the gentle sobbing of a grown man reached my ears. 'Are you all right?'

'I'm very happy,' he said, blowing his nose. 'But I am also sad. I'm pleased it is you who is buying the *Caillou,* yet sad to be losing her.'

'I understand.'

'Is it possible for you to come to Zeebrugge to sign the papers? I would like to put a face to her new owner.'

'I think we would both benefit from that meeting,' I answered.

'Will you change her name?'

'Yes,' I said, feeling guilty as I spoke to this older man that I felt I already knew so well. 'I shall call her the *Lily Jade*. Lily after my mother, and jade from the colour of her hull.'

'*Lily Jade,*' he repeated.

There was a moments silence before he said something I didn't understand.

'It sounds good even in Flemish.'

****

'I've made up my mind,' I said to Malcolm as soon as I returned to Shoreham on Monday morning. 'I'm going to buy the ship.'

He stood with his hands on his hips. 'Was there ever any doubt?'

The edge of my excitement was blunted. I had expected a more enthusiastic response to my announcement.

He grinned, and then laughed as he took my hand, his left fist punching my shoulder. 'Congratulations! That's fantastic news, but you should have seen the look on your face just now.'

'You rotten bugger!'

'Now, now. Is that the way to speak to a friend about to take you out for a celebratory drink?'

I smiled.

'Right, come on then. You can tell me all the news on the way to the pub.'

'It's a bit early.'

'It won't be by the time we get there. I can't imagine you going anywhere before visiting the *Caillou*. You only came here first because my house is between the station and the ship.'

I nodded. 'You're right of course; and a true friend. Thank you, Malcolm.'

In silence we drove down to the wharf and pulled up alongside the green hull. A plastic bag had caught on the back-spring, flapping noisily in the stiff breeze. I removed it, the sound of the wind in the rigging more pleasant to my ears.

'So when do you buy the *Caillou*?' he asked, interrupting my thoughts.

'The *Lily Jade*,' I said, turning to face him. 'I'm changing her name. Lily after my mother, and Jade from the colour of her hull.'

'The *Lily Jade*,' he said thoughtfully. 'I like it.'

It was another half-hour before we sat down in the pub. 'I'm catching the ferry from Dover on Thursday,' I told him. 'I'm going to Zeebrugge to see Jacques Kessel and sign the papers.'

Over lunch we discussed my research into available cargo on the island and in the West Country and, by the end of the meal, encouraged by an extra bottle of red wine, Christopher Bowden and the *Lily Jade* were a shipping company to rival Cunard.

Chapter Two

A light rain was falling as the train from Ostend followed the coast towards Blakenberge near Zeebrugge, and I wondered if Jacques Kessel would really welcome the man who was about to take away the small ship he treasured.

The old house, with its pale-blue stucco, backed onto the beach. Warm sunshine had dispersed the earlier cloud and the front garden was a blaze of colour with red roses mingled between clumps of yellow and white flowers I'd never seen before. The mixture of bright colours reflected my feelings as I knocked on the front door, which had a leadlight porthole.

'Captain Bowden.'

'Jacques? How did you know who I am?'

'You are English. Need I say more?'

He smiled and offered his hand. 'I'm sorry,' he said, 'that was not polite. I have mixed thoughts about this meeting. Please come in; I really want us to be friends.'

He led me to a backroom with a large picture-window overlooking the sea. It seemed so right for an old seafarer. He was much as I expected, with a full head of white hair, but his skin surprised me. It was tanned, as most seamen are, but although he was obviously in the latter years of his life, it was smooth. The sea usually gave its followers a wrinkled, leathery appearance, but Jacques Kessel could easily have been a man twenty years younger had it not been for the stoop of his shoulders and the need of a walking stick.

'Please sit down, Christopher. May I call you that?'

'Indeed you may Jacques. Thank goodness you speak such good English. I don't know your language – can't say anything except "Bonjour, comment allez-vous?"'

He laughed. 'I am fine, thank you for asking. By the way that was French, but never mind.'

He placed two cognacs on the table between us before sitting and taking a deep breath. 'I would like you to know why I am selling the *Caillou*.' His eyes seemed distant and the hard set of his mouth gave his face a troubled look. I began to wonder if I wanted to hear his story.

'Like you, I was a seafarer,' he began. 'Not naval vessels, cargo ships. Then the war came and many of the big ships fell victim to the U-boats. My brother-in-law, Laurens Oostermeer, owned the Dykendam Shipping Company, which operated out of Rotterdam, mainly to the Mediterranean with small vessels of two or three thousand tons.'

The name "Oostermeer" sounded familiar, but I didn't know why.

'Laurens was smart, too smart for the Nazis. He managed to send most of his ships away from Europe before the ports were taken. He sent them anywhere, as long as it was away from Europe. Only one was sunk by a U-boat. They must have looked too small for the captains to waste a torpedo, especially with their shallow draft.'

'Laurens made me master of the *Wassenhoot* and allowed my wife, Beatrice, to come with me. We left Rotterdam two days ahead of the Germans, and three weeks later arrived in New York. The *Wassenhoot* was too small and too slow to be used in convoys back across the Atlantic, so we steamed up and down the East coast collecting cargoes to be sent to England. When the Americans commenced building the Liberty ships, we spent most of our time taking materials to Wilmington and Savannah to fit them out. Beatrice was living on a ranch in up-state Virginia with friends of Laurens Oostermeer's agent in Wilmington, and I managed to go up and see her most times we were in port.'

He nodded and smiled as he looked at me, remembering those days.

'They were good times, Christopher. Even during the cold winter of January 1941 we could see each other and we were safe. Then came Pearl Harbour and suddenly the Americans were focused on the Pacific. We were sent to the West coast and I didn't see Beatrice again until February 1944, when we were sent back East to help with the supplies for the push into Europe.'

'Didn't you have any leave?'

'Some, but not enough time, or money, to travel across America.'

'At least you were both alive.'

'Thank God. We felt very lucky and almost stayed in America after the war, but when Laurens Oostermeer called his ships home we both felt the need to see our families. Beatrice had not heard from her parents and I wanted to see my sister, Fleur, who was Laurens' wife.'

He poured me a second cognac, and then paused for a moment when he noticed his was untouched. In a single swallow he emptied the glass, as if he needed courage, and re-filled it before continuing.

'By Christmas 1945 all of Laurens' remaining ships had returned to Rotterdam. He still had twenty vessels; almost half his original fleet, but several were not worth repairing and he set about building new tonnage. Because I was family, instead of putting me on the beach he offered me the *Caillou*. She had survived the war but was far too small to be in Laurens' plans for the future.'

'You were *given* the *Caillou*?' I asked, shaking my head. 'I've never heard of anyone being given a ship.'

'Neither had I. It seemed Beatrice and I were destined to lead a charmed life, and so we did for the next four years. The *Caillou* made good money until early in 1949, when repair bills and competition from newer vessels reduced our income considerably. In spite of the setbacks we continued until those terrible blizzards in February last year.'

His eyes grew misty.

'Beatrice caught pneumonia and I lost her; the only woman in my life for over fifty years. I blamed myself for being away on the *Caillou* when she needed me.'

'You shouldn't have blamed yourself.'

'That's what everyone said, but it was six months before I could go back to sea. That was last August. Then four weeks later my beautiful daughter Giselle…'

He glanced at a photo on the dresser that showed a blonde lady in a white dress hugging a tall man with dark hair. I recognised the wheelhouse and knew it had been taken on the *Caillou*. When I looked back, tears were rolling down his cheeks.

'…Giselle and her husband, Brian, were killed in an air crash when they were visiting their son, Simeon, in South Africa.'

'Your grandson?'

'Yes; he's still out there working for the diamond company, De Beers.'

He dried his eyes.

'I'm so sorry Jacques; I don't know what to say.' Nothing could have prepared me for what was to follow.

'Now it's Fleur I feel for,' he said.

'Fleur?'

'Yes, after the murder last Christmas.'

Suddenly I remembered where I had heard the name Oostermeer. 'Laurens?'

He nodded.

The news had been full of the vicious, unprovoked attack on the Dutch shipowner at home during a raging storm just before Christmas. His wife had survived because she was staying with family elsewhere.

'Your sister, she was...?'

'Fleur was spending a few days here, trying to talk me into going to Rotterdam for Christmas.'

'But why...?'

'Why was Laurens murdered? I wish I knew. There was no money in the house, I know that now. It seems whoever killed him was looking for something special, because they left all of Fleur's jewellery and the silverware.'

'You said there was no money?' I shouldn't have asked him such personal questions, but I was intrigued to hear about the crime that had been in all the papers.

'No; we all thought that must have been the motive but it turned out Laurens was not only, as you would say, penniless, but he was also deeply in debt trying to pay off his new tonnage. All he had were the ships, which were not making the quick profits he had hoped for.'

'How did Fleur cope with that?'

'That's the odd part. Laurens had always told her... and I never told the police this; he told her she would always be comfortable; that he had provided for her, but we don't know how. If a letter was left somewhere, we never found it.'

I was stunned.

'Now it's just Fleur and I,' he continued. I'm too old for the sea, and we need each other.'

'You still have your grandson, Simeon?'

'Yes, but he's still in South Africa. My grand-daughter, Katherine, is closer; she lives in her parent's home in Kent, but I only see her occasionally because of her work. So now Fleur and I must look after ourselves. She has sold all the ships, plus her home in Rotterdam, to pay the bills, and will come to live here with me.'

We signed all the necessary papers after agreeing on a price, and he poured one more cognac to celebrate the deal.

'Look after the *Lily Jade,* Christopher.'

I was surprised when he used that name.

'Yes, the *Lily Jade*. She's yours now.'

* * * * * * *

By Sunday I'd returned to Malcolm's house in Shoreham with a big grin, waving papers in my hand.

'Well, Captain Christopher Bowden,' he said, 'you're going to be a busy man.'

'And I'll enjoy every minute of it.'

He picked up his car keys. 'I expect you want to go down and see your new purchase?'

I nodded.

He took a bottle of red wine and two glasses from a cabinet. 'Daresay we should celebrate when we get aboard?'

As we sipped the wine sitting on the hatch aboard the *Lily Jade* I related the remarkable story told to me by Jacques Kessel.

Chapter Three

During the next three months most of my capital was used up. While I organised the necessary papers to change the name and the port of registry, I asked Scotty to check out the engine room.

The man from Aberdeen, who had been a friend of my father and the family since before the war, had sounded extremely sceptical when I told him I had bought a ship. He grew even more wary when I asked him to check the engine over and offered him the job as engineer. I knew he had been retired for several years, but had been at a loose end since his wife died two years ago.

When he first saw the *Lily Jade,* his natural dour, Scots apprehensiveness came to the fore. 'Did ye really pay good money for this old tub?'

'Hang on; you haven't even been aboard yet.'

'Not sure I want to,' he said, shaking his mass of curly, white hair. 'Can't imagine she'd be any better below. Certainly not good enough to make the regular run you've got in mind.'

'How about you have a look, before you draw all these conclusions,' I said, somewhat irritated.

He shrugged his shoulders. 'Ok, if that's what you want.'

I was on the bridge sorting out the charts when he came to see me an hour or so later. He smiled, revealing a gap in his front teeth as he announced the *Lily Jade* was a "bonny lass", who would be just fine once he replaced a piston in the engine and installed a new salt-water pump; plus a few other bits and pieces, which he didn't elaborate on, except to say, after which, *his* engine would be running like a sewing machine.

I shook his hand and promised he would have all those "bits and pieces" as soon as possible, realising I had just found my engineer; a person I could trust no matter where her new master took the *Lily Jade*.

On deck was a different story. A lot of work was needed to clean up the rust on the steel plates that formed the tank-top at the bottom of the hold. The derrick would need re-rigging, although some of the existing wires could be kept as spares, and the wooden row-boat that doubled as a lifeboat needed attention, as did several other items. I sorted out all the navigation equipment and the gear on the bridge myself, while four men from the Shoreham docks did the big jobs.

During the last week of August it seemed fairly certain the work on the *Lily Jade* would be completed by early September and I wrote to the old lady at the cottage in Colwell Lane to ask if the rooms were available. Although it was still summer holidays she had had a cancellation for two weeks and was more than happy for me to fill the gap.

I went back to the Isle of Wight to sign the final papers allowing me regular use of the berth in the port of Yarmouth and then, with the easy part over, I set about searching the local towns for the rest of my crew. I had Scotty for the engine room and myself on deck, but I needed one more qualified deck man, plus a general hand to do a bit of everything – someone to cook, help Scotty down below, or assist on deck if required. For four days I drew a blank as I asked around the pubs and shops in Yarmouth and all the villages between there and the capital, Newport.

On that fourth evening I sat on my bed at the top of the spiral staircase in the stone cottage and considered making a trip to the other end of the island, to the bigger towns of Ryde, Sandown and Shanklin. There were the boating fraternities in Cowes and Bembridge, but they were mostly wealthy people with yachts; not the sort who would want to get their hands dirty on an old coaster.

I tried to think of anywhere local I hadn't investigated. There was no town at Colwell Bay, only the beach.

The beach! I remembered a young man called Basil, who ran a business hiring out deck-chairs and rowing boats when I was a boy, and in my mind I could still see him by the slipway wearing an officer-style cap. I'd thought it looked important back then, but in reality I expect it came from a local shop. He used to tell me stories about ships and seemed knowledgeable about the sea. I wondered if he was still there, and if he needed a job.

Next morning, not overly confident, I walked down to Colwell Bay. It was the latter part of the season but many families were still on holidays. The two putting greens were full and there were children running around with ice-creams and candy floss. The gravel road crunched under my feet as the large rocks that once formed the supports for a pier came into view. On the slipway a collection of boats, canoes and rafts sat waiting for hire and my pulse quickened as a man in shorts and a tee-shirt wearing a nautical cap emerged from a hut and pushed a canoe into the water.

'Basil!' I called, but when he turned to go back into the wooden building where I'd been told all those sea-stories as a child the face was wrong and he was younger than Basil had been all those years ago.

'Can I help you?' he asked, when I appeared at the door.

Inside, the hut was as I remembered it. Old fishing nets hung across the ceiling, the bench covered in cuts from knives and on the walls souvenirs from around the world that included a Pontiac hub-cap and an elephant tusk.

Hanging on a metal chain in front of the window was a shining brass bell with some fancy rope-work attached to its clapper. It hadn't been there when I was a child, and for some reason it now had pride of place.

'Was it a deck-chair or a boat you wanted?'

'Oh, no thanks, I wondered if Basil Cole was still here.'

He looked at me curiously. 'Yes, Basil's here. He's in Freshwater at the moment, getting some clothes. He only arrived last month.'

'Basil Cole?'

'Yes. He came in July – from New Zealand.'

'Middle-aged man?'

'I think so; I'm just helping out here. I've only seen him once.'

I was disappointed. It seemed unlikely it was the same man I'd known as a boy. I thanked him and walked along the sea-wall wondering what to do next. I rounded the small headland, past the gun-emplacements from the war, into Totland Bay, where a paddle-steamer was berthed at the pier.

A footbridge crossed over the short steep road leading up towards Totland village. To the right, lush green grass stretched along the cliff-top in front of the houses overlooking the Solent. Still thinking of the Basil Cole I'd known all those years ago, I turned the other way and walked through the fields back to Colwell Bay.

The path finished just behind the putting green. As I went down the sandy steps cut into the grass a man walked past on the gravel road in front of me. He looked older, with grey flecks in the sides of his hair, but he also looked leaner.

'Basil?' I called.

He stopped and looked at me.

'Basil!' I called again, almost falling down the last three steps. 'I thought it was you.'

'Do I know you?' he asked.

'Christopher Bowden,'

'Bowden, Bowden – that rings a bell.'

'We used to rent a beach hut before the war.'

He smiled. 'Eric Bowden? I remember an Eric Bowden.'

'My father.'

'Telescope!'

'I'd forgotten you called me that.'

'Every ship that came up or down The Solent, you'd come running into the hut to use my old telescope. No wonder I didn't recognise you, you've grown a bit. It must be all of fifteen years since you were here.'

'Eighteen. Thirty-four was the last year we came.'

'Come down to the hut and tell me all your news.' Inside he lit an old primus-stove and put a kettle on. 'Tea?'

I nodded.

'So what have you been up to?' he asked, putting two tin mugs on the bench.

'I joined the Navy.'

'So did I.'

'I was invalided out two years ago.'

'What happened?'

'We were bombed in the Channel. Lost four men and I copped a piece of flying metal in the leg,' I said, patting my right thigh.

'Is it ok?'

'Not bad at all most of the time, however not good enough for the Royal Navy after the war. But what about you, I hear you've been to New Zealand?'

He looked away. 'There's a ship out there, you'd better have a look,' he said, passing me the old telescope.

I focused on a small cargo ship passing Hurst Castle, picturing the *Lily Jade* in my mind.

'After the war I felt it was time to make a fresh start.'

His voice sounded distant, as if he were immersed in his own thoughts.

'I went to New Zealand and found a job on a fishing boat up in The Bay of Islands. It was wonderful. Clean air, back at sea and enough money to be comfortable. Then I met Lee. She came from a town called Whangerai. We got on well right from the start; always together, we were almost ready to tie the knot. We'd even chosen some land, a section they call it out there, to build a home.'

'I couldn't make out the name,' I said, passing back the telescope.

'It's the *Alicarity,* one of Fred Everard's ships.'

'So, what happened?'

'It was mum,' he said, pointing up the road towards his parent's house. 'Dad died the year after I went to New Zealand, then four months ago mum had a fall and needed help – there was no-one here. I asked Lee to come with me, but she also had family ties. I got back last month.'

'Is your mum ok?'

'Frail, but she can get around slowly. My brother got back from Canada last week, so now we share the load.'

'What will you do?'

'Anything. Anything to earn a bit of money. I don't have much left after the trip back.'

'I'm sorry,' I said, feeling uncomfortable he'd poured his heart out to me.

'It's alright. I've resigned myself to being here as long as mum's alive. She'll be eighty-seven in November. In her condition I'm not sure she has too many years left.'

'And then?'

'Then?… then back to New Zealand if Lee and I can pick up the pieces. If not, maybe I'll go to Australia or Canada, if I can. They may not want anyone my age.'

The kettle boiled. 'So what are you doing?' Basil asked, making the tea.

'I've bought a ship.'

He turned round. 'You've bought a what?… Ow! That's hot!' He waved his left foot to shake off the drops of boiling water he'd spilt from the kettle.

'A ship,' I repeated.

His grey eyes stared at me, and he nodded as he pushed a steaming mug towards me. 'I'm not surprised, remembering you and that telescope.' He sat on an old stool. 'Tell me about it.'

I told him everything from the first time I had seen the *Lily Jade* and showed him the photographs of her. 'So now I'm almost ready for her maiden voyage, except I need a crew. That's why I came down; I wondered if you'd be interested in joining the *Lily Jade* as my number-one?'

He stared out of the window and gave the brass bell a gentle ring before looking back at me with a grin on his face. 'I don't know what to say. I feel honoured you should think of me – I'd be delighted.'

We shook hands.

'That's wonderful. Thank you,' I said.

'No, I'm the one who should be thanking you.' He stopped laughing. 'Just one thing, Christopher; when mum dies, if Lee still wants me, I'm going back to New Zealand.'

'I understand; but meantime we still need one more crewman, a general hand.'

He stood up and thoughtfully ran his finger around the top of the empty mug for a few seconds. Then he picked up an old dirk, and smiling, plunged it into the bench. Its blade went in half-an-inch, its vibrations audible around the hut as he let it go.

'I may be able to help us there, but no promises, mind, it's a long-shot. Someone who was here before I went to New Zealand. Let me ask around tonight. Can you come back tomorrow?'

I nodded. As I went back to the cottage I felt happy and confident it would work out, that everything was falling into place.

The next morning a chilling wind brought a shower of rain and with it the first hint of autumn, as I went down to the hut to meet

Basil at 10 o'clock.

He was waiting for me. 'Good morning, Chris. I think I've found our other crew-member.'

'You have?'

'Subject to your approval as master and owner.'

'When can I meet him?'

'Anytime this morning, he's at home in Freshwater.'

'A local man?'

'He is now. He arrived during the war after his ship was sunk by the Germans.'

'A seafarer, that's a good start. What was he at sea?'

'I've no idea.'

'I'll have to ask him.'

'Good luck.'

'What do you mean?'

'His name's Soo Wan Ling. Understands English perfectly, but doesn't speak it too well.'

'I'm not sure about this,' I said, having grave doubts about hiring an inarticulate Chinaman.

'I bet his English is better than your Chinese,' Basil said, still smiling.

'I daresay it is but…'

'Wait 'til you meet him. He's an incredible little man. Seems to have a sixth-sense about what is required and has it done before you ask him; at least that's what I've heard from people who employ him.'

'Doing what?'

'Anything. It appears he can do plumbing, carpentry, landscaping. He even made a set of curtains for a pub over in Shanklin.'

'Then we'd better go and meet this Soo Wan Ling.'

Basil took me to the butcher in the middle of Freshwater. 'He rents a room above the shop,' he explained. 'Mind you, he's seldom here, always off on a job somewhere on the island or over on the mainland. He built a hayshed on a farm near Dorchester last year.'

Behind the terraced block of shops we found a blue door backing onto the butcher and rang the bell. I heard someone running down the stairs inside. Soo Wan Ling seemed fit, if nothing else.

When he opened the door I liked him immediately. A wiry man with jet-black hair and bright green eyes, he had a beaming smile that showed a mouthful of yellowing teeth with several gaps.

'This is Captain Bowden,' Basil said.

Soo raised a hand above his head before saying "Chief" and bowing to me.

'You have to learn the sign language. The hand above the head was his way of saying "big". He called you "Big Chief".'

'Thank you,' I said, returning his compliment with a bow. Soo beamed an even bigger smile and ushered us inside.

The room at the top of the stairs was as neat as a pin, with a low bed on one side and, next to the window, a table was set with a place-mat and cutlery for the next meal. In the middle of the room four cane chairs surrounded a small coffee-table, upon which were three cups and a teapot with a wisp of steam issuing from its spout. By the time we'd sat down Soo had poured the tea and placed it in front of us.

'Would you like to come and work on my ship?' I asked.

'Please. Very much. I was seaman.'

'What can you do on a ship?'

'All things,' he said, spreading his arms.

'Engine? Steering? Cargo? Cooking?' I asked, miming to explain, which wasn't necessary as he understood perfectly and nodded enthusiastically to everything I said.

'What do you think?' Basil asked.

'I think you were right. The *Lily Jade* has her crew.'

'You come with Basil to the ship next Tuesday – ok?'

He nodded, we shook hands and he bowed.

'Next week Chris?'

'Yes Basil. She'll be ready if no new problems have cropped up during the last four days.' I took a piece of paper out of my wallet and scribbled Malcolm's address on it. 'Come to this address in Shoreham, it's near the station. Malcolm has a car and can bring you down to the ship.'

I looked at my watch. 'It's lunchtime and I think I should buy my new crew a celebratory meal.'

We went to the Colwell Bay Inn, a few doors down from my cottage. Basil and I washed the good food down with a couple of pints, but Soo would only have a tomato juice. I was to learn that was all he ever drank, apart from tea.

Returning to Shoreham on Friday, I went straight down to the *Lily Jade*. Painting of the hull was almost complete, as were the "bits and pieces" Scotty had talked about for the engine-room. Everything else, including the work in the hold, was finished. A feeling of nervous excitement made my fingers tingle, as I realised the dream of operating my own ship was about to become reality.

'Hi Malcolm,' I called as I entered the house. 'The *Lily Jade* is almost ready. I've just got to check that the last of Scotty's engine pieces will arrive on Monday.' He seemed quiet. 'Is something wrong?'

'No; well I hope not.'

'What is it?' I'd been thinking of nothing except the *Lily Jade* for weeks now and I hoped I hadn't upset him in some way.

'I've booked you a cargo.'

'You've what! – A cargo? – For the *Lily Jade?*'

'I hope you're not angry?'

'I'm... I'm astounded and delighted.' I started to laugh. 'It's fantastic, tell me all about it.'

'I was talking to a friend who works in the timber mill at the end of the dock, and happened to mention you and the *Lily Jade*. When I told him Yarmouth was going to be the home port for the ship he was intrigued. They send a truck every second day to the island.'

'There's that much demand?'

'More at times, but often they can't find extra trucks.'

'So is that the cargo – timber?'

He nodded. 'It might be a full load.'

'How do you know that?'

'I showed Peter the *Lily Jade*. It all depends on how much water and fuel you still have to take aboard.'

'Water we have, but there's twenty-five tons of diesel to come on Tuesday.'

'It didn't matter; he said there would be plenty to take.'

'When does he want to start loading?'

Malcolm passed me a slip of paper. 'He wanted you to ring him when you got back. Go on,' he said, pointing to the telephone.

'May I speak to Peter Dawson please? It's Christopher Bowden.'

'Captain Bowden, it's good to hear from you.'

That was the first time anyone, apart from Malcolm, had called me Captain and it sounded quite strange. In fact it was incorrect until Monday when the transfer papers were stamped by the harbour authority.

'I believe you have a cargo for me?'

'Indeed I do, if we can come to an agreement. Could you come round this afternoon?'

'I can come now if you like.' I said, excited at the thought of loading the first cargo aboard the *Lily Jade*.

A man about my age, Peter Dawson pushed a lock of sandy hair out of his eyes as he stood to greet me. 'I've never met a captain who owns his own ship.'

'Neither have I.'

'This is your maiden voyage I gather?'

'Both for the ship *and* the master.'

'Tell me, do you intend to make Shoreham a regular port-of-call?'

'I hadn't,' I confessed. 'However, I haven't really confirmed any regular route. The first few voyages will be somewhat an experiment, but I do know building materials are in demand on the island.'

'You're right. Let's call this a trial load to see how it works.'

I must have looked disappointed.

'But,' he said smiling, 'I think this could suit us both very well.'

Basil and Soo had just arrived at Malcolm's when I returned after helping Scotty load the diesel fuel the following Tuesday. 'I'm glad you've arrived,' I said, shaking their hands. 'I've asked Scotty to meet us in the pub for lunch.'

'Which pub?' Malcolm asked.

'The Lifeboat, of course, where we went the first time I saw the *Lily Jade*, and then after lunch I have a special job for all of us.'

They looked at each other and then back at me.

'I'll tell you about it over lunch.'

Scotty was already half-way through a pint of bitter when we arrived. 'I could nay wait any longer,' he said, revealing the gap in his front teeth – the result of a fight in a far eastern bar before the war.

'Scotty, this is the rest of our crew, both from the Isle of Wight. Basil will be my number-one, and Soo. Soo does everything. Cooks, paints, can steer the ship and even knows about engines; so he can give you a hand down below.'

Scotty shook hands, but looked at Soo mistrustingly. 'Oh aye? Well, we'll see about that.'

I bought four pints and a tomato juice. 'Now for the big news. Malcolm has found a cargo for our maiden voyage. It's timber from the mill at the end of the dock and we move down to the berth at 0700 tomorrow.'

There was laughter and words of approval.

'Well done Malcolm,' Basil said, raising his glass.

'It was just a lucky meeting. But what's this job you have for us?' he said turning to me.

'The only remaining piece of preparation left to make the *Lily Jade* ready for sea.'

'Which is?' Basil asked.

'Paint her name on each bow and the stern.'

After lunch I went to the off-licence and bought two bottles of champagne, a crate of bitter and several bottles of tomato juice before we all squeezed into Malcolm's Rover for the short journey down to the dock.

We stepped over the bulwark onto the foredeck. 'If ye goin' to be swingin' that derrick around in the morning, I'd best give the generator a test run,' Scotty said, disappearing below.

Basil and Soo looked up and down the deck of their new home and smiled at each other.

'She good ship,' Soo said, and Basil agreed.

'I'm glad you both approve so far, now let me show you your cabins.' Inside, I opened the door of the centre cabin. 'Not exactly the *Queen Mary.*'

'Comfortable enough, Chris.'

Soo just nodded when he saw his cabin. He put his bag down and went into the tiny galley next door, where he looked around, smiling. 'I make good food here.'

'I know you will, Soo.'

Suddenly he looked serious. 'But now we must paint name. We find paint.'

Basil, Soo and Malcolm followed me up to a wooden box bolted to the deck next to the funnel. 'I've only made one stencil,' I said, wondering how we could all work at the same time.

'Soo fix. Is that ok, Captain Chris?'

I nodded.

'Then no problem.' Soo took a red handkerchief from one pocket and placed the stencil on top of it. From his other pocket he took a knife and made a nick in the material to show the height and width of the letters, before cutting the stencil in half.

'Here,' he said, passing me the word "Lily". 'Captain Chris start with this. Basil you take "Jade". Then you swap – ok? I do the stern. Under name I put "Yarmouth"?'

Again I nodded.

'You spell please.'

'I wrote it on a piece of paper. 'Half-size,' I said, folding his handkerchief over, ok?'

'Ok. Yarmouth half-size.'

By the time I'd got the paint and brushes Soo had rigged a small stage over the stern. 'That's one efficient crewman you found, Basil.'

'I know; we were lucky.'

Basil put a rope ladder over the starboard bow and we discussed the position of the name in relation to the stem-post. From the wharf I could reach to paint the name on the port bow while Malcolm helped the others by passing them paint and rags. Suddenly the sound of the two-stroke generator reverberated around the ship and I passed my paint brush over to Malcolm and took the opportunity to check as many lights and other electrical fittings as possible.

Afterwards we stood back to admire our work, but were too close to the ship to see its full effect, so Malcolm drove us to the other side of the dock. The name *Lily Jade,* in the same cream paint as the upper works, glowed against the green hull on the starboard bow and across the stern in the afternoon sunshine. Soo had done a perfect job, the word "Yarmouth" painted exactly half the size of the words

Lily Jade.

Back on board I opened one of the bottles of champagne and poured out four glasses. I was about to open a tomato juice when Soo stopped me.

'Very special time. I join you.'

It was to be the only time he had an alcoholic drink with us. I poured the fifth glass and led them up onto the foc'sle carrying the other bottle of champagne.

'To the *Lily Jade,*' I called.

'The *Lily Jade,*' they chorused.

'Hold this for me, Basil,' I said, passing him my glass. I leant over the bow and smashed the second bottle against the stem-post, the bubbles sparkling in the sunlight as they rolled down the green hull. The party went on for over two hours before Malcolm went home, by which time many photos had been taken of everyone all around the ship, even down Scotty's hallowed hall, the engine-room. It was the proudest moment of my life.

The four of us stayed aboard that night, although I barely slept at all. By 0400 I was up and quietly checking everything I could, making mugs of tea, which went cold as I thought of something else to do.

It was almost five when Soo entered the galley. He saw the pot of cold tea and shook his head. 'I make fresh hot and breakfast. No sail without breakfast!'

Scotty appeared at 0530, grunted what might've been "good morning" and was about to go below, when Soo put a plate of bacon and eggs and a mug of steaming tea in front of him. He smiled. 'If this is the way the *Lily Jade* is going to operate, it'll be a pleasure to sail in her.' He took a large mouthful of food and then waved his knife at Soo. 'And if you know about engines as well as you can cook, I might let ye come down below now an' again.'

Soo smiled. It was big praise indeed from Scotty.

The promise of a fine day pushed through the haze over France and cast shadows across the deck as I took my place on the bridge at 0700. To say I was nervous was an understatement. My palms sweated and my throat was dry. The mooring lines had been put on a bight so we could slip them from on board – all it needed was for me to give the order. It would be the first time I'd been in command of a ship, and the first time manoeuvring the *Lily Jade*. It had to be good: there had to be no mistakes.

'Are you ready Scotty?' I called down the voice-pipe for the third time.

'As ready as I'll ever be; that's if I don't fall asleep waitin' for ye to move.'

'Let go!' I yelled to Basil on the focs'le, before turning to make a cutting motion with my hand towards Soo down aft. They pulled the lines in quickly and a light breeze from the English Channel pushed the *Lily Jade* off the berth.

'Dead-slow ahead,' I called down to Scotty.

He didn't confirm the order, but beneath me the *Lily Jade* vibrated as the little diesel burst into life. I'd just given my first command as master of a ship, and now I felt the response as the screw turned. She moved, almost imperceptibly at first, down the dock towards the timber wharf at the end, where I would have to make a ninety degree turn to starboard.

As our old berth fell astern I felt a rush of adrenalin at being in command, followed by a feeling of panic for a moment, a thought I might not be capable of managing such a responsibility. It evaporated as the *Lily Jade* responded to my helm and engine movements like a docile kitten when we swung to come alongside the timber wharf, without so much as a scratch on her new paintwork.

'Finished with engines, Scotty.'

Although the log-book would only show it as a "shift-ship", to me it had been a maiden voyage. As the engine died a feeling of relief flooded over me.

The feeling was not allowed to last long. Within minutes a man from the timber mill came aboard and entered the bridge. I leaned out of the window. 'Basil, they want to start as soon as we're ready.'

'Ten minutes, Chris.'

By the time I'd glanced at the loading list, Basil and Soo had the tarpaulin rolled back and were removing the hatch-boards. The sound of the generator broke the silence and less than twenty minutes later the first pack of timber was lifted aboard. It swayed dangerously as Basil tried to slow the swing of the derrick and it tipped almost vertical. For a moment I thought it might fall all over the deck and the wharf in pieces, but the rope snotters held and it was lowered into the hold.

Late that afternoon, Wednesday 10th September, the *Lily Jade* was almost half-loaded when Malcolm arrived. 'You look exhausted,' I said.

'It's been a long day,' he admitted. 'Started at six this morning with the client, and then assisted the lawyer in court all day. Sometimes this consultancy work is worse than a full-time job. But enough of my work, how's the loading of that cargo I organised progressing?'

'Come and have a look,' I said, grabbing him by the arm, ignoring his fatigue. I was like a child with a new toy wanting to show it off to everyone.

'When will you sail?' he asked, looking at the hold half-full of timber.

'Friday morning. I want to make the maiden voyage in daylight, even if we finish loading tomorrow afternoon. The timber mill doesn't mind.' He nodded, but seemed strangely silent, which I attributed to the long day in court. 'But now we're going to the pub for tea. I'm glad you made it in time.'

'I wonder how she'll behave out in the Channel?' Basil asked, as we tucked into the pub food.

'She good ship at sea.'

'How do yer know, Soo?' Scotty said, downing the last of his pint.

'She good. I know.'

'If we get thrown about I'll blame you. Now, who's for another?'

By the time he returned with fresh drinks everyone was convinced the *Lily Jade* would be a comfortable ship at sea. Only Malcolm remained quiet.

'What's the matter Malcolm? You seem a bit down this evening.' It was Basil who put the question I'd hesitated to ask in case I'd offended him in some way

'To be truthful I'm jealous.'

'Jealous?'

'I've been involved with Chris and the *Lily Jade* ever since he first saw her, and with the rest of you for the past few days, but now…'

'Now?' I asked.

'Well, you're off on the maiden voyage – even if it is only a few hours along the coast, I just wish I could come with you.'

It had never crossed my mind. 'Well, why don't you?'

'I can't. You'll arrive in Yarmouth late Friday afternoon or early evening, won't you?'

'That's right,' I said, realising he must have been thinking about this for quite a while, if he'd taken the trouble to work out our arrival time at the island.

'The first train on Saturday morning won't get me home until eleven, and I'm meeting an important client at nine.'

'The last ferry doesn't leave until 8 P.M. We'll be there by then,' Basil piped up.

Malcolm shrugged his shoulders. 'But there's no train.'

Basil smiled. 'So what?'

'So how do I get home by Saturday morning?'

'You drive.'

We all stared at him. Suddenly Soo laughed and clapped his hands.

'Basil and I fix in morning.'

'When we've finished loading we'll put Malcolm's car on the hatch. Soo and I'll scrounge some timber from the mill to make a cradle to hold it in place, and we'll cover it with a tarpaulin from the foc'sle.'

Malcolm laughed and shook his head in disbelief, black hair falling down over his forehead. Then he looked at me. 'Is that all right, Chris? It's your ship.'

I clapped him on the shoulder. 'Wouldn't take no for an answer. It seems my crew is smarter than the Captain,' I said, turning to the others – 'thank goodness!'

'You'll no be including me in that statement. It never occurred to me.'

'You just keep the engine going, Scotty, to make sure Malcolm doesn't miss the last ferry.'

Loading continued the next day with only a slight hiccup when we had to replace one of the rope guys on the derrick after it frayed. Although it wasn't a new one I had thought it would've lasted longer. When we finished for the day there was less than two hours work to complete cargo and I organised with the Harbour Authority for us to sail at 1000 the next morning, which I calculated that would put us into Yarmouth by 1630 if we made the eight knots Scotty had promised me.

Friday dawned warm and still, with a thin layer of high cloud covering the sky. By 0900 loading had finished and Malcolm's Rover was on the wharf as all of us, except Scotty who was down below, set about covering the hold with the hatch-boards and a tarpaulin. Fifteen minutes later Basil swung the derrick out and lowered a large net onto the wharf. Malcolm drove his car onto it and we packed some bags of rags and an old mattress around it to protect the paintwork.

I saw the look on Malcolm's face as the net closed around the car. 'Don't worry; it won't come to any harm.'

'I know,' he said unconvincingly, as the Rover was lifted into the air

It landed on the hatch. 'There you are, no problem.'

He said nothing but I heard a sigh of relief. Soo unhooked the net and guided the derrick into its crutch on the bridgefront as Basil lowered it down.

We were a bit early and I needed to contact Harbour Control to find out if we could sail straight away. I jumped off the hatch and quickly climbed the steps up to the bridge. Immediately I wished I hadn't hurried. The dull ache in my right thigh became the stabbing pain I'd felt when that piece of metal had hit me as I'd gone towards the forward gun, and Malcolm's words about not returning to sea flashed through my mind. It was, however, a momentary thought. Nothing and nobody was going to spoil today, Friday 12th September 1952, the day I took *my* ship, the *Lily Jade,* to sea for the first time.

'Basil,' I called down to the hatch. 'We must sail before ten. There's another ship due in at twenty past.'

'We need to have the cradle around the car before clearing the harbour.'

Soo was already nailing pieces of timber into the hatch around the Rover. 'You go,' he called, waving his hand. 'I finish before open sea.'

'Malcolm'

He looked up at me.

'You go aft and let go.'

'But I... I don't...'

'Don't worry, it's easy. I'll help you from up here

There was a hiss down below followed by a thump as the diesel started. Behind me the funnel emitted a single cloud of black smoke, which hung in the still air. 'Chris? Are ye there?'

'Yes Scotty,' I called back down the voice-pipe.

'Aye, all ready below – *Captain!*'

'Thank you – *Chief!*'

I waved my hand in an upward motion towards the foc'sle. 'Let go Basil,' I called before going to the port side and looking down.

A nervous face peered up at me.

'Just behind you – the rope on the bits.'

Malcolm turned and pointed to the two metal cylinders fixed to the deck, around which the mooring line was attached in a figure-of-eight pattern.

'That's it, take the rope off.'

He uncoiled the line until only the eye was left on the bits.

'It's on a bight. Throw the eye off and pull it in.

Suddenly he understood. The rope snaked along the wharf and around the bollard as he pulled on the line. The *Lily Jade* had drifted a few feet off the wharf and it splashed into the water astern. Seconds later he looked up at me clutching the wet eye of the rope, his shirt and trousers stained by the dirty water.

'Well done!'

He laughed and wiped his wet hands on his trousers.

'Dead-slow ahead Scotty,' I called, as I made the first entry of the voyage in the log-book. "0942: Let-go from timber berth". There was a slight vibration from the engine and a faint churning of the water astern as the *Lily Jade* began to move ahead. I eased the helm to starboard, watching the stern until it was clear of the wharf as we swung to head down the dock at a sedate three knots. She felt sluggish compared with our move down the dock on Wednesday, due to the weight of the cargo.

'Car all safe, Captain Chris,' a voice called from the hatch.

'Thank you Soo.' He left the Rover, now with timber around its wheels and covered in a tarpaulin to head towards the bridge. 'Half-ahead Scotty.'

'Aye,' came a grunt from below.

The engine sound increased and a wisp of continuous smoke emerged from the funnel. Basil entered the bridge carrying a camera with Soo behind him. 'Here we go, Chris. Can I take a photo?'

'Must take history photo.'

I laughed. 'Of course you can.'

Malcolm appeared, still wet from his encounter with the stern line. 'Here, I'll take it, all the crew together.'

'Not quite Malcolm, don't forget Scotty, but take one now and we'll do some more out in the Channel.' He took the photo, which was to remain forever on the bulkhead behind the wheel. 'Thanks, and not just for the photo; you did well down there letting-go the stern line.'

Basil raised his eyebrows. 'We might have to sign him on as crew.'

We all stood in silence as I brought the *Lily Jade* round and headed towards the open sea, the red and green channel buoys passing down each side. She started to pitch in the low swell and a sou-westerly gusting up the Channel sent the first spray of salt-water over the bow as we turned to starboard and headed westwards along the coast.

There were footsteps on the ladder outside and Scotty slid the door open. 'Now don't ye go thumpin' into any big seas. I want to check a few things after Agnes has been runnin' for a few hours without her being knocked about.'

Basil, who had taken the wheel, looked around. '*Agnes?*'

'Aye, she's a bonny wee lass. Can you no hear her ticking away down there?'

'It's a great name for the engine,' I said, 'and yes, we'll avoid all the icebergs for the next few hours.'

'*Lily Jade* good sea ship. I tell you before. Now I make tea.'

'When are we due in Yarmouth?'

'Wait awhile, Malcolm,' I said. 'That'll give us a better idea of how many knots we're making.'

'Meanwhile,' Basil said, 'I'm going to check the deck-cargo; namely your car. So come over here and take the wheel.'

Malcolm stared at Basil in silence and then looked at me.

'Go on,' I said. 'It's easy and I'll be here.'

The wind had freshened slightly, but the *Lily Jade* took the swell easily, sending only the occasional spray over the foc'sle.

'All safe and sound,' Basil said, when he returned. 'I should've known Soo would have it lashed down tight.'

A few minutes later Soo returned with a large steaming pot and a tray covered with a tea-towel. 'Please eat. I go to make lunch, then come back.'

Basil took a mug of tea and a couple of sandwiches before smiling at Malcolm. 'The helmsman will have to wait until the rest of the crew have finished.'

'I don't mind, I'm enjoying this.'

'In which case you can have your smoko at the wheel,' he said, taking tea and sandwiches over to Malcolm.

'I'm going to have a quick look around,' I said to Malcolm after we had all finished. 'Do you want to come?'

'Most definitely!'

'Malcolm, do I detect a change of heart from the person who described the *Lily Jade* as a dirty old coaster the first time he saw her?'

'Being at sea is a lot different to Shoreham Docks.'

'Well, that's where ships tend to go, to sea!'

The "quick" inspection would have taken hours if Malcolm had had his way. 'Come on, I want to be back on the bridge for our first alteration of course and we haven't visited the engine-room yet.' Even I was a bit apprehensive at entering Scotty's domain for the first time at sea.

He stood amidst the moving machinery with an oily rag in his hand. 'There's a wee tapping in the second cylinder and a slight oil leak from the generator, but it's nay anything you should worry your little head about.'

'Thanks Scotty. I won't.'

He smiled. 'Aye, Agnes and I are goin' to get along just fine.'

We rounded Selsey Bill at 1230 and steered west-nor-west towards Spithead. 'We're making eight and a half knots, Malcolm. That'll put us into Yarmouth about four o'clock.'

Soo arrived with big plates of beef and stout pie, with mashed potatoes and peas. I wondered where he had found the stout.

'I find in alleyway. Case of Guinness.'

I laughed and called down below. 'Scotty, lunch is ready, and I think I've found something you mislaid.'

'Now what…?' said Scotty as he entered the bridge. 'My, that smells good.'

'Lunch Chief. Eat while hot.'

'Thanks Soo.' He took a mouthful. 'Well, I've no tasted beef pie like this since my old mum died. Now, Chris, what's this I've mislaid?'

'You're eating it!'

'Sorry Chief. Not knowing it was yours.'

'What's he talkin' about?'

'He pinched a bottle of your Guinness for the pie.'

'Take another man's booze? That's a criminal offence!'

He glared at Soo, who stood with his hand over his mouth.

Scotty roared with laughter, bits of pastry spraying from his mouth. 'But in this case I reckon the taste is vastly improved!' He went over, shook Soo's hand and clapped him on the shoulder. 'Don't take any notice of a silly old Scot.' He took him aside. 'You must tell me what herbs you used.'

As the two talked I checked our speed steaming up Spithead. The flood had come in and the *Lily Jade* making nine knots as we left Portsmouth on the starboard beam. Altering course for some traffic, I explained to Malcolm some of the rules for the prevention of collision at sea and put on a pair of sunglasses when the sun reflected off the water as we swung south-west for the last leg down the Solent to Yarmouth.

Soo and Scotty appeared. 'Sorry. I do dishes,' Soo said.

It was only then I realised the dirty plates were stacked up in the corner of the bridge. 'Where've you been?'

'Hey, Chris; a wee bit more respect for the Senior Second Engineer if ye don't mind!'

Basil's jaw dropped. 'Senior Second…?'

'Aye; he's fixed the oil leak on the generator and we've worked out the tapping noise in the engine, haven't we Soo?'

I had the distinct feeling Soo, and not "we" had solved the latter problem, but I said nothing. I just smiled.

Yarmouth came into sight and we got ready to tie-up. It was just after 4 P.M. as the bow of the *Lily Jade* approached the berth. Basil made a port spring line fast and I steamed dead-slow ahead to swing her round until the row of car tyres, acting as fenders along the port side, came gently into contact with the stone wharf.

'I really don't want to leave,' Malcolm said forty minutes later as we all stood by the Rover watching the Lymington ferry approach.

'You can come anytime, can't he, Chris?' Basil said.

'Of course,' I said, wondering what we would do for accommodation on a longer trip.

'Thanks, Chris. The voyage completed everything that has happened during the past few months. It's something I'll never forget.'

'Neither will I.'

When they called Malcolm to put his car aboard the ferry we were still arranging how to keep in touch, especially with any news he might have from the timber mill in Shoreham. 'If you don't hear from me when we're due in Yarmouth leave a message with the Harbour-Master,' I yelled as the gap widened between the wharf and the ferry, the wash disturbing the yachts moored in the marina.

'Right, the first round's on me.'

We all stopped waving to Malcolm and looked around.

'Just because I'm a Scot does'na mean I can't shout first. We're not all tight-fisted ye know!'

Laughing, we followed him towards the pub, our feet clacking on the cobblestones now covered in long shadows from the evening sunshine. As we had tea, discussing the day and the maiden voyage of the *Lily Jade*, relief and contentment overwhelmed me with the realisation of achieving my greatest ambition.

Chapter Four

'Captain Bowden? Are you there Captain Bowden?'

The voice interrupting my train of thought as I sorted through bills and nautical publications that Monday morning seemed to come from ashore. Opening my cabin door leading onto the deck by the funnel, I saw Jim Middleton, the grey-whiskered Harbour-Master, holding his cap in the strong wind blowing along the wharf.

'Ah, there you are, Captain Bowden. I had a message asking you to ring Shoreham. They say you know the number.'

'Thank you sir,' I called, waving acknowledgment. 'I need to come and see you; would later this morning be convenient?'

'Any time. I'll be stuck in the office until lunchtime: damned paperwork!'

'I know,' I said, pointing behind me. 'I've got the same problem up here.'

It was Monday 15th September and our first cargo of timber was being taken away on trucks as fast as we could discharge it. At the current rate there would be little left in the hold by the end of the day.

'The mill wants to know,' Malcolm said, 'if you're coming back to Shoreham. They could have another load of timber for you in about two weeks. They are very happy with the result of the first shipment.'

'But we only started discharge this morning?'

'They've already had telephone calls.'

'Well… I've got a part cargo for Weymouth, and then a full load of stone and clay from Fowey to bring back to the island.'

'So, what should I tell them?'

'Tell them two weeks will be fine. I'll call you when we get back from Cornwall.'

Everything seemed to be falling into place, not only with cargo, but also with minor things that made starting a shipping company easier, such as a fresh water connection on the wharf Jim Middleton organised when I saw him later that morning. One cargo on offer that day, which I regretfully had to refuse, was fifty sheep heading to the market in Birmingham. 'I'm sorry; we're not equipped to carry livestock yet.'

'That's a shame. Means I won't have my truck for three days,' the farmer had said shaking his head. 'I can't afford to hire another one.'

'I hate to refuse cargo,' I told Basil and Soo after he'd gone. 'We'll have to find a way to carry livestock, and quickly!'

Soo pointed to a sling of our cargo being loaded onto a truck. 'Timber. We use some of cargo. I make.'

'You can't steal cargo!'

'But you could buy some of it,' Basil said.

I pulled a face. 'Spending the profits already?'

They looked crestfallen.

I smiled. 'Sounds like a good idea to me,'

When I rang the mill they let me have the timber for next to nothing. We sailed on Tuesday and soon settled into a routine, Basil and I sharing the bridge work and building livestock pens with Soo, when he wasn't busy in the galley or helping Scotty down below. After a couple of weeks I was beginning to wonder who was helping who in the engine-room!

The weather was good and the *Lily Jade* performed faultlessly, as if she was pleased to be back at sea. Our trading route also settled down remarkably quickly, with a part cargo from the island for Weymouth and Fowey and a full load of sand and stone from Cornwall back to Yarmouth. Then up to Shoreham with produce before loading timber for the island. Within two weeks the livestock pens were completed and lifted onto the hatch where they were secured in metal shoes I had made up myself. As we started to carry livestock to and from the island, our other cargoes increased as well, to the point where it became impossible to complete the round trip in two weeks.

In mid-October we were three days late into the island with the timber cargo and I arranged to work cargo on Saturdays in Fowey and Yarmouth to maintain the schedule, starting the following week. I decided to use the last two days of that week to clean out the hold and tidy up all round the ship and by Friday the *Lily Jade* had been cleaned from stem to stern and her paintwork touched up. Everyone had worked hard without a break for the past five weeks and I knew they would appreciate a weekend off as much as I would.

As Soo put lunch out on the hatch I took some beers and a tomato juice from the fridge in the galley and joined them. They looked surprised. Usually we had a drink after cargo had finished, but not at lunchtime as we were always too busy.

'Thanks chaps for being a great crew,' I said, awkwardly.

'Thanks for having us on the *Lily Jade*,' Basil said.

'Enough praise. Time we all had a break. No more work until Monday morning.'

Basil nodded. 'It'll be good to have a couple of days with mum. She's become frailer during the past month.'

'How about you Soo?'

'It good. I check on flat and see friend in Shanklin.'

Basil poked him in the ribs. 'I bet he owns the pub where you made the curtains.'

Soo nodded.

Scotty shook is head. 'What a waste. He gets to spend a weekend in a pub, but only drinks tomato juice!'

'What about you Scotty? Will you go and see your brother in Southampton?'

'Aye, if you're not going to need the generator running? Will ye no be living aboard Chris?'

'No, now I've made Yarmouth the home port I'll spend the weekend looking around this part of the island. It'll do me good to get away from the *Lily Jade* for a couple of days. I've thought of nothing else for the past six months.'

* * * * * * *

I took a bus to Totland and went to a hotel that I'd noticed when I was looking for Basil. It was next to the path leading up from the pier and the area had seemed so peaceful I felt it would be ideal for a couple of days. From my window I could just see the Solent through the trees beside the wooden footbridge, but the weather was so good I wasn't going to waste any time sitting around in my room.

The warm afternoon sun made it feel more like summer than late autumn as I walked along the grassy cliff-top between the deciduous trees, whose leaves had turned shades of red and gold.

About half-way along the cliff-top I noticed a "For Sale" sign. It stood in front of a low box hedge alongside a white lychgate, behind which was a small manicured garden with rose bushes and silver birch trees. A cobbled path led to the front door of a house with two bay windows which, like the eaves, were a pale blue, contrasting with the freshly painted white stucco walls. Set into the roof was an attic room with a balcony overlooking Totland Bay. I must have stood staring at the house deep in thought for several minutes, as I never heard her approach.

'Pretty, isn't it?'

'Yes… yes it is,' I answered. The voice belonged to a young woman with shoulder-length auburn hair and a big smile, which showed a perfect set of white teeth.

'I'm sorry. I didn't mean to startle you.'

'That's alright, I was daydreaming.'

'About the house?'

'Yes.' We both looked back at the blue and white building. 'It seems so peaceful and inviting.'

'I think it's beautiful. I could live there.'

'So could I,' I said, noticing the white blouse and matching shorts that showed off her tanned olive skin.

'Maybe you'd better buy it.'

'Maybe I should.'

'Then you could invite me in to have a cup tea on that balcony. I think the view would be fantastic.'

'Of course I would.'

Her grey-green eyes sparkled. 'I'll hold you to that.'

'Buying it might be just a dream.'

'We should make dreams come true. Good luck.'

I watched her athletic body striding along the grass towards the foot-bridge before looking back at the house, thinking about what she'd said about dreams and buying it. It certainly couldn't do any harm to make some enquiries at the estate agent. I turned to look again at the young woman who'd put the idea into my head, but she'd disappeared. I hadn't even asked her name.

An old-fashioned black bell gave one loud ring as I entered the estate agent's office in Freshwater the following morning. The thin, bald man behind the desk extolled the virtues of the property, but seemed reluctant to divulge the price of the blue and white house and I had to ask him four times before he told me in a quiet voice, as if he were afraid someone else might hear. I asked him to repeat the figure, mainly because he'd spoken so quietly I assumed I'd misheard him – I hadn't.

'It's the location sir.'

'I understand,' I replied, still coming to terms with his answer.

'Nothing can ever spoil the view.'

I nodded, mulling over a price I considered way beyond my means. He was an astute little man, I realised later, as he turned the conversation away from the house by talking about the weather, how good it was for this time of year and then asking me about my line of work. Immediately my mind went back to Yarmouth and the *Lily Jade*. He listened carefully, asking only a couple of questions as I related the past six months of my life. I knew a lot had happened, but somehow it put everything into perspective as I poured out my thoughts to this stranger.

'What an exciting and hectic year it's been for you.'

'I hope it settles down soon.'

'We all need to settle down at some stage.'

He paused, his words reminding me of the house on the cliff.

'Would you like to see through the property, sir?'

I stared at him, but said nothing.

'It can't do any harm to have a look, sir.'

'I suppose not.'

The owner is away at the moment. Would three o'clock this afternoon be convenient?'

I nodded, wondering why I should bother, the price of the property being so high. I suppose it was curiosity as much as anything else. Then I remembered the young woman whose words were the reason I was here and I wondered what she would think.

By midday, under clear blue skies, I sat in the garden of the Dovecote pub, whose birds cooed gently under the eaves of its thatched roof. Eating my ploughman's lunch washed down with a pint of bitter, the ambience, not just of Freshwater, but the entire western part of the island seemed in tune with my thoughts and feelings and suddenly I knew it was the place I wanted to call home. Although I'd be early for my appointment there was a purpose in my step as I strode through the lanes towards the cliff-top at Totland.

The church clock struck two as I approached the village and ten minutes later I passed the gate to my hotel and stepped onto the spongy grass above the Solent, anxious to see the house again. A light breeze stirred the leaves on the oak and elm trees, sending dappled shadows across the white stucco that momentarily turned the pale blue trim almost navy.

I must have been there over ten minutes when I caught the flash of yellow in the corner of my eye. Although she was almost a hundred yards away, somehow I knew the person who had just crossed the foot-bridge was the young woman responsible for my return to the cliff-top that afternoon.

'Still looking at that house?' She laughed. 'I can't blame you, but you haven't been here all night have you?'

'No, I just took your advice.'

'My advice?'

'Yes, I went to see the estate agent this morning to find out more about it.'

'Are you going to buy it?'

'I doubt it. It's a lot more expensive than I thought it would be.'

'But you've come back.'

'The agent is going to show me through the house at three.'

She gazed wistfully through the gate. 'I wonder if the rest of the house will be as wonderful as the balcony with its magnificent view.' She turned to me. 'Maybe you'll tell me all about it?'

'Better still, why don't you come and see it with me?'

Her eyes widened. 'Do you mean that?'

'Of course I do… I'm sorry I don't know your name.' I held out my hand. 'I'm Christopher Bowden.'

'Kathy, Kathy Wembourne.'

'Do you live on the island?'

'Oh no,' she said, shaking her head and glancing back at the house, the sunlight showing golden strands in her waving auburn hair. 'I'm just down here for a week with my aunt. She and her husband have some business to sort out.'

'That sounds like a good break in this fine weather.'

'I came down to look after Grandpa, but I get out whenever I can. I found this spot a couple of days ago. It's beautiful… the trees, the cliffs, the sea.'

'Where are you staying?'

'In a little cottage near the Colwell Bay Inn.'

'The one with a bus-stop outside the front gate?'

'Yes, do you know it?'

'Very well. I stayed there a few months ago.'

A car pulled up alongside us and the agent got out. 'Good to see you again Mr Bowden. I have the keys, so as soon as you're ready.'

'This is Kathy Wembourne. She is going to look around with me; you know, the woman's touch. I'm sure she'll notice things men wouldn't even see.'

'Pleased to meet you miss. Neil Crompton, at your service.'

'Thank you, Mr Crompton.' She punched me gently on the shoulder. 'I didn't know I was an expert in house design!'

The garden was full of buzzing insects taking advantage of the warm sun and the late flowers. From beyond the house the aroma of over-ripe fruit wafted on the easterly breeze.

'… in the nineteen-thirties.'

Engrossed in the garden, I'd missed everything the agent had been saying about the house

'If you'd just wait a minute, I'll turn the power on.'

He disappeared inside and I turned to Kathy. 'What did he say about the house? I was looking at the garden.'

She smiled. 'I thought so. It was built after the first world war and the second owner added the balcony in the thirties.'

The agent returned. 'Please come in.'

Kathy and I entered a spacious hall where the timber matched the front door. Neil Crompton opened a coat cupboard to emphasize the space available.

'Oh, these are beautiful!' Kathy said, running her hand across one of a pair of glass doors etched in pink and green that allowed light into the hallway. They opened into the lounge-room, where large windows on the front and the side of the house overlooked the clifftop and the sea.

'Pity the wall-paper overpowers the doors,' I said, noting the embossed pink roses and green ivy covering the walls.

Kathy looked around the room. 'Yes, I agree; the roses would be better left in the garden.'

More doors led to a dining-room panelled in dark timber alongside the kitchen, which was painted a dull green. Both rooms seemed sombre after the sunlit lounge.

'The kitchen needs bringing up-to-date,' Kathy remarked. 'Most of the fittings here are similar to those Grandpa had before Grandma died.'

It was the same with the rest of the house. The bedrooms were spacious but dated, their main feature being the views. The smaller one looked over the back garden with its fruit trees, while the main bedroom at the front had the same view of the ocean as the lounge-room.

'Imagine waking up to this,' Kathy said, leaning on the window-ledge. 'I think I'd leave the window open every night so I could hear the sea.'

'Not in the winter you wouldn't, unless you don't mind getting saturated with salt spray.'

'I'm sorry. Here I am telling you what to do and it's nothing to do with me. I just got carried away with the house.'

'I'm glad you did. It's good to hear someone else's thoughts. Come on, we haven't seen the balcony yet.'

We climbed the wooden staircase leading from the hall up into the roof. The stairs curved back towards the front of the house into a large room with double doors leading outside.

'I'll be down in the car when you're ready,' I heard Neil Crompton say, his footsteps receding down the stairs.

We both stood in silence on the balcony and drank in the view. With the extra height we saw the sunlight reflecting off the waves in the Solent and our ears were filled with the rustle of the red and gold leaves in the trees on the cliff-top.

'I've changed my mind,' Kathy said, still gazing out over the sea.

'About what?'

'About leaving the window open in the bedroom downstairs. I'd make this my bedroom.' She turned to me. 'That's if I were you and *I* was buying the house.'

'I haven't made up my mind to buy it yet.'

Her grey-green eyes widened and she grabbed me by the arm. 'Oh, Chris, you must. It's perfect. It's the most beautiful house I've ever seen. Things like the kitchen can be fixed up, but where else would you get a view like this?'

She put her arm around my waist as she turned back to face the cliff-top. I responded likewise and pulled her towards me. 'I think you're right, I'd be a fool not to buy it.'

She smiled, and then suddenly reached up and kissed me on the cheek. 'I'm glad – congratulations.'

A line of dark cloud had appeared over the land on the other side of the Solent and the afternoon heat had become oppressive. 'Looks like a storm approaching. I'm glad we're not sailing tonight.'

'Sailing?'

'On my ship, the *Lily Jade*.'

'Your ship?'

'I own a small coaster trading up and down the coast.'

'A real captain? Of your own ship? No wonder this house appealed to you. Up here must be like standing on the bridge?'

'You seem to know a lot about ships?'

'From my mother's side of the family.'

The wind gusted, turned cold and I sensed the first drops of rain in the air. 'Come on. We'd best get downstairs before we get wet.'

Shutting the door, we ran towards Mr Crompton and the car. 'Do you want a lift back to the cottage?'

'Do you think he'd take me?'

'He'd better if I'm going back to his office to sign up for the house.'

Neil Crompton drove down the hill and pulled up opposite Colwell Lane. 'Thanks for all your help today,' I said, as Kathy opened the door of the car.

'It was a pleasure. Thank you for showing me your new home.'

I took her hand. 'Would you have dinner with me tonight? As a sort of celebration'

'I'd love to; after I've got Grandpa his tea. About seven-thirty – is that alright?'

'That's fine. The Three Bells at the bottom of the lane is a good pub.'

'I'll see you there.' Kathy shut the door and ran towards the cottage in the increasing rain.

'Right Mr Crompton, I'm ready to come back to your office and sign-up for the house.'

* * * * * * *

The storm had passed, but it was still raining and there was a cold wind as I walked down to the Three Bells. Inside it was warm and I sat in a nook beside the crackling log fire reading the papers Mr Crompton had given me. It was almost eight o'clock before the door opened and Kathy stood there shaking the rain off her umbrella.

'Sorry I'm late. Grandpa wasn't ready for his tea; he was discussing something with Aunt Vivian.'

'No matter, you're here now. I've signed all the papers for the house, although I've yet to work out how I'm going to pay for it!'

I ordered some red wine and Kathy raised her glass. 'To your home on the cliff-top. It should have a name. Something to do with the sea, considering you're a captain.'

'Or its peaceful feeling. This afternoon it felt… serene.'

'What's the name of the channel it overlooks?'

'The Solent. Why?'

Kathy clapped her hands. 'That's it then – how about, "Solent Serenity". Do you like it?'

'It's perfect.' I reached out and took her hand. 'Thank you.'

The sky had cleared when we left and a new moon shone brightly as we walked hand-in-hand up Colwell Lane. 'I've done too much talking tonight,' I said, ' I don't know anything about you, except I've had a wonderful day with a lovely lady who gave me the courage to buy a beautiful home.'

Kathy stopped. 'I should be thanking you for making *my* day, and I'm so pleased I could help.'

She put her arms around me and we kissed; much longer than just a peck and with more intensity.

'Congratulations. And I loved hearing about the *Lily Jade*. She sounds wonderful.'

We walked on, our arms around each other's waist.

'My life hasn't been as exciting as yours, with your ship and everything. I'm twenty-eight and work as a vet in Canterbury, where

I grew up and went to school. I remember the early years were hard after the Depression and then being at school when the war came. That's when I started going round the farms helping out with the animals. I seemed to have a flair for it and by the end of the war I'd managed to become a qualified vet. Now I've got some extra qualifications and one day I'll open my own practice… I love the work, and the animals.'

'No wonder you've got such a great tan, working outside.'

'You're not exactly a paleface yourself!'

We'd arrived back at the gate of Colwell Cottage and although I wanted to stay and talk to Kathy, the cold wind made the idea impossible. 'When are you going home?' I asked, delaying the goodbye.

'Tuesday morning. Tomorrow we have to go to Cowes and Newport on business, and they want Grandpa there. He's a bit of a handful at times, so I have to go along.'

'What are you doing on Monday?' I asked in desperation. I wanted to see her again.

'I don't know yet.'

'How about coming to Yarmouth so I can show you around the *Lily Jade*? It'd have to be in the morning though, we'll be sailing about two.'

'I'd really like that Chris. I'll come if I can, but I can't promise. Now I must go inside and get Grandpa ready for bed. Goodnight.'

We kissed once more and then she was gone. I walked up the hill into Totland, my mind full of "Solent Serenity" and the lady who had given it that name.

* * * * * * *

The others were already on board when I returned to the *Lily Jade* late on Sunday afternoon. The weather had broken and the odd shower swept across the ship, driven by a strong sou' westerly sweeping up the Solent.

'Knew you coming, so make fresh tea,' Soo said, the moment I stepped aboard and into Basil's cabin.

'How the hell did you… ? Oh, never mind. Thanks Soo, I could do with a cuppa.'

'He told us that five minutes ago,' Basil said, raising his hands. 'But don't ask me how he knew.'

'Telementary,' Scotty replied, pouring the tea.

'I think you mean telepathy Scotty.'

'Yeah, that too,' he said, biscuit crumbs spraying through the hole in his teeth.

'Did you both have a good weekend?' I asked.

Scotty smiled. 'Aye, had a wee session in the pub wi' my brother Saturday lunchtime.'

'A "wee session"?'

'Oh aye. We were home for tea by seven – I think. A bit late according to Bill's missus, but never mind.'

'But the pubs shut at three!' Basil chipped in.

Scotty winked. 'They shut the door.'

'How's your mum Basil?' I asked, changing the subject.

'About the same. I doubt she'll see eighty-eight, but at least she's in no pain and recognises everyone.' Soo returned with more tea. 'How about you Chris? Did you have a good time?'

'Captain Chris have big news. I tell by look in eyes.'

'You're too clever by half, Soo!'

'Well dinna' keep us in suspense, Chris.'

'I met a beautiful girl, who talked me into buying a house.'

There was a stunned silence.

'You're no goin' to tell us you're selling the *Lily Jade* and getting married?'

I laughed. 'No Scotty, I doubt I'll ever see Kathy again, although she may come down to the ship on Monday morning, and I bought the house as an investment for my retirement in the distant future.'

'See, big news. Me, no news. Flat ok. Pub curtains ok. Tomato juice bad. All watery!'

'Where's the house?' Basil asked.

'On the cliff-top at Totland. A blue and white building.'

He nodded. 'I know the one. Never been inside it, but the location is wonderful.'

'That's what the agent said before he told me the price.'

'Och, if the skipper needs to save money I can see the quality of the food going downhill. Tell me Soo, what gourmet meal can ye concoct from a loaf of bread and a tin of jam?'

Soo said something in Chinese. 'It good!'

'I knew I should'a kept ma big mouth shut. I can see we'll be on strict rations from now on.'

Soo looked thoughtful. 'Good, but strange taste – like haggis,' he said, smiling at the Scot.

'I don't think I fancy either,' I said. 'We'll stick to our usual menu, even if I don't know how I'm going to pay for the house.'

By 5 P.M. I'd caught up on paperwork and when I stepped out onto the deck beside the funnel the daylight was fading fast as dark clouds swept overhead. The wharf was wet from a recent shower and drips fell from the lamp-post next to the ramp used by the ferry. Beside it stood a large man wearing a French beret, smoke rising from a cigarette dangling between his lips. He appeared to be studying the *Lily Jade* and nodded when I looked at him. I returned the acknowledgement, but he pulled the collar of his serge jacket around his neck, flicked the butt into a puddle and ambled off the wharf.

The next morning I watched a bus pull up at ten o'clock, as I had at nine and nine-thirty, hoping Kathy might've come down to the

Lily Jade, but only a few passengers for the ferry got off. I glanced over the bridgefront. Basil and Soo were down below putting a net over some cartons to secure them before loading the final few boxes that were sitting on the wharf. With a sigh, I went back to my cabin and the fresh paperwork on the desk.

Twenty minutes later I heard the sound of the windlass as the derrick was swung out over the wharf to pick up the remaining boxes.

'Chris! Chris, can you hear me?'

Basil's voice sounded urgent as it drifted up from below me and I wondered what had happened. I had visions of cargo spilt all over the wharf, or worse a major problem with the derrick, but when I looked over the side he was smiling.

'This charming lady wants to know if she has permission to come aboard. I told her she'd have to wait for the Captain to personally escort her across the brow.'

Kathy stood beside him smiling at his words, her dark hair a contrast to the pale blue jumper and woollen skirt she was wearing.

'I'll be right down,' I called laughing.

'She came, she actually came!' I almost fell down the stairs in my haste.

'Welcome aboard the *Lily Jade.*'

Stepping onto the deck her hands gripped my shoulders tightly and we kissed, before she glanced, first into the open hatch where Soo was unhooking a wooden crate from the derrick, then up at the bridge and the green funnel behind it.

'She's lovely, Chris.'

I remembered Kathy knew a little about ships. 'Not exactly the *Queen Mary*, but yes, she's special.'

'She has character: feels almost alive.'

'You really do have an affinity with ships.'

'I saw quite a few like this when I was a child. She brings back memories.'

'Come on, I'll show you around.'

No matter how I tried to string it out, the *Lily Jade* was a small ship and a tour could only last so long. Scotty helped me a bit by telling Kathy technical details about the engine, however, it became obvious pistons and cylinders didn't interest her and we went back on deck.

Standing on the bridge, half watching Basil and Soo secure the last of the cargo, Kathy noticed to the picture on the bulkhead behind the wheel.

'Where did you get that, Chris?'

I looked at the print of the liner. There was something in the tone of her voice I didn't understand, something different from the carefree woman who had come aboard almost half-an-hour ago. 'It was there when I bought the *Lily Jade*,' I said, watching her.

Kathy stared at it before speaking. 'Oh, I see.' Turning back to the hatch with Basil and Soo, she stood in silence for a few moments. 'Thanks, Chris, it's been… just wonderful, but I'd best get back to Grandpa.'

I saw the big man with the beret again as I stared over her shoulder wondering what had changed her mood. Was it something I'd said?

'I'd best go,' she repeated.

'Yes… certainly, Kathy. I understand.'

I led her across the brow onto the wharf and took her in my arms, but her response was lacking her earlier passion, as was the kiss. 'I'd like to see you again,' I said, realising her mind was far away as I spoke. 'You know I'll be here, on the *Lily Jade.*'

'Yes, Chris… Thanks.'

As she walked along the wharf, the big man approached the *Lily Jade*. Kathy stopped and watched as he passed her and then turned to stare back at me. I was about to wave, when I thought I could see tears in her eyes. Before I could call out, she'd walked quickly, almost running, around the corner of the Harbour-Master's office into the town of Yarmouth.

The big man ignored me as he walked past and I wondered if Kathy knew him, as I couldn't think of any connection he might have with the *Lily Jade*.

'All ready to sail, Chris.'

'Thanks Basil.'

I took one last look along the wharf before going aboard, unlashing the brow and going to the bridge.

As we moved off the wharf I wondered if I'd see Kathy again. It seemed a strange way to end a relationship.

Chapter Five

The Indian summer of October came to an abrupt end and by the second week of November winter had arrived with a vengeance. Strong winds, fresh from the North Atlantic, tested the seaworthiness of the *Lily Jade* to the full as we plied up and down the Channel, but she never faltered. The cargoes increased as people along the coast became aware of our regular calls and the colder weather meant there was no problem carrying perishable goods; a cargo I would've had to refuse in warmer months as the refrigeration unit had been put on hold due to the loan restrictions placed upon me by the bank.

By Thursday 18th December the rush for goods before the Christmas break was over and there was only a half load of timber from the mill at Shoreham. Now the winds were coming down from Scandinavia, and, mixed with a few clear nights, the temperatures had dropped well below freezing, bringing the first flurries of snow.

At 0700 I stood on the bridgewing with a mug of tea as the rope around a pack of timber was hooked onto the derrick and Basil lifted it off the wharf. It was about five feet above the ground when the rope slipped along the snow-covered timber, causing it to tilt. The centre portion of the pack shot out and caught under the next pack on the wharf. Basil tried to stop the winch, but the handle jammed on a piece of ice and in the few seconds before he managed to kick the handle to stop, the *Lily Jade* heeled to port some fifteen degrees. The timber came clear and rose off the wharf with a jerk as the ship righted herself, but because the derrick had been lowered out over the wharf, most of the strain came on the topping-lift that raised and lowered it. There was a thud as the derrick jumped, followed by an ominous "crack" of a wire breaking.

'Basil! Look out!' I cried.

He saw the derrick starting to fall and dived to the outboard side of the foc'sle in an attempt to avoid the flying tail of the broken wire as it whipped around the winch drum. The pack of timber split open as it hit the wharf and above it a section of rail was crushed and bent as the derrick came to rest on the ship's side.

'Basil! Are you ok?' I called, running forward, despite the pain in my leg after jumping down the last few steps.

I called again as I went up the steps onto the foc'sle. When he sat up I was horrified. The right side of his face was covered in blood.

'I'm fine, Chris, except I banged my elbow a bit hard.'

'But your face…'

'What?'

He put his hand on his cheek.

'Bloody hell!'

I pressed one of my gloves against his face and gently wiped it. Then I laughed with relief. 'You'll live.'

'What happened? It doesn't hurt.'

'One strand of the wire caught you. It put a thin cut across your cheek to your ear-lobe, that's what's bleeding, your ear! Lucky it missed your eye.'

'Is everyone else alright?'

'Yes. Soo was on the brow. The jerk nearly threw him into the dock, he just got shaken about.'

'Scotty?'

'I haven't seen him. He was down below, but I bet he'll have some complaint.'

'Of course he will. We probably disturbed Agnes!'

'Come on, you daft bugger. Let's get you cleaned up, then we'll have a look at the damage.'

I was washing Basil's face and trying to put a bandage on his ear when Soo arrived with mugs of tea.

'Good you ok, Basil. I go fix derrick.'

'Thanks, Soo. We'll be out there soon.'

'It all ok. I tell Chief he must leave engine to help. He there now.'

'That's a first, Chris, someone telling Scotty what to do!'

'I bet he complained.'

'No. Only say very cold. So Soo make more tea.'

When we arrived, Soo was already up the mast threading a rope through the block, which would be used to lead a new wire into position, and Scotty had a large clamp with a piece of pipe on its handle, trying to prise the bent rail away from the derrick.

I picked up the end of the broken wire, wondering why it had given way, as it was fairly new. Closer examination showed the wire was still in good condition, but had broken very close to the end, where it was clamped to the winch-drum. I could see nothing wrong with the drum as I felt along its greased edge, until something sliced into my finger and I saw blood all over my hand.

Basil heard my yell and came over. 'Not you as well? One of us is bad enough!'

'There's something sharp near the edge of the drum on the casing of the winch,' I said, holding the piece of rag he'd given me tightly around my finger.

Basil carefully cleared away the grease to reveal a crack in the casing and the metal bent inwards. Because the wire had been sitting proud of its groove on the drum as its end led to the clamp, it had rubbed every time the drum had turned, cutting into the strands. The extra jerk on the derrick had been enough to snap it.

We turned our attention to the wooden derrick. Without it, we couldn't handle any cargo. In a couple of hours the topping-lift wire had been re-threaded through the blocks, made fast to the winch-drum and the derrick brought inboard, where it was lowered into its crutch. Amazingly, there appeared to be no damage. Admittedly the wire had snapped at the end, the friction as it slid round the winch-drum slowing the derrick's fall initially, but it would take time to check and test it completely.

Peter Dawson appeared on the wharf. 'Is everybody ok, Chris?'

'Yes, thank you. No more than a scratch and a cut finger. Sorry about the spilt timber.'

'Don't worry; we'll fix that. When are you sailing?'

'It looks as if we'll be here for Christmas, instead of on the island. It'll be easier to get any repairs done.'

'There's no rush. This load's not needed until after New Year. You and the crew best come for a drink at our break-up party tomorrow.'

'Aye, don't mind if we do,' Scotty chimed in, as he straightened part of the bent rail. 'Isn't that right, Chris?'

'I wouldn't dare deprive you of a free drink, Scotty; it'd be more than my life was worth!'

Soo announced he'd made a fresh pot of tea and we mustn't let it go cold.

'So we're staying here for Christmas?'

'Yes, Basil, but I know you are worried about your mum, so feel free to go as soon as we've cleaned up the mess outside.'

I turned to Scotty and Soo. 'What about you two?'

'Well... Bill, my brother in Southampton, did say come over 'cos our cousin Ian is comin' doon from Edinburgh.'

'Heavens! What does Jill – his wife – say about that?'

'Ooch... after last time we thought we'd best try sommat' else. Bill's booked a room in the pub for both of us.'

'And a very Merry Christmas to the landlord – he'll need some cheering up after having you there!'

'That's nay too kind, Basil.' Scotty tried, unsuccessfully, to look offended. 'But I expect Ian and I'll have a couple of celebratory drinks.'

Basil rolled his eyes. 'If it were only a couple!'

Soo had been very quiet. I put my hand on his shoulder. 'How about you, my friend?'

'Not knowing. No longer have flat. *Lily Jade* now home. I stay if allowed.'

'You and I, Soo. I wondered if I would have any power, but I'm sure the Chief will let his senior second engineer run the engine-room and the generator; won't you, Scotty?'

'I dunno know about that.'

'Well I do, Scotty. You're going to Southampton and Soo is taking charge.'

'It's your ship. I'll noo be responsible.'

Soo looked despondent at the Chief's lack of faith, until the Scot's face broke into a wide grin.

'What's the matter, Soo? You know as much as I do about Agnes and her ways. Just don't pinch my job; I've grown to like the *Lily Jade*.'

That evening only Soo and I were left aboard. As we sat in my cabin talking, him with tomato juice and me with a beer, I was to learn he was a complex man, but with simple needs and ambitions.

His childhood was hazy, with vague memories of a squalid existence in Shanghai as a young boy before the family set off on a ceaseless journey seeking a better life, which they never found. They had worked in the paddy fields before trekking to the remote towns along the Silk Road seeking a permanent home. When Soo was twenty they had returned to Shanghai, his parents unable to continue working on the land due to what he called "The Cough".

They'd found a one-room basement that the family had been

forced to share with four other people, and he and his sister had searched for work.

'She was fourteen,' he said. 'Told our parents she had a job in clothing factory. I knew better. No clothing factory pay the money she made. We spent most on medicine for our parents. I tried my hand at anything. Had many jobs, but nothing permanent.'

'After nearly three years my sister became ill,' he continued, with tears in his eyes, 'but it not the cough. It from men around the waterfront. Mother and father now unable to do anything more than feed themselves.'

'One day I walk along the Bund where ships working on river. There was a scream on one vessel and I saw man lying on the deck, his arm broken by block that fell from rigging. The ship was due to sail and needed another man. My family wished me luck and I left them, Shanghai and China.'

With tears in his eyes he relived those memories for a minute or more as I sat in silence, distressed by what I'd heard.

Then he smiled. 'It ok, Captain Chris.'

He had spent his life sailing on any ship that would give him a job, until he was torpedoed twice during the war and allowed to stay in Britain.

'Excited when I come to England. Have cousin here. He also work on ships. Thought him easy to find. But too many people, like China.'

'What do you want to do now?' I asked.

'Simple life. Food and bed for work.' He smiled again. '*Lily Jade*, she good work, thank you Captain Chris. Now have all I want.'

'I can't promise a job for life.'

'Long enough for Soo.'

'What do you mean?'

'Soo not so long to live. Have growth here,' he said, patting his stomach.

'We must get you to a doctor! To hospital, immediately!' I got up ready to take him, but he motioned me to sit down.

'Doctor say nothing he can do.' He patted his stomach again. 'All fine now, no pain. Doctor say ok for one or two years. He not knowing how long. I hope *Lily Jade* sail long enough.'

'I hope *not*. I hope you make a great recovery and outlive the *Lily Jade*.'

'Thank you, Captain Chris, but I happy just to be here as long as possible; to die with *Lily Jade*.'

He poured another tomato juice, took a scrap of folded paper from his pocket and tipped its contents, a fine white powder, into the drink. Stirring it he smiled, showing off the gaping holes between his teeth. 'Making Soo feel good. Like Chief drink beer.'

'Cheers,' I said, raising my glass. I never asked him what the powder was and I didn't want to know. I didn't care if it was illegal. If it made Soo feel good, that was fine by me.

Chapter Six

There was a squeal of brakes on the wharf, followed by the slamming of a car door. It was Friday afternoon, 19th December. Sun shone from a clear sky, but any warmth was dissipated by the strong wind sweeping in from the North.

When I looked over the rail I saw Malcolm standing beside his Rover. 'What are you doing here?' he said. 'I thought you'd sailed yesterday, until I saw the funnel when I drove into town.'

'We had a problem with the derrick.'

'That wind's bitter!' said Malcolm, when he entered the cabin. As he removed his coat something fell from the pocket. 'Oh, these are for you,' he said, picking two envelopes up off the deck.

I looked at the letters. One was postmarked Rotterdam and the other was from a firm of solicitors in London. I ripped open the second.

'At last!'

Malcolm looked up from the cup of tea Soo had brought him.

'They've sold mum and dad's house in London, and for a good price. That'll go a long way to paying for Solent Serenity.'

I poured a cup of tea and picked up the official-looking envelope from Holland. Inside was a single sheet of paper from the Politie, the Dutch police.

'You're very quiet. Is something wrong?'

'I don't think so. The Dutch police are coming to see me and the *Lily Jade* in January. It's to do with the murder of Laurens Oostermeer, a routine enquiry.'

I passed him the letter.

'Jacques Kessel told me about it when I went to Zeebrugge.'

'So, they've never solved the crime?'

'Apparently not.'

Malcolm returned on Christmas Eve. 'Basil rang. He wants to know if you're still sailing to Yarmouth on Saturday.'

'Yes, the derrick's been inspected and tested.'

'It's his mum, she's worse.'

I thought for a moment. 'What are you doing over the weekend?'

'You and Soo are coming for Christmas lunch tomorrow, but nothing else.'

'Fancy a trip? – On pay! I can see you would. I'll ring Basil and tell him to stay at home.'

Soo and I spent Christmas Day with Malcolm, who put on a lunch with all the trimmings. We also heard Basil's mum had rallied sufficiently to enjoy being with her family.

About 4 P.M. Soo seemed to be in pain. Malcolm was worried something had been wrong with the food.

'Nothing wrong. Food extra good, but no good for Soo.' He tapped his stomach. 'Captain Chris know. Soo fix with tomato juice.'

To his glass Soo added the contents of two pieces of paper he took from his pocket. One was the white powder I'd seen before, but the other contained minute grey granules with black specks, like finely ground pepper. Within fifteen minutes Soo's eyes were glazed and distant, although he remained completely coherent and the pain had obviously gone.

Because of our concern with Soo, Malcolm didn't mention what was on his mind until he came to the bridge when we were half-way to Yarmouth.

'Well, Malcolm, you've certainly earned your wages.'

'I've still a lot to learn; I couldn't call myself a seafarer.'

'I couldn't call myself a lawyer.'

'I know, and I'm concerned about that letter you got from Rotterdam.'

'Why?'

'I find it odd, out of character for the judiciary. I can't understand why they didn't ask the British police to contact you if it's just a routine enquiry.'

'You think there may be more to it?'

'I'd be surprised if there wasn't.'

'I've nothing to hide.'

'I know that, but…'

'But, what?'

'I don't know. Can I see the papers you signed when you bought the *Lily Jade?*'

'They're in my cabin, but surely everything is in order. All the maritime boards have agreed to the sale and the transfer fees are all paid.'

'As long as no-one else can lay claim to the *Lily Jade.*'

I stared out at the bow pitching gently into the swell. The thought of losing the *Lily Jade* was unthinkable; she had become that daughter I'd promised Jacques Kessel I would look after. I fetched the papers for Malcolm to examine and we were past Ryde when he returned them to me.

'Everything seems to be in order. I don't understand all the nautical terms, but they're all signed and stamped correctly.'

'What should I do now?'

'Try to have a legal representative there when the Dutch police come to see you.'

'Would you do it?'

'I've just said I don't understand all the nautical terms.'

'But you're a legal man, so why not?'

Malcolm shrugged his shoulders.

We left it at that and resumed his nautical training, which consisted of him taking the wheel while the Captain of the *Lily Jade* made cups of tea. Soo, it seemed, was occupied as senior second engineer.

We arrived in Yarmouth just before 1700. Already it was pitch-black, and the wind made it feel there was more snow on the way. Malcolm had no need to go home until Monday and suggested that we use his car, which had made another voyage, for transport over the weekend.

On Sunday morning Malcolm and I drove round to see Basil. His mum was not good. Christmas seemed to have taken its toll and she was unable to get out of her chair.

'Thanks, Chris for letting me stay home. It'll be a Christmas I'll always remember.'

'That's ok. I had an eager substitute.'

'Sounds as if I could lose my job.'

'Hang on, Basil,' Malcolm interrupted, 'I'm not exactly Horatio Nelson when it comes to nautical matters.'

'I'm sure you'd learn quickly.'

His voice sounded strange, but before I could comment he turned to me.

'I have to tell you, Chris, I received a Christmas card and a long letter from Lee. Depending on the situation here, it may not be too long before I'll be making plans to go back to New Zealand.'

I shook his hand. 'Congratulations. I understand, Basil. You told me that when we started.'

He smiled. 'Where are the others?'

'Down below in the engine-room. Agnes has a cough or something, so it's Doctor Soo to the rescue.'

Basil's brother, Kevin, appeared. 'Why don't you go out for a while; I'll look after mum.'

'Thanks, I'd like to see the house Chris has bought.'

I'd given them a tour of the house and we were standing on the balcony when the grey waters of the Solent turned blue and green as a pale watery sun found a break in the clouds. 'Is New Zealand as beautiful as this?' Malcolm asked.

Basil suddenly seemed far away. 'Just as, and more,' he said. 'The air is so much cleaner. The trees, the hills… everything looks clearer and the colours much brighter. You must come and see it one day.'

'The house is wonderful, Chris,' Malcolm said, as we went down the stairs.

'It will be when I've made all the alterations. Talking of which, while I've got you both here can you give me a hand to lift the new kitchen cupboards into place?'

'I don't know Malcolm, we've been caught again!'

'It might cost him lunch in the pub.'

* * * * * * *

On Monday morning Jim Middleton the Harbour-Master came aboard. 'Belated Merry Christmas, Chris. I expected you here for the festivities. We were hoping you and the crew would be at the yacht-club party.'

'We had trouble with the derrick, but it's all fixed now.'

'Anyway, here's all your usual mail and a couple of Christmas cards as well.'

Some of it was nautical publications, most of it was bills. The first of the two cards had a foreign stamp on the envelope, which I recognised as Belgian. Inside, the card had three sailing ships on it.

Dear Captain Bowden – Christopher,

How are you and the Lily Jade? *I think of you often and wonder how the* Caillou *is going. I know you are looking after her. I look out into the Channel and wonder if one of those specks could be my little ship going past. It is wonderful to have Fleur here with me; everyone needs company when they are old.*

Merry Christmas and safe voyages,

Jacques Kessel and Fleur.

As I picked up the other card I resolved to take a photo of the *Lily Jade* and send it to him. The envelope was post-marked Canterbury, but I didn't recognise the writing. The second card also had a sailing ship on the front, and inside, a short, unexpected message.

I'm sorry I left the way I did. I hope one day we can meet again.

Merry Christmas, Chris.

Thinking of you… Kathy.

The memories of our meeting on the cliff-top and the inspection of Solent Serenity together flooded back. I checked the card and the envelope, but there was no address. Just like the first time we'd met, Kathy had come into my life and then disappeared. At least this time there was the hope of meeting again, but when, or where, I didn't know. I would just have to be patient.

Chapter Seven

Late that morning the cloud broke up leaving everything bathed in sunshine. I took the opportunity to go ashore with my camera, and walked around to the foreshore on the eastern side of Yarmouth to take a photo of the *Lily Jade* for Jacques. I took several and was returning, thinking to finish the film with shots of the crew on board, when in front of me was the big man with the beret. He stepped out of a dinghy, tied it up and stood at the end of the wharf staring at the *Lily Jade* as he waited for the ferry. I decided it was time I deserved an answer.

'You seem fascinated by the ship?'

He turned; surprised he hadn't heard me approach. His steely grey eyes met mine.

He looked at the *Lily Jade* momentarily. 'She is a fine ship: and are you her Captain?'

'Yes,' I said, noting his Continental accent.

'I sailed on Dutch ships during the war – cargo ships to the Far East.'

'And now?'

'Now? Now I have no family or home in Holland. I stayed with friends in Portsmouth until last year when I moved to the island and took a place in Newport.'

'Why the interest in the *Lily Jade?*'

'As I said, a fine ship. I would be better off back at sea. Something I understand better than clipping hedges.'

After my time at the Admiralty I knew what he meant. 'Christopher Bowden,' I said, offering my hand.

'Jean Lubec. Keep me in mind if you need anyone. I'm a good seaman,' he added, smiling.

He turned and walked towards the ferry as it berthed. There had been something about that smile that I found unnerving, as if it held a secret I should know about. Then I remembered another mystery – Kathy's reaction when she'd seen him after visiting the *Lily Jade*. Back on board I re-read her Christmas card with an uneasy, yet unsubstantiated feeling, there was a hidden message she was trying to tell me.

****

New Year came, and with it the Dutch police, who arrived in Shoreham on 8th January. Malcolm was already in my cabin when they came aboard.

'Thank you, Captain for your co-operation. We shall not take any more of your time than is necessary.'

The senior officer was middle-aged and obviously a long-serving member of the Politie, while the eyes of his young accomplice flitted everywhere as he took a continuous series of notes.

'Can you tell me what this is all about?' I asked.

'Just a few routine questions, plus we shall have to search the ship.'

'Looking for what?' Malcolm interrupted.

'And you are sir?'

'Malcolm Chatwin, the Captain's legal advisor and I feel it's necessary for you to have a search warrant if you wish to examine the ship. It would be expected from the British police.'

The senior officer held up a piece of paper. 'I believe this will satisfy your requirements sir. Issued at Scotland Yard.'

'If you could tell us exactly what you are looking for,' I said, 'maybe we could help you.'

'Exactly, Captain, at the moment we are unsure. Firstly, what do you know about Laurens Oostermeer?'

I decided not to mention Jacques Kessel. 'I read about his murder; it must be a year ago.'

'And this vessel?'

'Yes, according to the documents, my ship belonged to him at one time; during the war I believe.'

'Did you ever meet him?'

'Laurens Oostermeer? No'

'Or his wife?'

'No, I've never met either of them.'

'Have you ever had any contact with the Dutch ministry of transport?'

'No, I've never been to Holland.'

'Thank you, Captain, you have been most helpful. Now if we could just look around the vessel?'

Their examination of the *Lily Jade* proved to be thorough. They almost pulled the tiny stores locker in the foc'sle apart before opening every cupboard in the accommodation and driving Scotty mad as they poked and prodded around "Agnes".

'She'll no like all this muckin' about. I hope she'll no get upset.'

'Easy Scotty,' I said, 'it's only you getting upset.'

Returning from their inspection they had a few more questions. Had I ever had a bank account in Holland? Was the *Lily Jade* the only vessel I'd owned or been involved with? When I told them all my previous nautical experience had been with the Royal Navy they seemed to lose interest and left almost immediately. We stood and watched as they walked along the wet wharf past the end of the timber mill.

'I'm none the wiser why they came all the way from Rotterdam,' Malcolm said, 'but I do know it was the Lily Jade they were interested in and not you, at least not at the moment. What they were looking for I have no idea.'

Those words repeated themselves time and time again in my mind after we left Shoreham. What were they looking for? Malcolm had promised to make a few discreet enquires through legal contacts in Holland and, although I had nothing to hide, I wanted to erase the shadow that now hung over myself and the *Lily Jade*.

* * * * * * *

Just over two weeks later on Saturday 24th January, I'd been to the post office in Totland to send off the photos of the *Lily Jade* to Jacques when I saw Basil coming up the road from the pier. Although it was cold, he appeared flushed and obviously didn't see me until the last moment.

'Basil?'

'Oh, Chris, it's you. She's gone, Chris – last night.'

'I'm sorry.' His eyes were red. 'You were very close, weren't you?'

He nodded and I thought the tears were about to return.

'Can I help?'

He shook his head. 'No, I just need to look up some phone numbers. There are several people I have to tell about mum.'

I went with him to the house, where he and his brother had things to sort out. 'Come down to the ship afterwards, if you want to,' I said. 'You may like to get out for a few hours.'

He arrived just after four and Scotty made a big play of arguing with Soo over something trivial down below, just to ease the tension. Then we all went to the pub.

I don't think any of us remembered much about that evening, not even Soo, who must've drunk pints of tomato juice laced with powders. I do vaguely remember Basil and I making sure Scotty didn't fall into the dock as he crossed the brow onto the *Lily Jade*, but nothing else.

When I awoke at 6 A.M. Basil had gone, leaving a note of thanks on my bedside table. We sailed to Weymouth and Fowey on Monday, leaving him to organise the funeral, which we attended when we returned the following weekend.

The mood aboard the *Lily Jade* during the next two weeks matched the miserable weather of rain, cold winds and sleet. It was 19th February and we were in Shoreham when Basil told me New Zealand House had organised a working passage to Auckland for him on the cargo ship *Port Napier*, sailing from London by the end of the month, and that he was to join immediately.

'I'm sorry to leave so quickly, Chris. It's not fair on you, after all you've done for me.'

'Go, Basil. Go and make your new life with Lee in New Zealand. One day I'll come out and see you both.'

'Please do. I'll never forget the *Lily Jade* and our times together. She's a very special ship.'

'To both of us.'

He took his bags across the brow to the waiting taxi, opened the door and then stood in the rain looking back to me.

'By the way, Chris,' he called. 'I hear there's a good seaman available who lives in Newport, a man called Jean Lubec. Thanks, and good luck.'

As the taxi disappeared towards the railway station, I wondered how Basil had known about the big man with the beret who kept coming into my life.

Chapter Eight

I didn't have to go looking for Jean Lubec. He came to me, knowing Basil had left. I felt uneasy, but I needed another crew member and a professional seaman like Lubec was hard to find.

'Welcome aboard Jean. I hope you'll be happy here.'

'I know I will, Captain.'

There was that smile again. I was sure I was imagining things, but it unnerved me. I think it unnerved Scotty as well when they met an hour later.

'Aye, it's good to meet you Jean. Well, with a big fella' like you on deck I'll no be needing to start the generator to work cargo. You could push that derrick around by hand. What do ye reckon, Chris? With the money we save you could send Soo up the road for a few extra goodies.' He laughed, and poked me in the ribs.

Jean smiled and Scotty stopped laughing.

'Ok, so ye need the power, but you have to admit there's plenty of ye?'

'True and it's been a great asset over the years, even if it got me into trouble ashore a few times.'

Soo arrived with tea and coffee.

'Hey, why the coffee?' Scotty asked. 'Are we getting short on tea?'

'New man Jean. He drink only coffee.'

'Do you?'

Jean nodded at Scotty.

'How did you know? You're like me, you've never met Jean.'

'I meet now. Hello Jean, I Soo. Please drink coffee while hot.'

'Good to meet you Soo. I've sailed with many Chinese crews.'

'See, Chief. Jean from Europe. He drink coffee.'

'I could do with your muscles down below Jean.'

'Hang on, Scotty,' I said, 'you can't have everyone down below, there's not enough room, for a start.'

'Yes, I know, but sometimes I could do with a strong person down there.'

Soo looked distraught.

'And what's the matter with you, you inscrutable Chinaman.'

'Chief no want me below. Me not strong like Jean.'

'Don't be daft; you know you're the second engineer. Apart from which, Jean here could never get to the pumps behind "Agnes". He's too big!'

Soo jumped up and down laughing. 'I catch him, Captain Chris. I catch Chief this time!'

I almost knocked over my cup of tea as I laughed with him. 'The tables are turned, Scotty.'

'And I thought we were friends,' Scotty said seriously, before breaking into a raucous laugh.

Jean remained quiet.

'Don't mind these two,' I said, 'it goes on all the time.'

'A Chinese officer, that's something new to me,' he said, smiling at Soo.

Soo stopped laughing, collected the tea things and left. Suddenly the mood had changed.

'Best I have a look around on deck,' Jean said, picking up his beret.

When he'd gone Scotty shook his head. 'Seems a nice enough chap, but somehow I find him a bit odd.' He shrugged his shoulders as he got up to leave. 'It's probably just me.'

After he'd gone I stood looking down at the wharf and I knew it wasn't just Scotty.

That afternoon we slipped the lines and headed out into the Solent. It was only four days since Basil had gone to London, but already I sensed a different atmosphere on board. Even Soo was quiet.

During the short run to Weymouth the big man seemed capable of running the deck side of the operation single-handedly. He renewed a rope on the brow, cleaned up the foc'sle and had the derrick up all ready for cargo as we approached the berth. As Basil had said, he was a fine seaman, but he seemed a loner. He didn't even join me for a cuppa.

The following morning in Weymouth he came to see me.

'Captain, may I go ashore for a couple of hours? I have some business to attend to.'

'Of course, Jean, and please call me Chris like the others do. This isn't the Royal Navy.'

Again, that smile.

'Thanks, Chris.'

The trip to Fowey and back to the island was uneventful, with little cargo due to the winter weather, and I hoped the cargoes would improve with the onset of spring as I still had the mortgage to pay on "Solent Serenity". Back in Yarmouth I went up to Totland and did a little bit of work on the house. When I returned late Sunday afternoon Jean was tying up a dinghy, as he had done the day I'd taken the photos for Jacques.

I caught up with him as he headed back to the *Lily Jade*. 'Is that your boat?'

'Er, no. It belongs to a friend of mine.'

He seemed thoughtful for a moment.

'I just went out to check his lobster-pot.' He smiled. 'Sorry, Chris, nothing for the table tonight.'

Slowly trade picked up, and as we plied up and down the coast life aboard settled into a routine. One Thursday evening in Fowey we all got together in my cabin and over a few drinks Jean began to relate stories of his life at sea in Dutch ships.

'Tell me,' said Scotty after several beers, 'those women in Panama, were they slim or fat?'

For the first time Jean laughed. 'They were slim, Scotty, and they adored all white men, especially those with Yankee dollars.'

'Aye, I can imagine that.'

'What can you imagine, Scotty?' I asked. 'The Yankee dollars or the women?'

'Och, ye know I'm a clean-living soul.' He looked disappointed. 'Why would ye ask such a question?'

Soo laughed first, and then we all joined him. 'Chief no catch us this time, Captain Chris.'

After that there were several evenings when we gathered in my cabin and listened to Jean's tales. He was a good story-teller who had travelled to all parts of the globe and his experiences of storms and exotic ports came to life, having us on the edge our seats one minute and collapsing with laughter the next. By comparison my days in the Royal Navy seemed quite mundane.

One, Monday towards the end of April, when we arrived in Weymouth there was an Austin Sheerline waiting at our berth. A woman with mousy hair, wearing an apple green coat and a hat with a feather in it stood by the rear door watching the ship berth. From the foc'sle Jean waved to her.

Leaving my cabin to visit the Harbour Master, I saw Jean engaged in conversation with the woman. They noticed me crossing the brow as I went ashore and their voices went quiet.

'Vivian, this is Captain Chris Bowden.'

'Pleased to meet you,' I said, shaking her hand. She had a firm and determined grip, which matched her facial features.

'Vivian and her husband live in Portsmouth. They've come down to take me out.'

Vivian saw me glance towards the car, which was empty. 'My husband is up in the town, we'll join him shortly.'

I nodded. 'I'll see you tomorrow Jean, goodbye.' By the time I reached the Harbour-Master's office at the end of the quay, the car had disappeared.

Waiting in the outer room it occurred to me Vivian and her husband had made a long drive from Portsmouth to see Jean in Weymouth. I was trying to calculate the distance when the door opened and the familiar face appeared.

'Captain Bowden, do come in.'

I forgot all about Vivian and Jean. It was none of my business anyway.

It became the one night each voyage when it was just Scotty, Soo and I aboard. Every second Monday when we were in Weymouth Jean always went ashore as soon as everything was set up for cargo the following morning. They were quiet evenings, apart from the odd quip between Scotty and Soo, and I know the three of us looked forward to those nights to reflect upon our times together aboard the *Lily Jade*.

During the days that followed, both in port and at sea, Jean Lubec continued to prove he was an accomplished seaman and I knew, not only was the *Lily Jade* in safe hands when he was on the bridge, but all the cargo gear would always be in perfect order.

Although they worked well together; when on deck, Soo just did as the big man asked without question – as if his authority to initiate changes had been overruled. Instead, his spontaneous inventiveness created homely touches inside the accommodation. We all got new curtains in our cabins, he knocked out a cupboard one corner of the galley to create a small mess room and from scrap timber he made a table and a bench seat that he covered in a Chinese-style material he got from, I know not where. Other items appeared as he turned the *Lily Jade* into "his home", which he had talked to me about that night in Yarmouth.

Chapter Nine

Malcolm came down to see me nearly every time we were in Shoreham, but early in May, it must have been about the 7th, he seemed excited as he entered my cabin.

'Have I got some interesting news for you!'

I raised my eyebrows.

'It's about those Dutch police.'

Soo came in with a tray. 'You need strong tea for important news you have for Captain Chris.'

'How did you …?'

'You come aboard all excited. Soo see.'

'Some things don't change,' I said, 'you can't fool Soo.'

'I wouldn't try.'

'Well?' I asked, after Soo had gone.

'It appears the Dutch minister for transport until last year, a man by the name of Peter Van Maarden, authorised payment of government funds to Laurens Oostermeer for the rebuilding of his fleet after the war. However, not all the funds reached Oostermeer's bank account and the files with the allocations have gone missing. Van Maarden can't account for the discrepancy and awkward questions are starting to be asked.'

'How does that affect me?'

'Van Maarden is trying to prove Oostermeer obtained the extra money under false pretences and spent it on... who knows what. It could be the reason he was murdered'

'But why the interest in the *Lily Jade*?'

'Because it once belonged to Oostermeer and was the only vessel of his not sent overseas that survived the war. Whoever murdered him found nothing, or not what they were looking for, so the Dutch authorities have been told to examine the alternatives.'

'But I only bought the ship.'

'I know, but Van Maarden is desperate to clear his name, or cover something up and is using his political influence to persuade the police to find a suspect and close the case. That's why I need to see every piece of paper you have relating to the *Lily Jade*.'

'You're serious, aren't you?'

'Deadly. Any connection they could find between you and Oostermeer could see you in trouble, or they might try to seize the ship.'

'Did anyone mention Jacques Kessel, the man who owned the *Lily Jade*?'

'I'm afraid he's had a pretty rough time from the authorities. He and his sister have spent a lot of time with the police.'

'His sister Fleur? She was Laurens Oostermeer's wife, you know?'

Malcolm's eyes widened. 'No wonder they've been the prime suspects. That's the direct link to you and why the Dutch police came over here.'

'Why would I be a suspect?'

'You're not. As I said in January, they came to see the *Lily Jade*, not you. It seems they have few options. Laurens Oostermeer and, as I now know Fleur, had one child, but he was killed in the war. The only people left with family connections are Jacques, Fleur and maybe her sister, Yvette, who lived in Austria for many years, but now no-one can find her, so she may no longer be alive. You, especially as you own the last surviving ship of Oostermeer's original fleet, are the next link, together with the companies who have bought the new tonnage.'

'Almost sounds as if I'm guilty until proven innocent?'

'Not quite, but give me all the papers concerning the *Lily Jade* again. I'll have a closer look at the details. Meanwhile, during the next ten days until you get back to Shoreham, look around the ship. Search everywhere, like they did.'

'Looking for what?'

'Old paperwork from before you bought the *Lily Jade*, or anything else that might give a clue as to what they're looking for. I have no idea what it could be.'

I remembered Jacques Kessel's words: "There was no money – it seemed they were looking for something special."

After we left Shoreham I started a systematic search of the *Lily Jade*. Although I told no-one what I was doing, it was inevitable Scotty, Soo and Jean would realise I was looking for something. After we sailed from Weymouth, Jean came up to take over the bridge as we passed the end of the Chesil Beach.

'Can I help you find whatever it is you're looking for, Chris?'

'The trouble is I don't *know* what I'm looking for, well not exactly. The Dutch police are looking for something to solve the murder of a man called Oostermeer.'

Jean stared for'd for several seconds without saying a word before picking up some small stones on the bridgefront. He put them in his pocket and a familiar clacking sound, I'd heard several times before, started as he jiggled them like worry beads.

'Did you know this Oostermeer?' he asked, still staring beyond the bow of the *Lily Jade*.

'Not personally, just that he once owned this ship.'

He turned and smiled. 'So, what are you looking for?'

'Anything connected with the *Lily Jade* when she was owned by him; possibly some old papers or a log book, anything to help the Dutch police understand I'm not connected with the crime in anyway.'

'Are you a suspect?'

'I don't think so, not at the moment, but a high-ranking government official is using his position to try and close the case.'

'I'll check my cabin. When we get to Fowey and the hold is empty we'll take Soo down and the three of us can search it thoroughly.'

The ever-efficient Jean I thought. 'Thanks, I appreciate the help,' I said, and left him clacking his stones. I went to find Soo and Scotty. I would be stupid not to enlist their help as well, which was proved by their reaction to the news.

'Soo and I'll check every wee nook and cranny down below. There'll no be anything hiding from us.'

'I check galley and all cupboards. No let foreign men put Captain Chris in jail.'

During the next week the *Lily Jade* was searched from stem to stern. It was on the way back to Yarmouth Scotty and Soo emerged from down below triumphantly waving some papers.

'We found these at the back of an old cupboard, Chris. Well, actually, Soo found them.'

'They slip down behind drawer. Very old. All in strange writing.'

'He means it's in German or Dutch or something. I can't understand it.'

At the top of the first page were some numbers, which may have been a date in August 1943 and below it there was a column of figures alongside some old-fashioned writing from a foreign country. I showed it to Jean, who said he thought it was German, but he could only make out a few words.

'It appears,' Malcolm said, a couple of weeks later, 'that the engineer of the ship had some work done on "Agnes" that was approved by the Nazis as they needed a vessel this size to take military equipment up the Rhine to Cologne.'

'Nothing of importance, but at least you've checked the ship and

I've passed on the useless information to Rotterdam. Now, maybe they'll leave you alone.'

We heard nothing more from Holland, and to be honest, I began to forget the whole affair. It was now the end of May, the cold weather was behind us and the *Lily Jade* was running eighty per cent full most of the time.

It had been a good voyage from Fowey and at 0530 on Monday 25th May, as we left the Needles lighthouse abeam to starboard, the sun was already reflecting off the calm waters of the Solent with the promise of the first hot day of the year. On the cliff top at Totland Bay I could pick out *Solent Serenity* through the binoculars and below it, moored to the pier, was a modern motor cruiser.

'Have a look at that, Jean,' I said, as the big man appeared with a mug of tea. 'There's a lot of money tied up at the pier this morning.'

The shining white hull and timber upper works reflected in the still water. She looked a powerful craft, certainly one I'd never seen before around the island.

Jean took a casual look; he'd probably seen many such boats in his travels and was about to return the glasses when he suddenly re-focused them and studied the vessel more closely.

'Nice looking craft. Looks more suited to Monaco than here.' He smiled and handed back the binoculars. 'Best I go and get the derrick ready.'

After he'd gone I took another look at the sleek vessel. I studied her fine bow line and then swung the binoculars aft. In the well deck at the stern I caught a glimpse of a woman who made my heart jump as she disappeared into the accommodation. The dark hair and silhouette of the face in the early morning light – for a moment I thought it was Kathy. I rubbed my eyes and looked again, but this time all I saw was a tall man, whose mane of silver hair shone brightly in the sunlight. He stood and stared at the *Lily Jade* as we steamed towards Colwell Bay and the final reach into Yarmouth. A woman's head appeared. It wasn't the one I'd seen before, but somehow it was vaguely familiar.

Soo served up breakfast for everyone after we berthed.

'Did you recognise that boat at the pier?' I asked.

Jean shook his head. 'I've never seen it before.'

Scotty and Soo looked bewildered. 'An expensive motor cruiser tied up at Totland pier,' I explained. 'I thought for a moment I'd seen Kathy, the lady I met last year when I bought the house.'

'Ye not sure?'

'It was only a quick glimpse, and I've never seen the boat before.'

'Och, Soo, I worry when the deck department start losing their eyesight, us down below an' all!' He laughed and toast crumbs sprayed across the table.

The day grew hot, the temperature climbing to an unseasonable eighty-two degrees, making work uncomfortable. Our clothes clung to us as we discharged china clay and pieces of sandstone and although we took turns to go down the hold, we were all exhausted when we finished at 1630.

I changed my clothes and caught a bus to Totland. The sea breeze that greeted me at the cliff top was welcome, but I was still looking forward to a bath once I reached the house.

With just a towel around my waist I pushed open the double doors and went out onto the balcony. The dust and sweat washed away, I stood smelling the perfume of the surrounding vegetation as I gazed out over the Solent. Suddenly, there it was, that motor cruiser cutting through the water at a speed I estimated to be over fifteen knots. It was too far away to see anyone on board and in a few minutes it disappeared around the headland into Alum Bay. It made me wonder again about the dark-haired lady I'd seen aboard her that morning.

It was late, but still light when I returned to Yarmouth and the *Lily Jade* that evening. Silhouetted in the last rays of the sun I saw a dinghy pulling away from the harbour and recognised the bulk of the person rowing. Jean Lubec was off to check his lobster-pot.

Chapter Ten

The long days of summer brought full cargoes and working hours that sometimes extended into the evening twilight and, although everyone seemed happy to be busy in the warm weather, Scotty and Soo had retreated into their shells. The overpowering influence of Jean Lubec had destroyed the team atmosphere we'd created when Basil was on board, no matter how hard I tried to restore it. Not that I could fault his professional ability. The man had the *Lily Jade* operating at maximum efficiency and would've even organised the engine-room if Scotty and Soo hadn't made sure no-one, not even I, invaded that domain.

During the next two months the *Lily Jade* plied up and down the coast almost without a hitch, the ticking of Agnes' pistons down below in tune with the clacking of the stones in Jean Lubec's pocket.

'Good morning, Captain Bowden. Did you have a good voyage back from Shoreham?'

'Yes thank you, sir.'

Initially addressing each other in an official manner after each voyage was a small piece of protocol the Yarmouth Harbour-Master and I had maintained since the *Lily Jade* started her regular route.

Protocol over, I continued. 'I managed to get that piece of stone for you Jim. I think you'll like it, the colour variations are just what you wanted.'

'Thanks, Chris. I've been looking forward to building that fountain in the front garden since Easter.'

I handed Jim Middleton all the regular paperwork as he passed over the mail. 'Can't you find anything except bills for me, Jim?'

'Just this.' He took a scrap of paper from under a brass weight shaped like a ship's wheel. 'Telephone numbers for you to ring.'

There were two numbers scribbled down. 'Do you know what this is about?'

'All I can tell you is the lady sounded pleasant but upset. She said it was urgent.'

'When did she ring?'

'Last Friday, 17th July.'

'No name or anything?'

'No, just the numbers. Go and use the phone in the other office, I think she'd appreciate the call.'

Jim had written "work" against the second number and as it was 10 A.M. on Monday I dialled that one first. A man answered and I gave him my name explaining I had a message to ring a lady at that number.

'That must be Katherine, just a minute.'

It was several seconds before I heard the receiver being picked up.

'Chris, is that you?'

'Kathy?'

'Yes, Chris, it's me.'

'I never twigged when that chap said Katherine. Thanks for the Christmas card. How are you?'

'I'm ok.'

'It's wonderful to hear from you. Are you coming down to the island?'

'Chris, can I ask you a question?'

'A question? Yes, of course.'

'Chris, where did you get the *Lily Jade?*'

'The *Lily Jade?* I bought her from a chap in Belgium.'

'You sent him a photo of her, didn't you? You sent a photo to Jacques Kessel?'

'Yes, Jacques. Do you know him?'

'He was my grandfather.'

'Your grandfather! Isn't that the greatest coincidence? It really is a small world. I…' Suddenly her words sank in. 'Did you say *was?*'

'Yes, Chris. He died last week.'

Jacques Kessel dead? It seemed impossible that wise, understanding man was no longer with us. 'I'm so sorry Kathy. What happened?'

'He was an old man, Chris. I think he'd lost the will to live. A lot had happened in his life recently.'

'You mean the loss of Beatrice?'

'He told you?'

'Yes, and I also know he's been hassled by the Dutch police over Laurens Oostermeer's death since Christmas.'

'How did you know …?'

'The Dutch police talked to me about it as well, so I had a friend of mine make some enquiries to make sure I wouldn't lose the *Lily Jade.*'

There was silence before I heard a deep sigh.

'Chris, I know I shouldn't ask this, but could you come to the funeral with me? I need someone at the moment and, from what you've just said, I think we should have a talk.'

'When is it?'

'On Wednesday, in Zeebrugge. We would have to catch the ferry from Dover tomorrow afternoon.'

****

As we sat on deck in the late afternoon sunshine during the crossing to Ostend, I sought the answer to something that had been puzzling me since I'd put the phone down the previous day. 'How did you know the *Lily Jade* had been owned by your grandfather?'

'I went to see him in June, when he first became ill. He always had lots of photos of ships, so I didn't take much notice. Also, they were in black and white so there was nothing to remind me about the colour of the hull or the funnel. There was a faded photo stuck on the front of one picture that showed Laurens Oostermeer giving grandfather a birthday present several years ago on the deck of a small ship. At the time, because I was worried about him, it didn't register. It was only last week when I heard he was dying, I thought about that visit and the photo came to mind. It was the present Laurens Oostermeer was giving him. It was the print of a liner, the one on the bulkhead behind the wheel on the *Lily Jade*.'

Kathy put her head in her hands for a few seconds and when she looked up a tear trickled down her cheek. 'I wish I could've seen him again before he died. What else did my grandfather tell you?'

'He wanted to meet me and tell me why he was selling the *Lily Jade*, the *Caillou* as it was then. He loved the ship and wanted to make sure I would look after her.' I related the story Jacques Kessel had told me that day.

'I don't understand why my grandfather was given such a hard time by the police.'

'It may be something to do with a government official by the name of Van Maarden. He, or someone else, is putting pressure on the police to wind up the Oostermeer case.'

'I wonder why? It was just a robbery that ended in murder.'

'But a strange robbery. Your grandfather said they didn't take jewellery or silver. They were looking for something special.'

'They must've been after cash.'

'Which they didn't find. Jacques told me Laurens Oostermeer was deep in debt. The new ships hadn't been paid off. There was no money.'

'I heard Fleur had sold all the ships.'

'Only to pay the bills.'

'Poor Fleur.' Kathy shook her head. 'How will she survive?'

'Your grandfather said Laurens had told her she would always be comfortable, but he didn't know what had been left for Fleur, it certainly wasn't money.'

'Maybe the robbers knew?'

'It's quite possible, but I don't think they found whatever it was. That could be the reason he was murdered.'

'Do you think this Van Maarden is involved?'

'Not directly, but I'm only guessing.'

The sun went behind a cloud and I put my arm round Kathy's shoulder to protect her from the cool breeze that swept across the water. Her head rested on my chest in silence for a while before she looked up.

'Thanks for coming, Chris. I felt so alone.'

She pulled my head down and we kissed as the sun reappeared. She smiled, the golden strands in her auburn hair shining in the early evening light. We kissed again, our tongues entwined and her hands squeezed my shoulders. We sat holding each other close for several minutes before Kathy asked a strange question.

'How well do you know your new man, Jean Lubec?'

'I know he's a first-rate seaman who has experienced life around the world; but how did you know he was a member of our crew?'

'I've seen him before. That's one reason I left in such a hurry that day in Yarmouth when I saw him hanging around the *Lily Jade*.'

'Is there something I should know?'

'I'm not sure. He's a friend of my aunt and I've never trusted her. I'm sure they're up to something. He came to see her at the cottage, when I first met you last year. He seemed... devious. Made sure I didn't hear anything.'

I remembered the lady from Portsmouth who arrived in the big Austin. 'Your aunt, is her name Vivian?'

'Yes, how on earth…'

'She came to pick up Jean one day, when we were in Weymouth.'

Kathy's eyes widened. 'When?'

'About the end of April, I think.'

'So that's why I had to bring grandpa down to Freshwater, after that meeting.'

I was puzzled. 'You came to the island?'

Kathy nodded. 'In May. That's when I found out Jean Lubec was working on the *Lily Jade*.'

I remembered the boat at the pier. 'So that *was* you I saw on an expensive motor cruiser at Totland pier?'

'I was only there for two hours. They wanted grandpa to look at something. I asked him what it was when I took him home to Canterbury, but he wouldn't tell me. I saw you go past, but Marcos ordered me inside.'

'A tall man with silver hair?'

'Yes, Vivian's husband.'

'Does he own that boat?'

'I think so – it's new.'

'He must have plenty of money. It'd be worth three or four times as much as the *Lily Jade*.'

'I wish I knew what was going on, Chris.'

'Why do they need your grandpa?'

'I don't know. He lives in Canterbury with me where I work as a vet. When I get a call to take him to see Aunt Vivian he always wants to go, but he'll never tell me what it's all about.'

As the Belgian coast became a firm line and buildings started to appear we stood by the rail, our arms over each other's shoulders watching the arrival at Ostend. It seemed we both had many questions, but no answers.

It was almost dark when the train arrived in Zeebrugge, and Kathy went to ring Fleur as soon as we'd booked into our hotel in The Kustlaan beside the railway.

'Fleur wants to see us. She asked if we could go back to the house after the funeral.'

We went to a little café on the Zeegeulstraat overlooking the canal where the street lights reflected in the water as we sat outside that warm evening. Over a light supper we talked about things other than the *Lily Jade* or why we were here in Zeebrugge. We spoke of our childhood, strange happenings at school and early days in our chosen careers of veterinary surgery and the Royal Navy.

A local church struck midnight. 'We must go, Chris. Suddenly I'm exhausted.'

We ambled back to The Kustlaan, arms around each other's waist. At the hotel, I unlocked her door before turning to take Kathy in my arms. I could feel our bodies in close contact, her perfume invading my nostrils and I forgot about everything except this woman who had aroused my senses.

She looked up. 'Thank you for being here, you gentle, kind man.'

We kissed again, long and passionately, our bodies pressed hard together.

'Dearest Kathy.'

She looked up 'Oh Chris, … Chris.' Holding me by the arms she leant against the door, which opened and she fell backwards, dragging me with her. We landed on the bed laughing, before locking in an embrace that threatened to squeeze the life out of both of us.

I took her head in my hands, gently stroking her cheek and the auburn hair that had fallen across it. 'Time for sleep, you gorgeous girl, before you drive me insane.'

'Permission to drive you insane in the near future, Captain?' she asked, giving me a mock salute and a wry smile.

'Permission granted... and insanity requested.'

* * * * * * *

The service was to be held in the nearby church on Heistraat in the centre of town and there was already a large crowd gathered in the square when we arrived the following morning. Jacques Kessel, it appeared, had been a man well regarded in the local community, which did not surprise me even though I'd only met him once. We found Fleur.

'Oh, Kathy, my sweet girl. Thank you for coming. As I said, I need to see you afterwards.'

'It'll be our pleasure. Fleur, please meet Captain Chris Bowden.'

'Captain Bowden, it's an honour and a privilege to meet you, knowing Jacques was so pleased it was you who bought the *Caillou*. He loved that ship.'

'As I do.'

'I know, and thank you for that, because it made Jacques' final days happy in the knowledge his precious ship was in good hands.'

'But you, Fleur?' Kathy asked. 'What will you do now?'

Fleur gave Kathy a hug. 'My dear child, let's talk about such things afterwards, at the house. Now I must go and talk to all these people.'

We were left alone holding hands and I started to study the architecture of the church, when suddenly my hand was squeezed so tight I almost cried out in pain.

'Chris!'

'Kathy, what's the matter?' I asked, looking down and pulling her towards me.

'Over there – that car, it's Aunt Vivian and Marcos.'

Stopped across the square, away from the church, was a silver Mercedes. It was a large convertible in immaculate condition with red leather seats, obviously obtained from the remains of the Third Reich. Standing by the driver's door was the tall man with a mane of silver hair, I now knew as Marcos. In the passenger seat, powdering her nose sat the lady I recognised as Aunt Vivian.

'Chris, I don't want them to see me. They haven't come here because they respected my grandfather.'

She clung to me, and I held her close, this woman I now felt was more than just a casual friend. As we watched, a young man with blonde hair approached the Mercedes and started a conversation with Marcos.

'It can't be!' Kathy stared in disbelief, forgetting she might be seen. 'It's Simeon!'

'Simeon?'

'My brother. I thought he was in South Africa. Grandpa got him a job out there when he was working for De Beers, the diamond company.'

I looked back at the ex-Nazi vehicle. The young man began to walk away from the car, and then suddenly, before I knew it, Kathy had left me and was hurrying to cut him off in a back street behind the square.

Following, I found them talking in a doorway on Zeemanstraat. It appeared to be an agitated conversation, with lots of arm waving and I decided not to interfere, pretending to look in a shop window. As Kathy returned to the square it was obvious her mind was far away as she passed within twenty feet of me, oblivious of my presence. Using another street, I went back to the church door and waved to her as she looked around for me.

'Is everything alright?'

She nodded, but I knew it wasn't.

Inside the church I sensed Kathy was using the silence to reflect on whatever had been said with Simeon.

To me the service seemed fairly simple, with just a couple of variations on a Catholic service in England, except I couldn't understand a word. Afterwards the casket was loaded into the hearse and followed by a car with Fleur and some close friends to a cemetery along the coast, close to Blakenberge, where Jacques had lived.

At the station we had twenty minutes to wait for the local train.

'Did you catch up with Simeon?'

'Yes, I think he was more surprised to see me.' She swivelled on the seat and clutched my arm. 'Chris, something is going on and no-one will tell me anything. Please don't leave me; I'm starting to feel scared.'

'I'll be here. Do you want to tell me about it?'

'As I said, Simeon was surprised to see me, but when I said I thought he was still in South Africa and asked him what he was doing here he told me it was private business and turned the conversation to general matters, such as my work and asking if I was still living in mum and dad's house.'

'That doesn't sound too scary.'

'It was when I mentioned I'd seen him with Marcos and Aunt Vivian. He became upset. He told me to keep away and not to interfere. Not to try and contact him, that there was nothing I could do. Then he asked about grandpa. After that he left me standing there, but at the corner he turned round, pointed a finger at me and yelled: "stay out of it Katherine, if you don't want to get hurt".'

From the station at Blakenberge we took a bus a couple of miles out of town, before walking along the gravel track towards the cliffs and the pale blue house I remembered, with the leadlight porthole set into the front door.

'Do come in, the pair of you.'

'Fleur, are you alright? It's not too soon is it?'

'My dear, life must go on. I knew Jacques was dying weeks ago, I did most of my grieving then.'

We sat in the back room overlooking the sea and Fleur brought tea for us and coffee for herself, together with a plate of home-made biscuits. 'Thank you both for coming. I know you have to go back to England so I really wanted to see you before I left.'

'You're leaving?' Kathy asked.

'My dear, this is Jacques' house and although I was fond of my brother, I couldn't live surrounded by ships and the sea; it would be a constant reminder of the same life I spent with Laurens. No, I shall go and live with my sister, Yvette.'

I almost mentioned Austria, but thought better of it. It would seem as if I'd been snooping on the family.

'She has a house near the town of Vianden in Luxembourg.'

No wonder, I thought, Malcolm's enquires had failed to find her in Austria.

'Now, Kathy, my dear, I want you to have all those pieces of jewellery and other family items Jacques would have left to your mother, Giselle. I know he would have wanted you to have them.'

I took my cup of tea, went to the window and stared out over the sea while the two talked about the family heirlooms. I thought about Jacques Kessel and what a wonderful house this was for an ex-seafarer. It crossed my mind to ask Fleur how much she wanted for it, until I remembered I was still paying off Solent Serenity.

That took my mind back to the *Lily Jade* and I wondered how the voyage to Weymouth and Cornwall was going. I wasn't worried; my little ship was in good hands. I smiled to myself, because I knew Jacques Kessel was up there watching over her as well.

'Captain Bowden.'

My thoughts were interrupted.

'Captain Bowden, while Kathy is looking through those boxes, would you come with me, please.'

I followed the sprightly old lady, who seemed to have complete control over life, into the hallway.

'Captain Bowden, would you like to have this picture of the *Caillou*? It seems only fitting since you now own her.'

She took the picture down from the wall and removed a small photograph stuck to the frame. 'I'd like to keep this; it's a good photo of Laurens.'

'Of course, and thank you. The picture will hang in my cabin as a reminder of the *Lily Jade's* early years.'

'Thank *you*, Captain Bowden. I know Jacques would have wanted just that.'

We returned to the back room, where Kathy had packed a small cardboard box. Fleur paused at the mantelpiece. 'One other thing, my dear, I want you to have this.'

She gave Kathy a silver cigarette box.

'I know you don't smoke, just like me, but for some reason it was special to Laurens and he wanted me to keep it. If he hadn't been so insistent I'd got rid of it years ago, but I didn't and I won't now, but I will pass it on to someone I know who will respect Laurens' wishes.'

Kathy turned it over in her hands and opened the empty box. 'Of course I'll look after it,' she said, passing it to me.

It was quite heavy and obviously solid silver. Around the edge the top had a gold inlay resembling a ship's anchor cable. In the centre was a hand-painted ceramic tile of a passenger liner, but without a name. Below it, etched into the silver were the letters P-O-S-H, except the engraving of the "H" was worn and it no longer looked like a capital letter. I felt it was a shame the engraving had been done at all.

Chapter Eleven

Half an hour later we were on the bus heading back towards Blakenberge and the train to Ostend. It was now Wednesday afternoon and it would be late by the time the ferry arrived in Dover.

'Are you going back to work tomorrow?' I asked.

'No, I had no idea what I would need to do when I heard about Jacques' death and decided to go to Belgium, so I took ten days leave. At least I still have some time off.'

'Would you like to come down to the island for a couple of days? The *Lily Jade* won't be back until Monday.'

There was a train from Dover to Shoreham that evening, so I rang Malcolm to say he would have two visitors. He was slightly taken aback when he found out one was a female, but sorted it out by putting himself in the attic.

Although we were both tired when we arrived, Malcolm got us talking, asking about Kathy's work and the *Lily Jade*. By the time we went to bed it was well after midnight and, although I can't speak for Kathy, I knew nothing until Malcolm woke me with a cup of tea at eight o'clock in the morning.

With the slow train to Portsmouth and the old steam-train from Ryde, it was mid-afternoon before we arrived in Freshwater. Kathy looked dishevelled and had smuts on her face from leaning out of the window as we'd crossed the island.

'I'm glad you had a trip on our island train,' I said, smiling. 'It's going to close in September.'

She wiped a hand across her face, dismayed at what appeared on it. 'Maybe that's not such a bad thing.'

It was warm, with a gentle breeze, so we decided to walk through Freshwater and up to Totland. I stopped at the butcher and bought some lamb chops for tea and then called in at the off-licence for a bottle of red wine.

'It's just as I remember it, that first day I met you.'

We were standing on the cliff-top outside the lych-gate of Solent Serenity. 'Well, come and have a drink on the balcony and see if the view is still as good as it was then.'

It was quite some time before we reached the balcony as Kathy examined the incomplete renovations and new fittings. 'You've done a great job, Chris, the kitchen is a dream. I wish I had one like it.'

'I'm sorry it's still a bit of a mess. I would have liked to have had it finished before you saw it.'

'You silly man! It's not a mess, it's wonderful'

We took the wine up to the balcony, but hardly noticed the view and it seemed no time before the bottle was empty. 'Maybe I should go and cook tea?'

It seemed a ludicrous suggestion when we could spend the time together in the early evening sunshine and she hugged me closer. 'Don't leave me, I'll come and help you… later.'

I found another bottle of wine and after a late tea we went back up onto the balcony to finish it. The last rays of the setting sun were reflecting off the water, not that we saw them until the final minute or two.

'Oh, Chris, look at the sunset.'

We stood in each other's arms watching the sky turn crimson and the sun disappear behind the cliffs of Alum Bay, leaving us in a soft half-light. There was no breeze. The sounds of insects hung in the air like a distant orchestra and after some time, in the increasing darkness, the moon appeared, creating an almost monochrome, ghostly scene.

Kathy pressed her body against me and I responded by putting my hands on her buttocks. 'I don't know about you, but I'm starting to feel almost insane tonight.'

She laughed. 'We'd best do something about that; we can't have you feeling half insane, can we?'

We went through the double doors and lay on my bed, our hands roaming across each other's body until, instinctively and gently, we undressed each other. For a few moments we lay naked listening to the sounds of the sea coming through the open doors.

Her tanned limbs took on the colour of deep honey, hard nipples silhouetted in the moonlight. My fingers caressed one and her hand slid down onto my stomach.

We turned towards each other. The intimate touch sent an electric pulse through me and I heard a sudden intake of breath from Kathy. Our senses flowed free as our bodies became one, unashamedly doing what is normally reserved for married people.

The next three days, until the *Lily Jade* returned from Cornwall went in a dream. Kathy and I walked along the cliffs, collected coloured sand at Alum Bay and explored the countryside. Most of all we enjoyed each other's company and became lovers.

* * * * * * *

'Well, I can only say a few days away seem to have done ye a world of good.'

'Thanks, Scotty,' I said, coming across the brow.

'Och, now I can see why, with such a pretty young lady following you aboard!'

'Flattery will get you everywhere, Scotty. How are you?'

'Oh, nae so bad, thank you, Kathy'

'I trust everything is alright?' I asked.

Before Scotty could reply Soo appeared with a tray of tea. 'Good you are back Captain Chris. Everything ok.' He shook his head towards Scotty. 'Except silly old Scot!'

'Ger' out of it, you little Chinese monkey!'

Kathy looked at me as I laughed. 'That's good,' I said. 'Nothing's changed.'

The next day we were sailing to Shoreham and, as Kathy still had a few days off, I suggested she made the voyage up the coast.

'Chris, you know I'd love to come, but not with that man Lubec aboard. I know it sounds stupid, I just feel it would destroy everything we've found together; don't ask me why.'

'So when will I see you?'

'Could we meet at Malcolm's house?'

I nodded. 'Of course, I'll call him now.'

'But I won't stay there, Chris.'

I must've looked puzzled.

'It'll be our last night before I go back to Canterbury. I thought I might book into a hotel; you never know what insane people might be around in Shoreham at night.'

I laughed and then gave her a big kiss. 'You're a trick and no mistake, Kathy Wembourne.'

When we arrived in Shoreham I was so busy I wasn't aboard when Malcolm came down to tell me Kathy was at his house.

'Where've you been? I felt sure you'd be knocking on the door at breakfast time to see if that delightful lady had arrived.'

'I made an appointment a couple of months ago to see the authorities about the dry-dock. The *Lily Jade* has been running almost a year now, her speed has dropped over a knot and Scotty has maintenance that must be done if we want to keep on schedule.'

'You're putting the *Lily Jade* into dry-dock here?'

'Yes, there aren't any facilities at Yarmouth and I want to do it in the lull at the end of the summer before people start wanting materials before Christmas. I had to check with the mill to see if we needed to do a double run with timber before going in, as the whole thing will take a week.'

Lubec came in. 'Ah, Jean,' I said, 'we're booked into the dry-dock after discharge on Wednesday 24th September.'

'We'll be ready,' he said, picking up the loading sheets.

I knew we would be. The efficiency of the man was starting to make me feel uncomfortable, as if he were the Captain.

'Are you ready to go ashore?' Malcolm asked, 'because I think someone will be rather anxious to know where you are by now.'

He smiled and I punched him on the shoulder. 'You're too clever by half.'

'Don't have to be clever to see the look on both of your faces.'

I had a quick word with Scotty and Soo, asking them to meet us at a local restaurant at 7:30 that evening, but not to mention it to Jean.

'Why not?' Scotty said, and I rolled my eyes in despair.

Soo poked him in the ribs. 'Hey, you no understand anything except Agnes. Today keep silly Scot mouth shut for Captain Chris.'

Scotty was so taken aback he was lost for words and I knew there wouldn't be a problem. 'Thank you, Soo.'

It was a Chinese restaurant Soo had told me about, so we let him order everything.

'I'll know who t' blame if I'm no able to get up in the morning.'

'Don't you trust Soo?' Kathy asked.

'With Agnes, yes. In the galley, yes. But this is different.'

The meal was exceptional, to the point Scotty actually apologised to Soo. I said I would note it in the official log-book as it would never happen again. The pair headed off back to the ship, still arguing about anything that entered Scotty's mind while I paid the bill and returned to the table.

'I'm going to walk Kathy home,' I said, 'don't wait up.'

Malcolm nodded, but said nothing.

Walking towards the hotel it was almost closing time for the pubs and patrons were leaving the Golden Eagle. A large man stumbled out the door. As he steadied himself on the brick façade and stared across the road at us I knew it was Lubec. Kathy hadn't seen him and I guided her round the corner towards the hotel.

Her room had a sweet woodland smell from a bowl of potpourri on the dresser and that night our insanity reached new heights, as we both used all five senses to arouse and inflame an ardour that seemed impossible to satisfy. Our energy was boundless, not one tiny part of our bodies failing to find a desperate need for the intimate attention it received in different ways.

Eventually, although I have no idea of the time, we fell asleep. Strangely, we awoke at the same moment, to discover it was only seven o'clock. Not that time seemed to matter, because we nearly missed breakfast.

We went down, ready to leave immediately after the meal.

Kathy took the silver cigarette box from her bag and put it on the table. 'Best make sure I've got my ticket,' she said, looking in her purse. Afterwards she picked up the box and looked at the design on the lid. 'I still don't know why Fleur gave this to me.'

'She trusted you to look after it.'

Kathy rubbed her finger across the engraving. 'What's the significance of "POSH"?'

'I assume it's the old phrase connected with shipping meaning, "Port Out: Starboard Home". Passengers going to India would travel on those sides of the ship to avoid the harsh tropical sun heating up their cabins. It became quite a ritual and a status symbol among wealthy people.'

'Strange to see it on a cigarette box,' Kathy said, putting it back in her bag.

We stood, rather than sat on the platform awaiting the train. That way it was easier to remain close in each other's arms. Neither of us wanted the train to arrive, but we knew Kathy had to go to Canterbury, and I to the *Lily Jade*.

* * * * * * *

Back at sea, heading along the coast, it seemed as if I'd never been away from the ship, that my time with Kathy and the trip to Zeebrugge was a figment of my imagination, until I reached up to secure a lanyard hanging from the flag box. There on my wrist I could still smell her perfume and started to relive the previous ten days. Jean came to take over the bridge, but wasn't in a mood to chat so I left him to it. I was happy enough with my own thoughts.

On Saturday morning in Yarmouth, Scotty burst into my cabin before 8 A.M.

'Good mornin', Chris. You seem a bit busy, so I'll take the papers over to the office.'

'Hardly busy, Scotty. It's yesterday's newspaper and a cup of tea.'

'Och, well, you read on. I got quite used to goin' for a bit o' fresh air while you were away.'

'You took the papers to the Harbour Master's office?'

'Aye, that Lubec might be a good seaman, but he's nae so bright with the figures.'

'Give my regards to Jim,' I said, as Scotty picked up the file from my desk.

'Oh, Jim's away for a wee while. His cousin's looking after the office.'

Scotty had gone before I had a chance to ask the cousin's name. When Soo served breakfast, he hadn't returned. 'I've never known him to miss food.'

'Ah, Chief has, how you say, big fish to cook?'

'You mean, "Bigger fish to fry"?'

'Ah, see, yes. Chief, he looking to make a move.'

'He's not leaving the ship? Soo, tell me he's not leaving the *Lily Jade!*'

'No, no. Chief like Soo. Never leave *Lily Jade*. Please, not to worry, Captain Chris. He tell you sometime. Everything ok.'

I trusted Soo implicitly and if he said, "everything ok" I was sure it would be… but I still had nagging thoughts at the back of my mind and I was none the wiser when Scotty returned mid-morning.

'Well, there you are, Chris. All the paperwork signed and up to date.'

I swear the big Scot almost did a jig in the middle of my cabin, before there was a knock on the door and he left to go below.

Jean came in and grunted we had some chilled cargo for Fowey and I'd need to turn on the cooling unit we'd put into a small area at the aft end of the hold.

'You seem upset about something, Jean. Do you want to talk about it?'

He looked at me for a few moments wondering, I think, whether to say anything. His arrogance won.

'Yes, I wondered how you know the Wembourne girl.'

'Kathy?'

'Yeh.'

'She just happened to be walking along the cliff top at Totland when I first saw the house that I bought and we got talking.'

'I've met the family, but she doesn't seem friendly, somehow.'

'Each to their own,' I said. 'We get on well together.'

'Not to put too finer point on it, Chris, I found her troublesome.'

He left and I was glad I'd never mentioned Jacques Kessel, or the fact Kathy had been with me in Zeebrugge.

Chapter Twelve

My workload increased in August as we sailed with full cargoes and, in addition, I needed to compile a programme for the dry-docking. Not knowing what we would find when the *Lily Jade* was taken out of the water meant I had to allow some time for unexpected work below the waterline. I didn't expect any major repairs as I knew Jacques had always kept the *Caillou* in top condition, but it was however, now over two years since her last docking and I expected extra cleaning would be needed, especially around the saltwater intakes. Certainly the zinc anodes to prevent corrosion to the propeller would need to be replaced.

It was also an ideal opportunity to sort out all the papers I'd accumulated concerning the *Lily Jade*. I'd been meaning to do it for some time as up until now everything had been put in a large drawer under my bunk that I really needed for clothes and linen.

I bought a small filing cabinet and began by sorting the papers into groups, such as certificates, original builder's specifications and the maintenance programme for the forthcoming dry-docking. Slowly over a period of almost a month I managed to put everything into a chronological order of type and date.

Each time we arrived in Yarmouth, Scotty seemed anxious to take the paperwork over to the Harbour Master's office. I was so busy with the dry-dock programme and ordering the necessary equipment such as paint and anti-fouling, I'd forgotten what Soo had said about "a big fish".

'Morning, Chris. I see you're busy so I'll take the paperwork over.'

It was Monday 17th August. 'Hang on, Scotty. I'll come with you.' He stood looking at me as if I'd threatened him with a knife. 'Is something wrong?'

'Och, well no – of course not.'

He was strangely quiet as we walked along the wharf, and I was about to say something when I saw some corrosion around the upper pintle on the rudder and my thoughts became caught up with what work would be needed there.

From the inner room of the Harbour Master's office I heard a strange female voice and wondered who was talking to Jim's cousin. There was the sound of the telephone receiver being hung up and then a middle-aged lady appeared at the doorway.

She looked businesslike in a dark green skirt and a white blouse with a lace collar. The round face with a fresh complexion had a wide smile below neatly permed salt-and-pepper hair.

'Scotty, how've you bin?'

'Aye, I'm fine, thank you, Fiona.'

She looked towards me. 'An' this mus' be Captain Bowden.' She held out her hand. 'Fiona Parkinson, Jim's cousin.'

The lady, whose accent announced a connection with Yorkshire, was efficient and sorted out the paperwork quicker than Jim had ever done.

'Right,' she said, 'time for a cuppa!'

I got the impression Fiona Parkinson was not a woman to be refused. During the next twenty minutes I found out she was not only efficient, but also possessed a wealth of nautical knowledge when she asked about the *Lily Jade* and my time in the Royal Navy.

It finished as quickly as it had begun, with Fiona Parkinson deciding tea-time was over. She left for an appointment in Cowes and we found ourselves walking back to the ship.

'Well, Chris, what do you think of Fiona?'

Scotty had a big smile on his face and suddenly I realised what Soo had been talking about. I stopped and grabbed his arm. 'You and Fiona?'

'Well, I'd like to think she has some feelings for me.'

'I'm sure she has. Good luck to both of you.'

'Ah, Chris, she's a wonderful woman. I knew it when we first met and I said I was the engineer.'

'I bet you said, *Chief Engineer*?'

'Aye, but then straight away, she wanted to know about Agnes. Fiona knows all about marine engines, Chris. She worked at Swan Hunter's yard in Newcastle with the big Doxford diesels during the war.'

'Fiona might teach you a thing or two.'

'She already has. It's a pity she had to go to Cowes; I wanted to invite her aboard. I've been cleaning up down below for a week now.'

'I can see this is serious.'

'Soo thinks it's a bit strange. I told him it was the big clean-up for the dry-dock. He doesn't know about Fiona.'

'Soo knows exactly what is going on. He knows all about you and Fiona, he told me.'

'You knew?'

'Not exactly. Soo told me in his roundabout way, but it didn't make sense until this morning.'

'I should've have realised I couldn't fool Soo.'

'Why don't you go back this afternoon and invite Fiona over for a drink after work?'

Scotty went straight down below to give Agnes a final polish. It was less than thirty minutes before Soo appeared at my cabin door.

'Captain Chris, you want I should make little foods for later when

Chief's lady come?'

I laughed and shook my head in amazement, as I had done many times before, at this incredible member of my crew. 'Thank you Soo, some finger food would be wonderful.' I didn't know if Fiona was coming, but obviously, Soo did.

Fiona did come, and after spending almost an hour down below she and Scotty emerged deep in conversation about marine engines and it became obvious that was one passion they shared. Soo's food consisted of morsels that none of us had ever seen or tasted before, not even Jean with all his travels around the world.

'Scotty, you can't tell me you spend hours each week polishin' the brass on Aggie down there?'

'It's Agnes, Fiona and well, I have to admit she got an extra bit o' attention since you were coming.'

Fiona laughed. 'Oh, you sweet old thing. How do you put up with him Captain Bowden?'

'If he plays up I send Soo down to sort him out.'

'That little Chinese monkey!'

Soo looked at him, and then dropped his eyes before going to get the tray with the finger food.

Fiona pushed Scotty in the shoulder. 'That was a bit harsh.'

Soo took the tray around to each of us. 'Chief, you no try this one yet,' he said, pointing to a pastry covered titbit.

'Och, I suppose he's ok, especially when it comes to food.' He took a bite and two seconds later started coughing, his face going scarlet. 'What…!'

'I catch Chief! I catch Chief!' Soo cried, jumping up and down. 'See miss, Captain Chris right. I sort out Chief.' He took Scotty a glass of water. 'He be ok. That food meant for me. It warm.'

'Warm!' Scotty spluttered as he took the water.

We were all laughing.

Fiona patted his arm. 'Oh dear, I think you need someone to be lookin' after you.'

'Thank you, Fiona. Life is dangerous around here – but it's fun.'

Two hours later Scotty walked arm in arm with Fiona to end of the wharf. Watching them from the deck outside my cabin, a breeze wafting in off the Solent and the radio gently playing "in the cool, cool, cool of the evening", I felt content with the *Lily Jade* and her happy crew.

The big man crossed the brow and headed down the wharf. Even he'd enjoyed himself. The dinghy was dragged down to the water and a rhythmic soft splash could be heard as the oars left ripples in the calm waters of the harbour. Jean Lubec was off to check his lobster-pot.

Scotty and Fiona hadn't noticed him. They were otherwise occupied – and they weren't discussing marine engines! I wondered how Kathy was, and wished she could've been here this evening.

* * * * * * *

Because we were so busy the days passed quickly until about the middle of September when, with the first cool wind of autumn, the cargoes dropped off and I made my final preparations for the dry-docking.

After discharge on the Wednesday morning we moved up the wharf and, painstakingly, the Harbour Master and I positioned the *Lily Jade* in the middle of the dry-dock alongside the timber mill. We put out lines fore and aft, the gates were closed and the water level started to go down. Scotty had come up on deck and the four of us eased back on the mooring lines as the *Lily Jade* followed the water level down. When she sat on the blocks at the bottom of the dock we made the lines fast and placed spars between the dock wall and the ship's side as a precautionary measure. I certainly didn't want my ship falling over. We met Malcolm at "The Lighthouse" for a quick bite of lunch and by the time we returned all the water had gone, leaving the *Lily Jade* high and dry, surrounded by several men who were erecting stairs and scaffolding around the hull.

Malcolm looked upwards. 'It's a weird feeling to be walking under the *Lily Jade*. She seems so much bigger.'

'That's because you don't realise how much of a ship is normally under water.'

Jean had gone for'd, while Scotty and I, with Malcolm in tow, had started at the aft end. Soo's first job was to inspect the saltwater intakes. I'd decided we should start in different areas as one of us might spot something we may miss as a group. At the moment the thick marine growth on the hull prevented any close inspection of the plating, but the hoses to sand-blast it clean were already being lowered into the dock.

'Ooch, this is nae too good.'

Scotty and I had climbed some steps to examine the corrosion I'd seen on the rudder pintles. Both the upper and lower points that acted like hinges for the rudder needed an overhaul.

'We'll unship the rudder and do it properly, Scotty.'

He nodded his agreement and we headed for'd, meeting Jean amidships

'A couple of plates near the bow will need some work, Chris. How much, it's hard to say until the weed is cleaned away.'

The plates Jean referred to had been pushed upwards into the hull. 'Looks as though she's sat on something.'

'You're right, Scotty. There are plenty of places where ships like this sit on the mud at low tide, but I reckon the *Lily Jade* found a mud flat with a rock in it.'

The following day the hull was stripped back to the bare metal and after another inspection I was relieved to find no other defects apart from routine maintenance. I arranged for the rudder to be unshipped and the two bottom plates to be replaced, and by Friday morning anti-fouling to deter marine growth was being applied.

'We'll be finished by two,' the dockyard foreman said. 'Then we'll see you on Monday morning.'

'There's nothing we can do over the weekend,' I told the others as we had a cup of tea, 'so we might as well enjoy ourselves. I suppose you'll be going to see your brother, Scotty?'

'Well, maybe not. Fiona is back down at Jim Middleton's place for a week, so maybe I'll pop down to the island.'

Soo made an impression of frying a fish and I laughed.

'What's he doin'?'

'Never mind, Scotty, but take these.' I tossed him a bunch of keys. 'You might need somewhere to stay. You can use Solent Serenity.'

'Won't you be going there?'

'No, not this time. I'm going up to Canterbury,' I said, watching Jean Lubec's reaction to my news from the corner of my eye. He nodded almost imperceptibly.

'Jean,' I said, turning to face him. 'Any plans?'

'I'll go down to Portsmouth. My friends there need a hand to move some equipment.'

So, I thought, he's going to see Vivian and Marcos.

Sitting quietly in the corner of my cabin looking at the deck was the man I should've considered first. 'How about you, Soo?'

'Soo have nowhere to go. He happy to stay on *Lily Jade*.'

'I'm sorry, Soo, you can't while she's in the dock.'

I was about to offer him a trip to Canterbury when Malcolm spoke.

'Come and stay with me, Soo and we'll go for a drive somewhere. It'll do me good to get out of the house.'

'You sure Mr Malcolm? Soo not want to be a bother.'

'It's fine. We'll have a great time.'

'Thank you. Mr Malcolm and Captain Chris good friends.'

There seemed no more to say and an hour later the *Lily Jade* was left alone in the dry-dock.

****

I'd rung Kathy from the timber mill that morning as soon as I'd heard there would be no further work until Monday. I heard her laugh and clap her hands when I said I was coming to Canterbury.

'The quickest way is for me to go from Brighton to London and catch a connection from there. It just means I won't arrive until about eight tonight.'

'Oh, Chris, that's so long. Hang on a minute.'

The heard the receiver put down and it was about half a minute before Kathy returned.

'He says yes, Chris. He says yes!'

'Who says yes, and why, Kathy?'

'My boss. He says I can borrow the firm's estate car and come to pick you up. Take the twelve-thirty train from Brighton to Hastings and I'll pick you up at two o'clock.'

Malcolm, with Soo in the back of the car had taken me into Brighton and now the train was only ten minutes away from Hastings, the smoke from the engine hanging in the cuttings where the track passed through the South Downs.

The Morris Minor with its wooden window frames smelt of sheep, I think, but it could've been goats or any other animal. On straight parts of the road we held hands and a few times I leant over to kiss Kathy on her cheek.

'Careful, Chris. I really want to return the car in one piece.'

'Ah, sanity prevails,' I said.

We laughed.

'I've never met a sea captain before; we don't get many in Canterbury.' Gerald Griffiths was an affable man in his forties. 'I hope you're not thinking of taking this young lady on a voyage around the world, we need her here.'

'I might, if she said yes.'

He shook his head. 'That might be the last time you get the car Miss Wembourne. I should watch out for this one.'

'It won't happen tomorrow,' I said, 'the ship's in dry dock.'

'Well, that's all right then, off you go and have a great weekend. I'll close up.'

Hand in hand we walked away from the centre of town and down a lane with stone walls where the long boughs of several oak trees hung across the road. At the bottom of the hill we came to a gate with a broken hinge that Kathy swung open a short way before it stuck in the mud. Set back from the road a single storey white house sat in open fields previously hidden by the oak trees. It seemed a little run-down with paint flaking off the windows and the front porch.

'This used to be the surgery, but when the new building opened we started using this as a recuperation centre because it has five acres of open land at the back. Slowly, I'm renovating the place and Gerald has said I can live here as long as I keep it available for the surgery.'

'But I thought you lived at your parents' house?'

'I did, but it's quite small and Grandpa has hobbies he tends to spread everywhere. I go and see him most evenings, but he likes the place to himself and, quite honestly, I prefer to be here. At least I can fix it up as I like it and it's so convenient for the animals.'

'You love animals, don't you?'

'Adore them; more than people usually, present company excepted.'

We left our shoes in the small wooden porch and Kathy opened the door. Inside I stepped into another country. Large white floor tiles with a geometric pattern spread down the hallway between the sandstone coloured walls trimmed with blue woodwork. Two bronze urns sat by the doorway on each side of the entrance.

'I love the Italian style, if you hadn't guessed. One day I want to go to Tuscany.'

'You didn't mention that at Solent Serenity?'

'That was already a beautiful English cottage. This was nothing, so I could develop it in any style.'

'I can see why you enjoy living here.'

Kathy led me to a large room at the back with the kitchen in one corner. Here the colours included splashes of orange. One wall had new windows and curtains with a pair of doors in the centre that opened onto a courtyard, half of which was paved in terracotta stone slabs, the remainder being covered with rotting, discoloured timber. In the centre was a muddy circle.

'That's as far as I've got, Chris. It's a slow process and I can only afford a few materials at a time. I'll do the main bedroom and the bathroom next.'

'It's incredible!'

'Let's have a drink outside before the sun goes down.'

As we sipped our red wine, Kathy's vision of sandstone walls around the courtyard with a central fountain guarded by dolphins would normally have seemed out of place in the Kentish countryside, but in the afternoon sunshine the undulating land and a copse of evergreen trees on a nearby hill made it look and feel like a small piece of Italy.

It was almost dark when Kathy asked if I'd like to go with her to visit Grandpa. 'He's fine now, not like last year when I first met you. He'd had a fall then and we wondered if he would need permanent care, but although he's bounced back I still like to check on him.'

We walked up the lane and into a road behind the High Street. Number 47 was a small semi-detached house with two rose bushes in its tiny front garden.

Kathy unlocked the front door and opened it. 'Grandpa, it's me, Kathy.'

Standing in the narrow hallway I noticed a picture frame containing two photos on the wall above a small table. One was of a shiny gem that looked like a diamond; the other showed a dull, larger stone. Kathy saw my interest. 'The big one is an uncut diamond and the small one is a piece of it after Grandpa had worked on it.'

She looked down the hallway. There had been no answer and she called again.

From a back room a tall, thin man appeared carrying a screwdriver and the metal carriage from a model railway. His thick, white hair stood up at various angles and his Adam's apple bobbed up and down behind a collar that was three sizes too large and sported a green tie with the head of a giraffe.

'The bogies came loose,' he said to no-one in particular, looking down at the carriage.

He looked up again and suddenly the dark eyes that had seemed so distant sparkled. 'Kathy, my darling girl, it's wonderful to see you.'

He came over and gave her a hug and a kiss. 'And this is? No, let me guess. You're the Captain of a ship? Kathy met you when we were at the Isle of Wight last year?'

I nodded, astounded at the change and the alertness of the man who had been immersed in his train set.

'Do you like model railways?'

'I never had one,' I admitted.

'Well, come and see mine!'

Kathy motioned me to follow him. Four tables filled the back room leaving only a narrow walkway around them. With the agility of a man in his thirties' Kathy's Grandpa got down on his knees and crawled into the small space at the centre of the tables.

'Watch this... I'm sorry I didn't catch the name, I'm Frank,' he said, holding his hand out over a model station with four platforms.

'Chris.'

'Watch this, Chris!'

He flicked some switches and trains began to move along the tracks that at times disappeared behind mountains or into tunnels. Frank watched the movement intensely and became oblivious to our presence for almost a minute. Only as a train passed in front of me did he remember we were there.

'Ah, Chris, time for sunset.'

He flicked more switches and then turned out the main light to reveal trains and stations illuminated in the dark, but this time he remembered we were there and gave us a detailed description of the whole layout.

'He has a shed full of woodwork as well,' Kathy said, as we strolled back down the lane. 'He's a wonderful old man and I love him dearly.'

'Did you say he was with De Beers?'

'Yes, in South Africa. He was one of their top diamond cutters and got Simeon his job out there. But now Simeon's back.'

I sensed tautness in her voice. 'Don't you get on with your brother?'

'I always used to. We were inseparable as kids; it's just since that meeting in Zeebrugge. Something strange is going on.'

'You told me he asked if you still lived in your parent's house.'

'Yes, that's it, where Grandpa is living.' Kathy stopped and grabbed my arm. 'Didn't I ever tell you?'

'Tell me what?'

'About mum and dad. They went out to see Simeon in 1950; two years after Grandpa retired and came home. Their plane from Johannesburg crashed in the desert on the way to the mine. It was three months before they found the bodies.'

When I saw her face I realised a wound had been re-opened. It wasn't my fault and I didn't want to sound patronising, so instead I just put my arm around her shoulder as we walked slowly under the boughs of the oak trees.

Saturday dawned fine, with a light breeze. Kathy and I set to work ripping up more of the old timber in the courtyard and laying the remaining slabs of terracotta stone. We'd stopped for lunch when Kathy went to answer the door.

'Grandpa, what are you doing here?'

I came down the hallway as Frank spoke. He sounded slightly agitated.

'Vivian wants me to go and see her, I don't know why.'

'Will you be all right travelling alone?'

'Yes, my sweet girl, I'll be fine. You shouldn't spend your time fussing over an old man. I'll see you when I get back. Good to have met you, Chris. You take care of my little angel.'

'I certainly will, Frank.'

He went to the waiting taxi and with a wave, he was gone. I put my arm around her waist as Kathy stood staring at the gate and the empty lane.

'As I said before, Chris, something's going on. Grandpa knows, but he won't tell me.'

I took her hand and we went back to work. By four o'clock we'd laid all the available stone slabs and three-quarters of the courtyard was complete.

'I'll have to order more stone.'

'Plus the fountain, you'll need that next so you can run the power line to the house.' I turned her towards me and lifted her face upwards. 'Meanwhile, enough is enough. You go and get cleaned up while I stack this old timber.'

Afterwards, I went and had a bath myself. When I returned, Kathy had taken some large cushions outside and, in the late afternoon sun that caught the golden lights in her hair, we sat sipping a glass of red wine admiring the fruits of our labour.

She rested her head on my chest. The fragrance of freshly applied perfume invaded my nostrils as I kissed her neck. Kathy sighed and pressed my hand against her breast before reaching under my shirt and letting her fingers stray across my stomach and then down to my groin.

The warm sun and the mellowing effects of the red wine had created feelings that couldn't be ignored. Soon scents of the autumn countryside wafted across the fields to mingle with our nakedness. The tanned limbs of Kathy's silky-smooth skin enveloped me and she gave a slight moan, her firm nipples quivering as I teased them with my tongue. With increasing intensity our feelings transported us to a new plateau where our bodies were thrust together in mutual delight. Insanity had never felt so sane.

We awoke late on Sunday morning and after breakfast strolled up to the copse of evergreens. Low cloud was beginning to build-up to the west and a cool wind drifted up from the South Downs. 'I'll try to come back and help you finish the courtyard.'

She pulled my lips to hers. 'Just come back, Chris.'

The lunch and the atmosphere in "The Woodlark" lost a little of its perfection with the knowledge I had to return to Shoreham and the *Lily Jade*. All too soon the bus departed to Dover leaving the sight of Kathy waving good-bye imprinted on my mind.

Chapter Thirteen

Malcolm had a grin on his face when he met me at Shoreham station that evening. 'What's up?' I asked.

'You'll find out when we get home.'

'Nothing drastic, I hope?'

'Soo'll tell you.'

The dining table was covered in a crisp white cloth and a stack of small plates stood beside half-a-dozen wine glasses.

Scotty and Fiona arrived. 'What's all the fuss about, Chris? Fiona and I got a message to catch an early train.'

'Except we've bin choppin' and changin' trains 'cos the early one stopped at Southampton.'

'I've no idea. Malcolm knows, but won't tell.'

There was another knock at the door and Malcolm entered the room followed by Peter Dawson, the manager of the timber mill.

'Hi, Chris. What's the big occasion?'

'I was hoping you'd tell me.'

Malcolm headed towards the kitchen. 'Soo'll be out in a moment. He'll tell you all about it.'

Seconds later the door opened and Soo appeared carrying a large tray of his Chinese finger food. 'Welcome back, Captain Chris and Chief. Also good to see lady friend of Chief and Mr Dawson.'

He hardly looked at us, which seemed odd; but it was a large tray he was carrying.

'Hey Soo! If you've been up here cooking, who's down at the *Lily Jade* looking after Agnes?'

I was about to remind Scotty the *Lily Jade* was in dry-dock and no-one was needed to look after Agnes, but Soo spoke first.

'Agnes?' He gazed at us with a blank look in his eyes.

'Yes, Agnes; or have you forgotten you're the Senior Second engineer on the *Lily Jade?*'

'Ah… yes, Agnes. Agnes… she fine lady, very good, all ok.'

'Chris, I think he's lost the plot. Soo doesn't seem to know Agnes is…'

The kitchen door burst open and we all stood in stunned silence. There were now two identical Chinamen standing there.

There was a big flash of light.

The man who had just appeared started jumping up and down. 'I did it. Mr Malcolm said no, but Soo did it. I fool Captain Chris and Chief! Also Chief's lady, Fiona and Mr Dawson.'

Malcolm clapped his hands. 'Well done, Soo and I've caught them all on camera. It should be a great photo.'

Soo came and grabbed my arm. 'Please, Captain Chris. I like you meet my cousin, the one I tell you about.'

Soo Hong Ling had the same nervousness about him our Soo had had when I first met him. We'd have to get to know him very well to avoid such a deception again as they appeared identical, even to the parting in their hair.

Scotty rubbed his eyes. 'Fiona, that pie I had for lunch, I think it was off, my eyes have gone all funny, or are there really two Soos?'

The spontaneous party kicked on into the evening. It was after nine o'clock when I noticed our Soo sitting quietly in a chair holding his side. 'Stomach?' I asked.

He nodded.

'Tomato juice?'

Again he nodded and when I brought the drink he produced two sachets. I didn't know what the powders were but I felt sure members of the medical profession would be interested in the immediate results they had on what I imagined to be an ulcer of some sort.

The next morning we all went down to the dry-dock and the *Lily Jade*. The only person missing was Jean Lubec.

'I'm sorry, Chris,' he said when he came aboard at midday. 'Had some business to attend to last night and missed the last train from Portsmouth.'

He knew I wasn't pleased, but I didn't make a big thing of it, considering the efficiency of the man. By Tuesday afternoon the painting was finished, the dry-dock equipment was removed and we tidied up around the deck. As Scotty and I stood at the end of the dock in the late afternoon sunshine, the *Lily Jade* looked like a new ship, resplendent in her fresh coat of paint.

Soo appeared on the focs'le. 'Captain Chris. Can Soo get camera from your cabin to make photo of *Lily Jade?*'

Why hadn't I thought of it? 'Of course, Soo.' We took several shots with Scotty, Soo and I in the foreground as a memory of that week.

'Slow astern, Scotty.' It was Wednesday morning, the dry-dock had been flooded and it was time to resume our trading along the coast. Half an hour later the first pack of timber was lowered into the hold. Our life settled back into the old routine, except now I seemed to spend a lot of money in call-boxes phoning Canterbury.

It was a quiet night in Fowey a few weeks later and, as had become the habit, we sat around in my cabin telling stories over a few drinks. Invariably it was Jean Lubec's tales of exotic ports and his experiences around the world that held our attention.

'Missed a ship in New Orleans once,' he said, his steely, grey eyes becoming glazed as he remembered. He nodded and suddenly the eyes were bright again.

'No ships about, so I took a job on a stern-wheeler to Saint Louis and back. I was only a deck-hand, but I could see the whole trip was a gambling cruise for the rich folk from the southern states. One night in Memphis I was asked to stand in the gaming room to look after any trouble-makers.'

An obvious choice for the job I thought, as the big man continued.

'They had a competition where the passengers threw darts at a set of playing cards to score points depending what they hit. It was pathetic. Half of them couldn't even hit the board behind the cards. I'd had a few drinks down below and fronted up saying I could hit any card from three times the distance with my seaman's knife. I was about to be sent back to my cabin, but several of the crowd clamoured they wanted to see it. I asked a couple of them which card they wanted me to hit and then they all started to take bets on me. It was such a success I was asked back every night for the rest of the trip.'

'Are ye still any good at it?'

'Not sure, Scotty, I haven't done it for a long time.'

I could see what was coming. Scotty staggered to his feet, disappeared and returned with a pack of cards.

We went outside and Soo found a tube of glue to stick some of the cards onto the timber bulkhead at the aft end of my cabin.

Jean Lubec went to the rail behind the funnel almost twenty feet away, took his knife from its sheath and stood staring at the cards barely visible in the faint deck lights. 'It's been a long time.'

'Ace of spades,' said Scotty.

A moment of concentration was followed by a thud. None of us had seen the knife travel from Jean's hand until the blade had hit home into the timber. The handle was still waving slightly as we all looked at the tip of the blade, which had pierced the centre of the black shape on the white card.

'Not as rusty as I thought,' Jean said, shaking his head as he retrieved the knife.

Soo stared in amazement. 'Must see more. Red one this time.'

Again the knife flew faster than we could see, bisecting the diamond as it came to rest.

'Ooch, maybe that's too easy for him,' Scotty muttered.

Jean was laughing and obviously enjoying himself. 'Your turn, Chris. Pick a card.'

'The top mark on the three of hearts.'

Jean nodded. 'That makes it a proper test.'

The tip of the blade landed in the upper heart on the card. It wasn't quite in the middle, but it was still so impressive we all went quiet for a few moments.

Jean sensed the mood and put his knife away. 'Enough of that nonsense, it's getting cold out here.'

By the middle of November the weather had turned nasty, with cold winds and rain announcing the oncoming winter, spray rattling on the wheelhouse windows as we left the sheltered waters of Weymouth harbour to head down the Channel. As the *Lily Jade* rolled in the westerly swell there was a clatter of something falling off the window-ledge in front of me. I knew what it was. I picked up the small stones that were rolling around on the deck by my feet and looked at them. They were all the same size and tan, white, or black with white spots. I knew they belonged to Jean, and put them in an old tobacco tin he used as an ashtray.

Coming up to take over the bridge, a cigarette hanging from the corner of his mouth, he took the stones from the tin and tossed them in his hand, gazing towards the twenty miles of shingle that formed the Chesil Beach. I followed his gaze, but saw nothing of interest.

He put the stones in his pocket and the familiar "clack, clack, clack" commenced as he jiggled them. 'Ok, Chris, I've got her.'

He turned and gave me that disarming smile as I left the bridge.

Chapter Fourteen

For the rest of the month the *Lily Jade* carried full cargoes of goods people wanted for the festive season. I'd rung Kathy at least once a week, often from Malcolm's house, but there had been no opportunity to see each other since the dry-docking in September, and now it was less than four weeks to Christmas.

As we approached the berth in Shoreham on Tuesday afternoon, 1st December, I could see a solitary figure standing on the wharf. Even in the fading light I recognised her hair from half way down the dock, but couldn't believe she was here until I focused the binoculars on the tanned face with its slightly turned-up nose.

She took the bow-line from Jean, putting it on the bollard without saying a word to him, before coming aft waving and laughing.

'Kathy!' I called down, almost laughing with excitement. 'How are you? How did you manage to get down here?'

She smiled. 'I'm fine, Chris, I'll tell you all about it in a minute.'

'Miss Kathy,' a voice below me piped up. 'You must've known.'

'Known what, Soo?'

'Soo have sore leg. Didn't want to jump on wharf,' he said, passing her the rope.

'What happened?'

'Silly Soo slip. Bang leg on stove. But ok now.'

'You should look after your crew,' Kathy said, waving her fist at me and laughing.

I leant over the bridge-wing so I could see the wiry Chinaman, who was also laughing. '*Silly Soo* should tell me if something is wrong!'

Five minutes later we stood in the middle of my cabin, our bodies close and our lips locked together. I thought I heard a noise and looked around, but saw nothing. We sat down on the tiny settee and almost immediately there was a knock on the door.

'Too late for tea. Better to have early wine,' Soo said, placing a bottle of red wine and two glasses on my desk.

I realised I had heard a noise, but Soo had waited outside until we were ready.

'Thank you, Soo,' Kathy said, 'what would we do without you?'

'Without Soo I couldn't operate the *Lily Jade*.'

He left without a word, but smiling.

'So, what brings you to Shoreham?'

'You, you daft, delicious man. Why else would I come?'

'But how…?'

'I worked on an emergency all over the weekend a couple of weeks ago so I asked for today off. I have to be back tomorrow afternoon.'

We sipped our wine and I gave her a peck on the cheek. 'Thank you for coming,' I whispered. 'I felt a bit out it of last week.'

'What do you mean?'

'Fiona came down to see Scotty and we all had a great day, except I kept wishing you were here. But you're here now my sweet girl, so everything's fine.'

'Captain Bowden?'

The voice calling up from the wharf belonged to Peter Dawson, the manager of the timber mill. I stepped out onto the deck and looked down.

'Can you come over to the office for a minute?'

I waved and returned to Kathy. 'Business calls, I'll be back soon.'

She took me in her arms. 'I might not let you go, we haven't got a lot of time.' She kissed me on the cheek. 'Ok, off you go then, but don't be long.'

'Are you all right, Chris?' Kathy asked, when I returned.

'Yes, I think so. Why do you ask?'

'I thought we might go out for a meal?'

'Of course, but what's that have to do with me?'

'Well, I've booked into that hotel again and…' She felt my forehead. 'I thought so; I think I feel a touch of insanity in you tonight.'

'You cheeky girl!' I said, laughing and smacking her bottom gently.

Our "insanity" that night allowed my mind to be certain, in a sane and level-headed way, that I wanted to spend the rest of my life with Kathy.

We dined in "The Lighthouse" and as we walked back to the hotel I held Kathy close, afraid I could lose her into the cold night air; that she might evaporate; that I would lose the one person who meant more to me than anything else in the world, even the *Lily Jade*. I couldn't let that happen.

Entering our room, away from other people, that fear born from desire intensified as we embraced and kissed long and hard. I sensed a similar urgency from Kathy, her hands sliding down to the bottom of my back, trying to pull me closer.

My fingers began to undo the buttons on the back of her blouse, strangely without the fumbling that had occurred on previous occasions. I stroked the bare flesh of her shoulders, my mind so intent on the smoothness of her skin I didn't notice her unbuttoning my shirt until I felt her soft hands on my chest. The blouse slid from her arms and fell to the floor as my fingers teased her firm nipples through the thin lace of her bra.

Kathy flung her head back, the dark hair hanging clear of those tanned shoulders. 'I want you, Chris – *now*' she breathed. 'Let's not waste a moment of our precious time together.'

Rapidly the pile of discarded items on the floor grew as we peeled off each other's clothes until Kathy stretched the elastic of my briefs, freeing my passion and allowing our naked bodies to be pressed together in an odyssey that invaded our senses.

After our second session of intense insanity, I almost proposed to Kathy, but somehow I felt that occasion deserved a more romantic and memorable location than the bedroom of a Shoreham hotel.

Again we were late for breakfast. 'They'll be talking about us if we're not careful.'

'I think they already are,' I said, nodding towards the two waitresses who were giggling to one another.

Kathy turned and then suddenly looked down both sides of her chair. 'I've left my handbag upstairs. I feel uncomfortable without it.'

As she left I began to think where and when I could ask Kathy to share the rest of her life with me. When would I see her again? I didn't know, the thought bringing back the fear of losing her.

I wandered across to the buffet and picked up a copy of the *Daily Telegraph*. The headlines were about the Prime Minister hosting a meeting of envoys from Commonwealth countries and casually I turned several pages, not reading anything thoroughly until I saw a photograph of a car being pulled out of a canal. I'd nearly turned the page when I thought the car looked familiar. The picture wasn't great and half the car was still in the water, but when I took the paper to the window, the big old Mercedes jumped out at me. The article said the driver had drowned, but the police were investigating suspicious circumstances and the name had not been released.

'What are you doing over there?'

I went back to the table and gave Kathy the paper pointing to the photo.

'What's this?'

'Have a look and tell me if you recognise anything.'
'A car being dragged from a canal.'
'Not any old car.'
'My God! Is it?'
'I don't know, but there can't be many Mercedes Benz' of that type around.'
Kathy started to read the article. 'Was anyone killed?'
'Just the driver, but it doesn't give a name.'
'Or whether it was male or female,' Kathy remarked.
'I hadn't thought of Vivian.'
'We're probably mistaken and it's nothing to do with them.'
'I expect so.'
'Grandpa will find out soon enough. I'll ask him how they were when he comes home from Portsmouth.'
'Is he there now?'
Kathy nodded. 'He's been going down there every couple of weeks, but he still won't tell me why.'

Breakfast arrived and it wasn't the right time or place to propose to Kathy, apart from which talk about the car and its driver had created the wrong atmosphere.

Back on the *Lily Jade* we were greeted at the door of my cabin. 'Special brew of tea for special Miss Kathy. Also for Captain Chris for clear thinking to make good decisions.'

Soo, as usual had been ready and waiting and I almost felt as if he could read my mind. The morning passed quickly and I hadn't been able to escape the attention of the timber mill or Peter Dawson. All too soon it was time to take Kathy to the station.

There had been no quiet moment, romantic location or not, when we had been alone and I could've asked Kathy to be my wife. My only chance left was going to be the platform at Shoreham station just before the train whisked her away in a cloud of smoke and steam. I was determined to take that opportunity.

'Miss! Miss! Jimmy Parkhurst just took my lunch-box'

'Miss, can Jennifer and I sit together on the train?'

'Miss, will we get a chance to see the engine?'

We'd passed through the ticket barrier at the station. Far from finding a quiet place to ourselves, it was almost impossible to find anywhere to stand without being jostled by the crowd of schoolchildren which seemed to stretch all along the platform.

'Let's try to find a spot at the end,' I suggested.

Kathy nodded and slowly we worked our way through the throng of excited children. At last I could see some empty platform with uncut grass near the signal-box, but at that moment the mournful sound of an engine's whistle sounded in the distance and we were engulfed in a tide of youngsters running to see the arrival of the train. Surrounded by the chattering children I only had a chance to give Kathy a short hug and a kiss.

'I love you Kathy.'

She squeezed me tightly.

'Oh, Chris I...'

The doors were opened and we were nearly separated in the rush as people piled aboard.

'... I can't tell you how I feel. I adore you, my wonderful man.'

Kathy was hustled onto the train and as she stood by the open window we held hands for a few seconds. The sound of doors slamming up and down the train faded and the guard waved his green flag.

'Kathy, I wanted to ask...'

The whistle of the engine drowned out my voice.

'What was that, Chris?'

There was a rattle of couplings as the train jerked forward accompanied by a hiss of steam from the straining engine. It was too late.

'I'll tell you next time.'

Still holding her hand I ran along the platform as the train gathered speed.

'I love you, Kathy,' I called, and she gave my hand a kiss before letting it go.

Her reply and her smile were drowned by the doleful sound of the whistle and smoke from the engine. Suddenly Kathy was gone. Alone on the platform I repeated the words I'd planned to say to the most wonderful woman I'd ever known, but only the sparrows in the hedgerows surrounding the station heard me.

As I left to return to the *Lily Jade* I wondered how long I'd have to wait to propose to Kathy, and if by then the magic between us would still be the same. Then I remembered Christmas was less than four weeks away and the *Lily Jade* would be tied up for several days. A perfect time for us to get together. I realised what I'd just said to myself, Christmas was less than four weeks away… and I hadn't got Kathy a present yet! I made a mental note to go to the shops in the morning.

Chapter Fifteen

The next morning I was having breakfast when a fresh pot of tea was put on the table. 'No thanks, Soo, I've had enough.'

He looked up at me and smiled before disappearing into the galley. A minute later Malcolm arrived looking tired, but excited.

'Good morning, Chris. I've got some interesting news for you, but first could I have a cuppa? I was too busy to get one this morning.'

I pushed the pot and a clean cup towards him. 'Soo's just made this, and when I said I didn't want it he just smiled. Obviously it was for you.'

'But how…?'

'Don't ask. I don't think I'll ever work it out. Now what's your news?'

'My friend in Holland has been asking questions and, although it's not been made public, it appears this Van Maarden might be involved in several dubious schemes. It seems certain now a substantial amount of the money allocated to re-build Laurens Oostermeer's fleet after the war went missing. There is also a rumour Van Maarden's involved with some underground mob dealing in precious metals or narcotics or something and in some way it's connected to Laurens Oostermeer's death. Then yesterday a man drowned after crashing his car into a canal in what seemed like an ordinary accident until it was reported in the paper, when suddenly the police raced around suppressing any of the details.'

'Kathy and I saw that. I never told you but we saw Kathy's Aunt Vivian and her husband Marcos with a similar car in Zeebrugge last July.'

'Did you say the man's name was Marcos?'

'Yes, I don't know their surname. Why? Do you think it was him?'

'My friend wasn't sure, but it sounds similar to the name he told me and he thinks the death may not have been an accident, but linked to the criminal underworld.'

'Kathy is going to ask her Grandpa if he knows anything about it.'

'I'd tell them not to get involved if I were you. If Marcos was killed because he upset professional criminals, any questions could put Kathy or her Grandpa in danger or get them involved with the Dutch police, who have slammed the lid on the accident and anything to do with it.'

'It's that serious?'

'It appears so. Not even the top people in the legal profession can get an inkling of what's going on.'

'Do you think Van Maarden's involved?'

'I don't know of course, but I wouldn't be surprised.'

'I must ring Kathy and tell her; talking of which, I need to buy her a Christmas present. Can you give me a lift up to the shops?'

'Sure.'

'The trouble is I have to go over to the mill, so I won't be ready for half-an-hour.'

'That's not a problem. I've got no appointments until three o'clock, after you've sailed. I wouldn't mind looking round the shops for a change. I don't go often; it's a bit boring on your own.'

It was only as I walked up to see Peter Dawson I remembered I was also going to look for a ring. Malcolm, it seemed, would be the first to know of my intentions.

I only had a couple of hours, but luckily we walked past a shop called Manteris just after we'd parked the car. I recognised the sign from one of their shops in Canterbury, where Kathy had stopped to admire a moss green outfit in the window, remarking how much she liked it. I knew her size from looking at her clothes at the hotel in Shoreham, so it was just a few minutes later Malcolm and I left the shop with not only the outfit, but also a matching pair of shoes and a bag.

'That didn't take long,' said Malcolm. 'What shall we do now you've finished shopping?'

'Well, actually, I haven't finished,' I said, stopping outside a jeweller three doors down from Manteris.

'What else do you need?'

I looked in the window full of watches, rings and bracelets. There was nothing that caught my eye and we moved on down the street. 'You'll know soon enough.'

I started looking in the window of a big jeweller in the middle of town, a window that was full of rings. 'I'll have a look in here,' I said.

'What do you want from…?'

It was then he noticed what was on display.

'Chris! Are you going to ask…?'

I nodded.

'That's fantastic, that's…'

'I know,' I said, laughing at the look on his face.

'She's a wonderful girl. You're a lucky man, you…' He shook my hand. 'Congratulations, Chris, I know you'll both be very happy.'

'Congratulations to you as well. That time you actually managed to finish a sentence. You should've seen your face.'

'What do you expect with news like that?'

We went to many shops and time was running out. If it hadn't been for Malcolm, who knew where to go, I'd have never seen enough to be sure I'd chosen the right one. As it was, we retraced our steps several times to have a second look in three shops before I decided on a diamond and sapphire ring from the window where I'd told Malcolm about Kathy and me.

'Just over three weeks,' I said, as we headed back to the car. 'I don't know where I'll be seeing Kathy but it won't matter, it's going to be a very special Christmas.'

'If she comes to Shoreham we'll have a big party, if you like. I wouldn't want to take up precious time you could have together.'

'A party would be wonderful.'

I looked at the ring as we walked along the street, seeing Kathy's face in my mind. 'Nothing could spoil this Christmas, Malcolm. It's going to be the best ever, the one I'll always remember.'

As I went back aboard the *Lily Jade* I saw Lubec down the hold and wondered if he knew about Marcos. I hadn't told anyone about Malcolm's news and I certainly wasn't about to tell him.

When I'd tried to ring Kathy from Malcolm's house the line at the surgery had been engaged and there had been no answer at her house, so when I went up to the timber mill to collect the papers for the voyage to Yarmouth I asked Peter Dawson if I could use his phone. 'I want to ring Canterbury; I'll pay for the call.'

'It's your girl, isn't it?'

I nodded.

'Be my guest,' he said, pushing the phone towards me.

I rang the surgery and Gerald Griffiths answered. 'She's not here today, Chris. Something to do with her Grandpa.'

'He's not ill, is he?'

'I don't know. Kathy came in this morning, obviously concerned about something, but didn't elaborate except to say it was to do with her Grandpa. She apologised for letting me down, especially after having the past two days off, and then she left. I'll tell her you called.'

I put the phone down feeling flat. Maybe she'd heard about Marcos and… and what? I asked myself.

'Did you get through?'

'Yes thanks, Peter, but Kathy wasn't there.'

'Never mind I'm sure you'll catch up soon. Have a good voyage and ring me from Fowey about the cargo before Christmas.'

I rang Kathy at home from Yarmouth, but there was no answer the first time. I tried again that evening from the phone box near Solent Serenity, relieved when I heard her voice at the other end.

'Kathy, my sweet girl. How are you?'

'Oh, Chris. It's so good to hear your voice.'

My heart skipped a beat to hear her so happy. 'How is Grandpa? Gerald at the surgery said you had to take Wednesday off?'

'He's fine. We're both fine.'

Her voice had suddenly changed. The zing had gone and it had the tone of someone making a report. I wasn't sure what to say.

'Oh, I'm glad. Did you have a good trip back from Shoreham?'

'It was ok.'

Something was wrong but I wasn't sure how to handle it over the phone. I wanted to take her in my arms and tell her everything would be alright.

'What plans do you have for the weekend?'

'Nothing, just catching up. Look, Chris, I must go, Grandpa hasn't had his tea yet.'

'Oh… right.'

'Bye, Chris.'

'Kathy?'

It was too late. The phone had gone dead. I looked at my watch. It was 9 p.m. It seemed strange to me Grandpa hadn't had tea when he usually ate about five.

A Handful of Pebbles

Normally I would've spent the night at Solent Serenity and done a few small jobs about the place, but the phone call had unnerved me so much my mind started to imagine all sorts of terrible things and I decided to go back to the *Lily Jade*.

The ship was quiet. I think Scotty was ashore and I heard Lubec snoring as I made a mug of tea. It was a cold night with a strong wind, but I put on a coat and took my tea out to the lee-side of the bridge. Low clouds were sliding across the sky with a crescent moon darting in and out between them. The wind seemed to whip over the bridge-front and I pulled the collar up around my neck. Even though the temperature was close to freezing I stood there for quite a long time before going to bed.

Chapter Sixteen

The next morning we were working cargo and I was sorting out fresh paperwork, when Scotty appeared after nine o'clock looking somewhat worse for wear. 'You look a bit fragile, Scotty.'

'Had a wee session with Jim Middleton last night.'

'A wee session?'

'Aye, nothing serious. We were talking about Christmas.'

'So what time did this "wee session" finish?'

'Och, I'm not sure. Maybe two or three.'

'As long as Agnes is ready.'

'Agnes is in better shape than I am'

'Thank heavens for that.'

'Fiona's coming down on the twenty-second, so do we know what's happening over Christmas?'

'I have to talk to the mill from Fowey, but I think they'll want us to bring a load of timber to Yarmouth to be discharged between Christmas and New Year, so we'll be tied up here until 4th January.'

'That's great – Fiona and I'll have a bonny time. How about you?'

'I need to speak to Kathy.' I didn't mention last night's phone call.

'Oh, this is for you,' Scotty said, taking a crumpled piece of paper from his pocket.

'This is our clearance to sail signed by Jim Middleton; except it's blank.'

'Aye. Jim thought he might not be feeling a hundred per cent this morning, so he gave me that. Fill in the figures and give him his copy when we get back.'

'You two could end up in a lot of trouble.'

'Only if you tell Fiona, please don't tell Fiona!'

'Never mind Fiona; what about the authorities?'

'What authorities? Jim's the authorities.'

I knew when I was beaten. 'Thanks anyway.'

'It's nought, but remember, don't tell Fiona or we'll both be better off dead.'

The subject was never mentioned again.

We sailed to Weymouth where Lubec, as usual, had his day off. When he returned he had a grim look on his face and I wondered if he'd seen Vivian. He didn't say hello, going straight to his cabin where he remained until we sailed.

We cleared Weymouth harbour, and as we steamed past the end of the Chesil Beach I heard the "clack, clack, clack" of the stones in his pocket as he came onto the bridge to relieve me.

'Usual position, Jean. Making about eight knots.'

He nodded but said nothing, the stones continually being twirled by his fingers.

Scotty was having lunch when I came down. He tapped the table with his knife and pointed it upwards before trying to speak with a mouthful of food. After trying to swallow too quickly and having a coughing fit he finally found his voice.

'What's up with Jean? He ignored me when I said hello, and then when I made a joke about eating too many snails makes a Frenchman go deaf, he called me a silly old Scots fart and told me where to go in language that even made me cringe.'

'The fact you called him a Frenchman didn't help the situation, because he's Dutch.'

Scotty shrugged his shoulders. 'What's the difference? They all come from over there.'

'It's like someone calling you English or Welsh, however, that's not the real reason he got angry. He's upset.' I told Scotty what Malcolm had said in Shoreham. 'It seems it was probably Marcos who drowned in the canal and I think he's found out from Vivian while we were in Weymouth.'

When I rang the timber mill from Fowey they confirmed a cargo to be taken to Yarmouth before Christmas to ensure builders would have stocks immediately after New Year. It would only be a part cargo and I decided to arrive in Shoreham a day early so we could be back in Yarmouth by the afternoon of Thursday 23rd. I rang Malcolm and told him.

'I was hoping you'd be here and Kathy was coming down, so we could all have Christmas together.'

'I'm going to call Kathy from Yarmouth, it's better I ring her at home during the weekend rather than keep interrupting her at work and if she can come down to the island how about you make another voyage on the *Lily Jade?*'

'I don't want to spoil your time with Kathy, especially if you've just popped the question.'

'It won't be a problem, there are two bedrooms at Solent Serenity, or you can use my cabin on board.'

'I'll bring the car down and we can all have transport.'

It sounded as if Christmas had been organised to perfection.

****

The atmosphere on board during the day in Fowey and on the voyage back to Yarmouth lacked the Christmas spirit. Jean Lubec was still sullen and Scotty just wanted to get ashore or anywhere away from him. The altercation between them seemed to have destroyed some of the harmony aboard the *Lily Jade* and I didn't like it. Even Soo was quiet.

Back in Yarmouth I went over to the Harbour Master's office to ring Kathy. It was now 20th December, just five days to Christmas. 'No reply, Jim. I'll have to try again later.'

'I'm going home, Chris. I don't usually come in on a Sunday, but I don't mind when it's you and the *Lily Jade*. Here, take the spare key to the office and call from here, don't try and use the public phone; it's developed a reputation for cutting people off.'

That evening I returned to Jim's office. Inside it was quiet. Not even the wind that was whining in the rigging of the boats in the harbour penetrated the old brick building.

'Kathy, my sweet girl. It's so good to hear your voice.'

'Chris, how are you?'

She sounded tired. 'Are you ok, Kathy? You sound worn out.'

'I am a bit tired. It's been a hectic week what with… with the run-up to Christmas and everything.'

'Christmas is why I rang. When shall we be able to see each other? I wondered if you could come down to the island or should I come up to Canterbury?'

'Oh, Chris.'

There was a muffled sound at the other end as if the mouth-piece was covered.

'Kathy?'

There was no answer and for a moment or two I thought Jim's phone had gone out in sympathy with the public call-box.

'Kathy?' The muffled sound returned. 'Kathy are you alright?'

'Chris, it's about Christmas. I'm sorry, Chris, but I won't be able to see you.'

Her words hit me like a sledgehammer. What had happened? Why? 'But, Kathy…'

'Chris, it's just something that's come up and I need to sort it out.'

'Can I help?'

'No, no, Chris. No!'

'So when can I see…? When can we…?' I spluttered, my mind reeling over the possibility I could lose Kathy. What had I done to upset her? How could I make amends?

'I don't know, Chris. I'll leave a message with Malcolm or Jim Middleton when I can.'

'Soon, Kathy, make it soon.'

'When I can, Chris.'

'I love you, Kathy.' But it was too late, she'd gone.

I sat in Jim's office, the telephone receiver still in my hand. I felt numb. So many questions entered my mind, but I had answers for none of them. I only knew that at the moment, my world and its dreams had been shattered and I had no idea if I would ever be able to pick up the pieces. It was a comfort the old brick building was so solid. No-one could have heard me moaning, 'why, why, why.'

I went back to the *Lily Jade* and my cabin, fortunately meeting no-one on the way. As I put my coat in the wardrobe I saw Kathy's green outfit and the box with matching shoes. I fingered the material, trying to visualise her wearing it. From the drawer of my desk I took the small box containing the ring and opened it. I sat staring at the six diamonds surrounding the sapphire, wondering if I'd ever get to place it on Kathy's hand.

Putting it away, I made a mug of tea, and taking my jacket went to the lee-side of the bridge as I'd done another night. The bridge of a ship, any ship, but especially the *Lily Jade* was the one place I felt in control of any situation and, at the moment, to try and be in control of myself, but I could think of nothing except Kathy and the phone call. The air was cold and I gulped down the tea while it still had some warmth in it.

I never heard him arrive, but suddenly, Soo was there with two mugs of tea – one for him, the other to replace the empty mug in my hand.

'Soo tell Captain Chris a story.'

It was a statement, not a request or, would I care to listen.

'Many years ago family live in South China near Guilin on river Lei. One day son take boat out fishing but no return. Father upset. Worried about son and boat. Many days he wondered what had happened.

'Then stranger come with big men. He say second son done bad things and he owe stranger money. Father say he not responsible for second son's actions as he grown man. Stranger say second son told him he had no money, but father have boat so they had come to take it.

'Father say he has no boat and tells stranger go and see. Stranger very angry when he find no boat, but he and big men go away.

'Two days later first son come back with boat. Father was cross until he hear first son know about second son and stranger and he not want father to worry. That why he went with boat so stranger couldn't find it. He was loving son trying to protect father.'

I looked at Soo, wondering why he'd told me that story, but he just took my empty mug and left. Suddenly I felt very tired. It wasn't until the next morning I realised he'd drugged me.

* * * * * * *

On the voyage to Shoreham if Lubec was in a better mood or Scotty less impatient to see Fiona, I didn't notice, nor did I care. I had enough trouble coping with my own thoughts, never mind anyone else's. Whether they noticed my mood, I don't know, but Soo certainly did as he gave the breathing space I needed.

'Good morning, Chris. I think I'm looking forward to my next voyage. I've been listening to the weather reports and it seems I may find out how good a sailor I am – they're forecasting lousy weather.'

I'd been looking at the latest Admiralty Notices to Mariners, checking for any alterations to buoys or lights when Malcolm arrived. 'Hi Malcolm,' I said, turning around.

'My God, Chris, What's the matter? You look terrible.'

I motioned him to shut the door and sit down before I told him about the phone call to Kathy. 'I don't know what I've done or not done, Malcolm,' I said, as he sat there in stony silence. 'Or how to put it right.'

'I don't know what to say, Chris, except you and I are much the same in some ways.'

I looked at him questioningly, hoping he had an answer to at least part of my problems.

'In our professional roles as a lawyer or a ship's captain, there isn't a situation we can't handle, usually easily. But emotions and understanding other people's thoughts is another matter all together. I can only suggest you try to tackle it from the professional angle. For me, that would mean waiting to see if any more evidence came to light. For you, maybe it's like waiting to see the first blink of a lighthouse to ascertain your position. It's not much help I know, but at the moment I think you just have to be patient. Time usually has the answers.'

I took a deep breath. He was right of course. In my usual manner I'd set off at a hundred knots, trying to resolve everything immediately. 'Thank you, Malcolm. I needed someone to say that.'

'It looks as if I won't be making the voyage now.'

'Why ever not?'

'I just thought you might...'

'Might what?'

'Well, you know, want to be alone or something.'

'More than ever I need someone like you around, someone other than the crew of the *Lily Jade*. Please Malcolm, come and spend Christmas with me at Solent Serenity.'

I was glad we had only a part cargo from the mill as the weather forecast was so bad I would never have risked putting Malcolm's car on deck. We left a hollow in the middle of the timber that allowed the hatch boards to cover the Rover after it was lashed down.

The voyage that normally took just over six hours lasted until Christmas Eve morning, the *Lily Jade* punching into a force eight gale sweeping up the Channel. Malcolm, it appeared, would have made a good seafarer as he was the only person aboard who seemed to enjoy getting soaking wet as he was thrown about when the *Lily Jade* pitched and rolled, shipping green water over the bow. The only time he got upset was when a wave pushed open the door and soaked his trousers while he was sitting on the toilet.

I put out extra lines when we arrived as the weather report was just as bad until after Boxing Day. We opened the hold and as the Rover landed on the wharf Scotty came across the brow. Under his raincoat he wore a sports jacket over a green shirt with a tartan tie. In his hand was a small suitcase.

'You're quick off the mark,' I said.

'Aye; there's no point in keeping a good woman waiting for no reason.'

I winced, thinking of Kathy, but I hadn't told Scotty she wasn't coming in case he felt he should stay, and I didn't want his Christmas ruined as well. Instead I tried to make a joke.

'Have you got the kilt to match the tie?'

'Aye,' he said, tapping the suitcase. 'I would nae be goin' out half dressed yer know. Only this weather stops me wearing it now.'

Even Lubec nodded understandingly as another blast of winter wind blew across the wharf, and I wasn't about to get into what Scotty wore under his kilt.

'I've left the Senior Second in charge,' he called over his shoulder as he walked towards a car that had just arrived. The driver wound down the window enough to wave to us.

'Hi, Fiona,' I called. 'Merry Christmas.'

'Same to you and Kathy.'

Again I winced.

After stowing the derrick, Jean Lubec had gone to get changed as he was going to see his brother in Newport. Until he'd told me ten days ago what he was doing I'd had no idea he had a brother, much less that he lived on the island.

Back on board I tidied up the little bit of outstanding paperwork and got ready to go to Solent Serenity. When I went down Malcolm was talking to Soo.

'He says he feels important, to be looking after the engine-room.'

'You're more than just the Chief, Soo,' I said. 'You're also the Captain.'

He blushed. 'Not like Captain Chris. He better.'

'Thank you, Soo, but remember you don't have to stay aboard. You can come with Malcolm and me.'

'No, no. This Soo's home. *Lily Jade* is home. Soo like to be here looking after *Lily Jade*.'

'Ok, Captain Soo. Ok Chief Engineer Soo. The ship is in your hands.'

Soo burst into raucous laughter, unable to speak for nearly a minute. He wiped tears from his eyes and looked at us. 'Captain Soo!' he exclaimed, and burst into laughter again.

'Remember we're coming tomorrow morning to take you home for Christmas dinner.'

He nodded and stopped laughing. Neither of us had mentioned Kathy, but somehow I felt he knew she wasn't coming. 'Thank you, Captain Chris. Captain Chris and Mr Malcolm very kind.'

I left the *Lily Jade* knowing she was in the best possible hands.

On the way to Solent Serenity we called at a farm where I'd organised to pick up a plucked turkey and some fresh vegetables. When we arrived I lit the fire and started showing Malcolm the work I'd been doing around the house.

'Enough of work, Chris; you've earned a bit of time off. Let me get you a drink.'

Chapter Seventeen

We sat and talked all evening. The subjects included films, the latest music, shipping and the legal profession; but never, and I was grateful to Malcolm for it, he never mentioned Kathy. We became so engrossed in conversation that at times I even forgot my feelings of despair for a little while. The fact we also drank too much may have had something to do with it.

The clock in the hall struck twelve.

'Merry Christmas, Chris.'

'Thank you, Malcolm, and to you.'

'I've got a present for you, but do you think we should wait until Soo is here?'

'Soo! With all that's happened I forgot to get Soo a present! What can we do?'

'Don't panic, Chris.' Malcolm poured us another drink. 'Let's think, what would he like the most?'

'The *Lily Jade*,' I said, laughing.

'I believe she's owned by someone else who wouldn't sell her for the world.'

'Maybe for Kathy…' After all evening with Malcolm being such a thoughtful friend, it'd been me who had mentioned her name.

He nodded. 'Let's think what your relieving Master and Chief Engineer would want for Christmas,' he said, immediately changing the subject. Suddenly a big grin appeared on his face.

'What are you thinking?'

'What size clothes do you think Soo would wear?'

'Clothes?'

'Yes, say a jacket or coat.'

'He's rather thin and short. I'm not sure, maybe about the size of a young teenager.'

'That's what I thought. Have you got any material left over from the renovations? Curtains or the like, but it must be yellow or gold.'

'What've you got in mind?' I asked, now intrigued as Malcolm's grin got bigger.

'You try to find the material while I get something from the car.'

I rummaged around in the cupboards at the back of the kitchen, but anything I found was the wrong colour. Then I remembered a small gold cushion I'd bought for the chair in my bedroom. It had been too bright and I'd put it away in the top of the wardrobe. It was brand-new, but I couldn't imagine how it would become a present for Soo.

I took it back to the kitchen where Malcolm was holding a bag from a menswear shop. 'That's perfect,' he said, when he saw the cushion. 'As long as you don't mind cutting up the cover?'

'Would you like to tell me what you've got in mind?'

From the bag he took a black jacket. 'I bought it for my nephew who's fourteen. Do you think it'd fit Soo?'

I nodded, still not understanding.

'We'll make Captain's braid from the cushion cover and stitch it on the sleeves.'

'That's brilliant, Malcolm!' I said, going to get scissors and the sewing basket that'd been left in the house by the previous owner.

It was twenty to four on Christmas morning before we finished. I hadn't seen Santa Claus, but he'd certainly arrived for Soo. Both of us were tired, but happy when we got up just four hours later and started to prepare the dinner. By ten the basics were ready and Malcolm drove down to pick up Soo.

'Captain Chris have beautiful house. It palace. All full with beautiful things.'

I hadn't realised Soo had never been to Solent Serenity; an oversight on my part.

'Can watch for *Lily Jade* from here,' he said, when we were on the balcony. 'But Captain Chris no watch. He must be on board in command.'

'You've been told,' Malcolm chuckled.

'Captain Chris is cold,' I said. 'Let's go down to Christmas dinner.'

Malcolm poured two glasses of wine for us and a tomato juice for Soo. I'd cut off a branch from the conifer in the garden and placed it beside the fireplace as a Christmas tree and beneath it were three parcels – presents for Malcolm and I from each other and Soo's jacket.

Soo watched as Malcolm and I exchanged presents, before I picked up the third parcel. 'This is for you, Soo. Merry Christmas.'

'For Soo? Cannot be for Soo.'

'Read the tag,' Malcolm said.

His eyes were misty when he looked up. 'Captain Chris and Mr Malcolm too kind. Treat Soo too well.'

'Soo deserves it,' I said.

Malcolm opened his present, a model kit of a ship.

Soo clapped his hands. 'Ship like *Lily Jade!*'

He was so excited I wished I'd thought to give it to him. Malcolm must've had the same idea. 'Would you help me put it together, Soo?'

'It for Mr Malcolm.'

'We'll do it together.'

Malcolm had given me two books, "Uncommon Law" and "More Uncommon Law" by A.P. Herbert. 'They'll show you how the law can be a big ass,' he said.

I flicked one of the books open, read a few lines and burst into laughter.

'Law funny? Not serious?'

I nodded. 'Is Soo going to open his present?'

Carefully, he unwrapped the jacket and lifted it out of the paper. 'This mistake,' he said, when he saw the gold braid. 'This Captain Chris's jacket.'

'No mistake,' I said, holding it for him to put on. 'This is for Captain Soo and Chief Engineer Soo when he's looking after the *Lily Jade*.'

He stared at his arms before suddenly leaving the room and there was silence for a couple of minutes. 'Where's he gone?' Malcolm asked.

We found him in the hall standing in front of the mirror shaking his head. I put my hands on his shoulders. 'Now Soo is a real Captain and a real Chief.'

At one o'clock we sat down to Christmas dinner, Soo still wearing his jacket. On our plates Malcolm and I each found a small intricate carving.

'Merry Christmas, Captain Chris and Mr Malcolm. Just little thing. Soo say thank you.'

'Did you make these?' I asked.

'Soo make from big fish bone. For Captain Chris it love charm for happiness. For Mr Malcolm it good luck charm.'

I vowed to get a gold chain and wear it around my neck forever, despite what people might say. I didn't hear what Malcolm said, my thoughts were with Kathy.

We ate too much and half-an-hour later Soo went quiet, clutching his stomach. I didn't ask, I just poured a tomato juice and watched as he took two sachets of powder from his bag and stirred them into the drink. He drank the concoction, the effect immediate, if not a complete cure.

'We must take you to see a doctor,' I said.

'A special doctor,' added Malcolm.

'No good. Nothing can do. Soo been to big doctors.'

After twenty minutes he was obviously still in some pain and drank another tomato juice with one powder.

'I go for little walk. Just few minutes with stretching. It fix.'

He was still wearing his Captain's jacket as we watched him walk across the road to the cliff-top. 'He'd better be back soon,' Malcolm said. 'He'll freeze to death out there.'

Ten minutes later Soo returned with a worried look on his face.

'Does your stomach still ache?' I asked.

'No, no. All fixed, all ok.'

'Is something else wrong?'

'Soo not sure.'

Do you want to talk about it?'

'No, it nothing.' He smiled. 'I silly Soo. We have good Christmas in palace of Captain Chris. It cold outside. We stay in warm.'

After tea Malcolm took him back to the *Lily Jade,* when he refused my offer to stay at Solent Serenity saying, Captain Soo must go look after his ship. I realised I was no longer the sole owner of the *Lily Jade,* despite what the paperwork might say.

The front door slammed as Malcolm returned. 'Sorry, Chris, the wind got it, it's blowing a gale out there.'

He came into the kitchen, rainwater dripping from his coat. 'Pour us a drink, I need to talk to you,' he said, disappearing back into the hall before I could say anything.

'Thanks,' he said, taking the glass of wine from my hand and heading towards the chairs by the fire. 'Come and sit down. Something happened to Soo this afternoon.'

'He's not still ill, is he?'

'No, his stomach is fine, but something happened when he went for that walk on the cliff-top.'

'Such as?'

'I'm not sure. Maybe he heard or saw something. I doubt anyone spoke to him, but I noticed the look on his face when he came back – it was one of disbelief, as if he'd seen a ghost. You were in the kitchen and by the time you saw him he'd hidden most of it, but he was still jittery.'

'Are you serious about this?'

'Extremely. Think about what he said to you at the time.'

'I remember asking if his stomach was better because he didn't look the best.'

'And he said he was fine, but had something else on his mind. When you asked about it, he said it was nothing.'

'I remember that.'

'Then he went on about how cold it was outside, and how we should stay in the warm.'

'Soo's never worried about the cold or the rain.'

'I think he was trying to stop us going outside in case we saw what it was that upset him.'

'Any idea what it might have been?'

'I tried to question him in the car, but he knew I'd tell you anything he said, although he did let one thing slip out.'

'Which was?'

'You may not believe, or like what I think he meant.'

'Try me,' I said, now bewildered and slightly apprehensive.

'I asked why he didn't stay here, and he said he must protect Captain Chris and the *Lily Jade*.'

'Protect?'

'He laughed it off immediately, saying now he had his jacket and was Captain Soo he could look after the *Lily Jade* and all of us, but I'm sure he meant what he said the first time. He thinks you're in danger.'

'Who or what would threaten me?'

'I've no idea, but if Soo thinks you're in danger I'd be taking the thought seriously.'

I had to agree with him. I'd never fathomed out Soo's sixth sense, but I did know it had always been right. 'Let's go and look outside.'

We put on our coats and I grabbed a torch. Outside it was pitch black with an overcast sky and the wind, as Malcolm had said, was blowing a gale. On the cliff-top we looked each way and then out across the Solent, but the rain was so heavy I could barely see the flashing light on Hurst Castle.

'This is hopeless,' I said.

I didn't sleep well and when I awoke early on Boxing Day morning the wind had died away and the rain had eased to a drizzle. I was clearing up the breakfast dishes while Malcolm sorted out some tools to help me fit a new wardrobe in the second bedroom when someone pounded on the front door. As we went to the hall the pounding started again and there was the unmistakable sound of Scotty's voice.

'Och, Chris, wake up ye lazy sassanach!'

When I opened the door Jim Middleton was standing there with him. 'What the blazes…?'

'Ye'd best get down to the *Lily Jade* straight away.'

'What's happened to the *Lily Jade?*' I asked, horrified at his words.

'The ship's fine, Chris,' Jim said, 'but the police are there and Soo, we understand, won't let them aboard until you arrive.'

Malcolm had grabbed his car keys and our coats. 'How did you know about this?' I asked, as we ran towards the Rover and Jim's car with Fiona in the driver's seat.

'A phone call,' Jim said. 'I think Soo found my number and told the police to ring it.'

At somewhat more than the speed limit we raced through Totland and down the hill past Colwell Common. Less than ten minutes later we swung up onto the wharf at Yarmouth.

The scene that greeted us was bizarre. The brow had been taken in to prevent anyone going aboard and standing on the deck glaring at the group of police, was Soo. He was wearing his jacket, making sure everyone could see the gold braid, and brandishing a large knife from the galley.

'Excuse me, sir. Do you have anything to do with this ship?'

'Yes, officer, I do. I'm Christopher Bowden, owner and Master.'

'Can you talk to that crazy Chinaman so we can come aboard?'

'He's not crazy, but yes I can talk to him.'

I hadn't said a word to Soo, but the brow was already back in place and the knife had disappeared. 'You can come aboard now, but I hope you've got a good reason for disturbing people at this hour on Boxing Day morning.'

I stood on the deck as the four of them came aboard, each wary as they passed Soo, now smiling broadly.

'It good you come, Captain Chris,' he said, as they went up the steps.

I said nothing. I just put my arm around his shoulders and nodded before following them up to my cabin, which became extremely crowded with six people in the confined space.

'Who is this, sir?' asked the uniformed policeman, the pencil poised over his notebook pointing towards Malcolm now sitting on my bunk.

'I'm Malcolm Chatwin, Captain Bowden's lawyer,' he said curtly.

'Captain Bowden,' said a plain clothes officer turning towards me, 'why did you feel the need to call your lawyer before returning to the ship?'

'He didn't,' Malcolm said. 'I was staying with him; but before you ask any more questions we'll see some identification, please.'

I wondered if irritating the man was a good idea, but I was thankful to have Malcolm with me. Reluctantly, it seemed, they showed me their papers, ignoring Malcolm until I called him over to examine them with me. Apart from the uniformed sergeant there were two detectives from the Metropolitan Police in London and one from the Dutch authorities in Rotterdam.

'We need to ask you and the crew some questions and also search the vessel.'

'If you have a warrant,' Malcolm cut in.

The detective rummaged in his brief-case and produced a slip of paper that he passed to me. 'I trust you'll find this in order, sir' he said, looking at Malcolm.

I gave it to Malcolm who nodded.

'Very well gentlemen; fire away, we've nothing to hide,' I said, noting the change of attitude seemed to catch the detective off-guard. They took particulars of the crew and as an after-thought, also of Malcolm.

'Captain,' the man from Rotterdam said, 'has this ship ever traded to Amsterdam?'

'Not since it came into my possession.'

'Or any other port in Europe?'

'The ship has not left the English coast since I became the owner.' The next few questions were the same as I'd been asked back in January, and I remarked on it.

'We needed to check your answers, sir. Now do you know a man by the name of Pradera?'

When I said no he asked to see the log-book for the past six months and while he was looking at it Scotty burst into the cabin.

'Soo's collapsed!'

'Who are...?'

'Where is he?' I said, interrupting the man from Rotterdam.

'Down in the galley. He was making some tea when he clutched his stomach and collapsed.'

I didn't hear what the detective said, as Malcolm and I stumbled down the stairs. Soo was lying on the deck curled up in a ball

'He's still breathing,' Jim said.

'Sit him up Jim.' I felt in the pocket of Soo's old jacket hanging on the door to the galley and found a sachet of white powder that I tipped into the glass of tomato juice Malcolm had fetched.

'Wait, Malcolm, don't give it to him yet.' There were no more sachets in the jacket but I knew he'd have some more somewhere. I went to his cabin and at the foot of his bunk was the duffle bag he always carried when he went ashore. There in the first pocket I found more small packages. 'Here we are!' I cried, unfolding a scrap of paper; but its contents were white. 'No good,' I said, 'it's the wrong one.'

I returned to the cabin and checked the bag again. In the base, under the plastic insert, I found what I was looking for – the black pepper-like powder.

Soo had come-to, but was groaning as we put the glass to his lips. Immediately the eyes opened and his body stiffened until he recognised me. His eyes closed again as he sipped the red liquid. He'd drunk half the glass when his hand rested on mine, the eyes opened and a thin smile appeared. 'Thank you, Captain Chris,' he whispered.

When he'd finished the potion Scotty carried him to his cabin and placed him on the bunk. I closed the door. 'They're going to search the ship, Scotty,' I said, quietly. 'We mustn't let them find Soo's drugs. Empty the duffle bag and have a good look around, he must have more somewhere. White and black powder. Take it all down below and hide it somewhere safe.'

'Aye, Chris.'

'Malcolm and I will try to delay the search as long as possible, or you can bring up a pot of tea if you're ready.'

'Is the Chinaman ok?' the second detective asked as I closed my cabin door.

'He's resting.'

'You realise he may face charges of threatening policemen with a dangerous weapon?' the first one said.

I stood up and pointed at him. 'And I'll take you to the highest court in the land if he doesn't recover!'

'Easy sir, I don't want to have to caution you as well.'

'Excuse me,' Malcolm butted in, 'would you mind telling me what happened when you arrived at the *Lily Jade?*'

'We don't have to tell you anything.'

'I know that, but if you charge Soo I shall be representing him in court and you'll have to answer the question then.'

'It doesn't matter,' his colleague said, 'you might as well tell him. We all know the Chinaman appeared with a knife and stopped us coming aboard.'

'We saw no-one on board until we started to walk across the gangway, then the Chinaman appeared from inside wielding the knife and wearing a jacket that gave us the impression he was the Captain. He said, "who you" or something and when I told him we'd come to see him, the Captain, he said "no-one board *Lily Jade*" and approached us waving the knife. So we retreated back down onto the wharf.'

'Did you show him any identification?'

'We told him we were policeman.'

'But you didn't show him any identification?'

'I wasn't going near that madman while he had the knife.'

'The only reason he had the knife was because he'd been preparing food in the galley when he heard you come aboard. Was the uniformed policeman with you?'

'No, he was parking the car.'

'That meant Soo had no idea who you were and he was just protecting his employer's property. What did he do when you said you were policemen?'

'He yelled out a telephone number and said get Captain Chris.'

'We came as soon as we were informed of the situation and have been co-operative since then…'

'And will continue to be,' I interjected.

'As Captain Bowden says, and will continue to be, so I suggest you forget any thought of pressing charges against Soo, because, I can assure you I would crucify the prosecution in any court.'

'Shall we continue with the real reason for your visit?' I asked, trying to deflate the escalating tension.

They agreed and the Dutchman, who had been silent during the discussion about Soo, resumed his questions. There was nothing new except some names and the history of the *Lily Jade* years ago. I couldn't help him with anything apart from the fact the ship had been given to Jacques Kessel by Laurens Oostermeer after the war. He seemed interested in that, but I got the impression he thought I was trying to hide something.

Scotty appeared with a tray of tea and biscuits. 'This is Scotty, my engineer.'

'Aye, I look after Agnes.'

'You have a female in your crew?'

We laughed and the detective looked confused. 'It's the name I've given the engine,' Scotty explained.

They asked Scotty some questions and his answers confirmed everything Malcolm and I had said.

'We'll need to question Mr Soo and the other crew member, Lubec.'

'Jean Lubec will be back in the morning, by which time Soo should have recovered. One thing I don't understand,' I continued, 'and you don't have to tell me, but why was it necessary to come down at this time on Boxing Day morning?'

'We were acting on some information received, Captain Bowden. Senior people thought it required immediate action.'

They searched the ship for more than two hours, opening every drawer and cupboard. They checked any container, be it a pot in the galley or a drum in the foc'sle. By noon they seemed fed-up and ready to go home, as if they had wasted Boxing Day. After a conversation on deck they announced they would return in the morning to see Soo and Lubec.

'If you need to have another look around the ship I don't mind,' I said, 'but understand we'll be discharging cargo.'

'Thank you, Captain Bowden.'

They left and I went to see Soo. He was awake and cheerful, but looked somewhat pale.

'I sorry, Captain Chris.'

'What for?'

'Trouble. I make trouble.'

'You did not. Captain Soo looked after the *Lily Jade* just as he said he would. Captain Soo is my number one man.'

Soo smiled and some colour returned to his face. Scotty appeared. 'Do ye need another juice?'

Soo nodded and when Scotty returned with a glass he had two pieces of folded paper. 'This is the last one of black powder,' he said to both of us. 'I could nae find any more in the duffle bag.'

'Do you have some more, Soo?' I asked.

'I hide. No-one find.'

'Aye, you hide bloody well.'

'Soo show.'

We followed him into the galley and he took down two large containers from the rack above the table.

'But the police looked in all those,' I said.

He opened the one marked flour and showed us.

'Flour?' asked Scotty.

Soo nodded before spreading a plastic sheet on the table and emptying the container. Buried in the flour was a tobacco tin that he dusted off and passed to me. After replacing the flour he did the same with the second can marked rice which revealed a similar tin.

'At least I'll know what's happened if I feel ill after a bowl of ye rice, ye cunning little monkey.'

'No good for Chief. He act strange with powder.'

'He's strange enough now, Soo,' I said, 'without you adding to it.'

'On that note of confidence I shall resume my Boxing Day festivities with Fiona and Jim.'

As he left Malcolm came in having made some more tea, and we sat down with Soo still sipping his juice.

'What did you make of it all?'

Malcolm shook his head. 'Whatever it is, it's a lot bigger than I imagined, and obviously highly political with this Van Maarden and maybe others. By the way, the man Pradera they asked about was Marcos.'

'Marcos! Do you think he and Kathy's Aunt Vivian are involved?'

'They must've had some reason for mentioning his name.'

'But why the *Lily Jade*? They've searched her twice now.'

'I'll get my friend over there to ask some more questions, but I think he may come up against a brick wall. Certainly they think the *Lily Jade,* and therefore you, are involved in whatever it is.'

'Is there anything I should do?'

Malcolm thought for a moment. 'Do you need to keep the papers concerning the sale from Jacques Kessel on board?'

'Only the certificate of registry which is displayed on the bridge.'

'In which case, I'll lodge all the other correspondence in a safe deposit box in the bank, just in case someone becomes nosey.'

'I'll get it ready for you before we sail. Thanks for sorting it all out today; otherwise they might've taken Soo to court.'

'They still might, so let me know if anything happens when I'm not around.'

Malcolm and I insisted Soo came back to Solent Serenity for the rest of the weekend. I used some of the vegetables from the farm to make a soup, which he ate before we got him into one of the single beds in the back bedroom. It had been the worst attack I'd ever seen Soo suffer since I'd known of his condition.

'I must get him to a doctor.'

'It's Boxing Day, and we're on the island, where I doubt you'd find a specialist at the best of times.'

'In which case, I may have to send him to London.'

'I'll make some enquiries when I get home.'

Talking of Soo reminded me. 'We never went out this morning to try and find what it was that frightened Soo last night. Let's have a look while he's asleep.'

We went over to the cliff-top and stood in the drizzle looking along the grass where I'd first met Kathy, down at the empty Totland pier and across to the mainland trying to find something that could've upset Soo or threaten me.

'See anything?'

'Nothing, Malcolm. You go back inside, I'm going into Totland to ring Kathy.'

After hearing the unanswered ring of the telephone in Canterbury my mood matched the cold wintry weather sweeping up the Channel as I returned to Solent Serenity.

'I gather Kathy wasn't home, judging by the time you were out and the look on your face?'

'I wish I knew what was going on. I'm worried about her, Malcolm.'

Soo joined us, but he was obviously still feeling weak. We all had some soup and after a cup of tea he went back to bed. An hour later, exhausted, Malcolm and I followed suit. It hadn't been the Christmas I'd envisaged a week earlier.

The following morning Soo's stomach must have recovered as he demolished a large breakfast, but he still seemed upset.

'I go. Get some fresh air,' he announced, taking his jacket and opening the front door.

I thought no more about it until Malcolm came downstairs. 'I went to see where Soo went.'

'And?'

'He went over to the cliff-edge and stood looking down at the water for quite some time before walking along the road towards the village.'

'Why would he go to Totland? It's Sunday, the day after Boxing Day and nothing will be open.'

'Unless he just went for a walk?'

Once again Kathy's words: "There's something strange going on", came into my mind.

'Last time he went out there,' Malcolm continued, 'he came back looking as if he'd seen a ghost.'

'We saw nothing yesterday afternoon, but I suppose we could go and have another look.'

At the front gate we looked down the road to see if Soo was returning, but there was no-one in the mist rising from the grass as the sun melted the overnight frost. From the cliff-top we looked down over Totland Bay with the sunlight reflecting off the calm water. It would have been pleasant to stand there a lot longer if it hadn't been so cold.

'Malcolm nudged me in the ribs. 'Look! Down there.'

I looked in the direction he was pointing, towards the pier, but saw nothing.

'There's someone behind the ferry office.'

A few seconds later a lone figure appeared from behind the cream building and stood by the rail looking into the water. Even with my good eyes it was impossible to see who it was at this distance until the person moved and immediately I recognised the distinctive short step, which was almost a jog, as he went to peer over the rail along the side of the pier. 'It's Soo!'

'I wonder what he's looking for?'

'Maybe,' I said, 'he's looking for whatever scared him the other night.'

'In which case we'd best not mention we saw him unless he says where he went.'

As we walked back to the house I wondered what on earth could've been down at the pier on Christmas night.

Chapter Eighteen

'Och, let me take ye up to the pub for lunch.'
'Scotty, we're working cargo!'
'Aye; but I'll no be seeing Malcolm for Hogmanay; and we'd no be long, just a quick bite.'
'He did offer to pay, Chris.'
'I know, Malcolm and that's a worry in itself.' Scotty didn't have a go at me for what I'd said and I wondered if there was another reason he wanted to go to the pub. 'Well, alright; but just one pint.'
'Aye, just one.'
Now I knew he had an ulterior motive – Scotty would never agree to just one pint.

Malcolm and I sat next to the fire in "The Old Yawl" wondering what Scotty had to tell us as we waited for him to get the drinks.

'Happy New Year, Malcolm, and you Chris.' After a sip of his drink Scotty put down his glass and fumbled in his pocket. 'Thought you should see this, Chris,' he said, putting an envelope on the table. 'I found it yesterday when I was trying to find Soo's stash of powders.'

It was a doctor's report from a specialist attached to Guys Hospital in London. It said he had examined Soo and confirmed the diagnosis of a doctor E. Chang in Southampton that a growth had re-occurred after a stomach operation in March 1951. He was unacquainted with the powders Doctor Chang had given him, but suggested Soo use them when necessary to relieve the pain as the condition was inoperable and unfortunately, there was a life expectancy of approximately two years. It was dated 16th October 1951.

Silently I passed it to Malcolm.

'I know it's very personal and we should nae be reading it, but I felt you should know, Chris.'

'Thanks, Scotty. I already knew something was wrong, but none of the details. What Soo said one evening about hoping he could stay on the *Lily Jade* for the rest of his life now makes sense.'

'It's nae fair. He's such a terrific little chap.'

'Is that why you abuse him all the time?'

'Och, it's just a wee bit of fun.'

'Fun you must keep going,' Malcolm said. 'You must never let him know you've seen this letter; everything must seem normal if he's to enjoy whatever time he has left.'

'Apart from which, he's winning the battle of wits anyway.'

Scotty smiled. 'Aye, Chris, I think you're right.'

That night I made a small note in my personal diary: "Scotty went to the pub and had *one* pint".

The next day, 29th December, Malcolm had returned to Shoreham, the cargo had been discharged and after cleaning out the hold I was ready to shut down the *Lily Jade* until the New Year. Jean Lubec left almost immediately, catching the early bus to Newport while Scotty still had a small job to do on Agnes before heading to his brother's house in Southampton.

'What are you going to do, Soo?' I asked the wiry little Chinaman.

'I help Chief.'

The smile had returned and, for the moment at least, I knew Soo was feeling better. 'He's leaving tomorrow,' I reminded him.

'Me invited to Shanklin for New Year.'

'Don't tell Scotty you're spending New Year in a pub, he'll want to come with you!' When the two left the following morning I noticed Soo was wearing his captain's jacket under his mackintosh and I was pleased he was spending a few days away from the *Lily Jade*.

The ship was quiet; too quiet. I sat in my cabin, not seeing the grey sky outside, instead picturing her tanned limbs, dark hair and vivacious smile. I wished Kathy were here. My mind moved on, worrying about Soo and then puzzling over the events of Boxing Day.

I sighed. Before I went to Solent Serenity I had to sort out those papers for Malcolm. Perhaps a cup of tea would motivate me. I'd just put the kettle on in the galley when I heard footsteps coming across the brow.

'Are you there, Chris?'

'I'm in the galley, Jim.' The grey bearded face of the Harbour Master appeared at the doorway. 'What can I do for you?'

Jim Middleton smiled. 'Other way round, actually; I've just had a call from Canterbury.'

'Kathy?'

He nodded.

'Could I...?'

'That's why I came over.'

I left my tea on the stove and followed Jim across the wharf to his office, where he picked up some envelopes. 'Take your time; I've got some letters to post.'

After two rings there was a click as the receiver was lifted. 'Chris, is that you?'

The sound of her voice was so intoxicating I almost forgot to reply. 'Kathy, my dearest girl, it's so good to hear your voice.'

'Thank heavens!'

'For what, Kathy?'

'I thought you might not want to talk to me after the last phone call.'

'I've wanted to talk to you every day, or better still, to see you.'

'I'm sorry about Christmas, Chris. It was going to be such a special time for us.'

'What happened? Is Grandpa all right?'

'Grandpa is fine, Chris, and there is nothing more I'd like than to be with you.'

'Can *I* come up to Canterbury? We're not sailing until after New Year.'

'No, Chris, not at the moment, but that's not because I don't want you here.'

'What's wrong, Kathy?'

'I'll tell you all about it one day.'

'I love you, Kathy.'

There was a muffled sound, almost like somebody crying, and then Kathy was asking about Christmas and everyone on board. '... and we couldn't get the jacket off his back.'

'Oh, how wonderful.'

Kathy laughed and for me *that* was wonderful.

'I would love to have seen Captain Soo.'

I went on to tell her the events of Boxing Day, after which she went quiet for several seconds.

'Chris, keep a place for me in your heart. I can't be with you at the moment, but I'm thinking of you; and Chris, be careful, I don't want anything to happen to you.'

The phone suddenly went dead, but whether she had hung up or the line had failed I didn't know. I felt elated, just the sound of her voice had given Christmas a meaning; a sense of love and belonging and yet, at the same time I was worried about Kathy and whatever was happening in Canterbury as well as the fact she'd told me to be careful. Be careful of what? I was sitting there with muddled thoughts when Jim Middleton returned.

'How did you go?'

'We had a great talk. It really made my Christmas, thank you, Jim.' I wasn't going to mention I was worried about Kathy. Instinctively, I knew the only person I could confide with, in that part of our conversation, was Malcolm.

I returned to the *Lily Jade,* made a fresh cup of tea and went up to sort out the papers Malcolm wanted. At the same time I decided to make a note of how our cargo figures at the end of the year compared with those for the previous year. I opened the top drawer of the papers I'd carefully organised just prior to the dry-docking and there on the top was the sheet I wanted with the figures for December 1952. I took it to the desk and ran my finger down the figures for each port, almost laughing to myself seeing the totals for the current year had doubled everywhere except for Fowey, which had still improved by sixty per cent. The figures had been helped by the amount of deck cargo we had carried during the last six months, something we hadn't done in the previous year, and I jotted down the tonnage on a separate piece of paper before returning the sheet to the drawer.

It was then I first noticed it. The sheet with the figures for 1952 had been sitting on top of the papers for the months of 1953.

I slid out the drawer and took it to my desk. Everything was out of order, as if the contents had fallen on the floor and someone had just thrown them back in. I re-arranged the papers and put the drawer away. Suddenly I felt hungry. Without Soo around I'd forgotten about lunch and was about to go down to the galley when something made me open another drawer.

The papers seemed in order until I thumbed through them and came to the records of the *Caillou* prior to Laurens Oostermeer giving her to Jacques Kessel. Some of the sheets had been folded and on one page the ink was smudged as if it had got wet. I'd read all these papers carefully when I'd acquired the *Lily Jade* and didn't remember any such blotch. A quick glance at the other drawer that contained records of cargo gear and correspondence with authorities regarding the new port of registration seemed to be in order.

Maybe the drawers had fallen out and, whoever had put them back had forgotten to tell me, and maybe I'd forgotten about the smudged ink.

Then I remembered the drawers could not have slid open at sea. There beside the desk was the locking bar I placed through the handles to prevent such a thing. As I ate a sandwich with my mug of tea I tried to come to terms with what I'd found.

My immediate thought went to the police who had searched the ship a few days ago, until I remembered I'd been with them when they looked through those drawers. It had been just after we'd got Soo to bed and being worried about him I didn't take as much notice as I might've, but I did remember they were methodical and meticulous about replacing everything as they'd found it. That meant it was one of the crew. I felt sad. Although there was nothing in those drawers I would've hidden from anyone my trust in people had been betrayed. Any of them had only to ask me for any of the papers or, if someone ashore had requested some detail when I wasn't there, tell me afterwards they had been to my cabin. I checked all my personal items, but nothing had been touched. I looked at the drawers again. Only two seemed to have papers that had been disturbed, and of those only the one with the records from the early days of the vessel had papers that were creased and completely out of order.

Scotty? Soo? Jean Lubec? Why would any of them want details like that and when would they have done it? It had to have occurred during the past four weeks as I'd checked cargo and other monthly figures at the end of November and everything had been in order then. Who else could've been alone in my cabin? I had nothing to hide but several strange things had happened during the past couple of months. I removed the file Malcolm had requested plus a few other papers, put them in a bag and sighed – it wasn't that important, except for the invasion of my personal space.

I wished Kathy was here, someone I could talk to about it. It had been so good to see her when she'd come down to Shoreham unexpectedly, even though we'd had only a few hours together, and what time there was being interrupted by people like Peter Dawson calling me over to the timber yard. I laughed to myself as I realised even Kathy had had the opportunity to rummage through the files and, although I couldn't remember a time, it seemed just as likely Malcolm could also be a suspect.

I put it out of my mind, deciding it wasn't worth worrying about and prepared to go to Solent Serenity. As I crossed the brow I was thinking of Kathy and had almost forgotten about the files until I remembered her last words on the telephone. "Be careful, Chris" she'd said, and that other time when she'd remarked. "Something strange is going on." Kathy was certainly right about the latter and now both she and Soo thought I was in danger.

Chapter Nineteen

For the next two days I immersed myself in the completion of the kitchen restoration. I fitted the last cupboard, cleaned up all the mess and then filled the shelves with the pots, pans and tins that had been stored in the shed outside, before fitting the trim around the edges. By Thursday evening it was done and all I needed to do was put a coat of paint on the narrow piece of wall between the cupboards and the door-frame.

I couldn't find a small paint brush and was annoyed with myself for not bringing one from the ship. The radio announced there were only five hours to go before it was 1954. I'd forgotten it was New Year's Eve, the first one I would spend at Solent Serenity. It was a shame I would be alone instead of with Kathy as I'd planned and the lack of a paintbrush became a more than sufficient excuse to grab my coat and head to the pub. It was a clear, dry night and I decided to walk down to the Colwell Bay Inn next to the cottage I'd stayed in when I was first thinking of buying the *Lily Jade*.

There were a few familiar faces in the bar, among them a couple of people who had sent cargo on the *Lily Jade*. They were pleased I'd got the ship running and remarked how good it was to have the service available.

Their words, the warm fire and the alcohol made me happy and relaxed as I joined in the celebrations for the New Year. Suddenly it was 1954 and after a lot of hand-shaking and a final drink that got topped-up for an hour, the landlord escorted us out the door.

The street lights showed the grass on the common covered in frost that sparkled like the stars in the clear night sky, but I didn't notice the cold until I reached the middle of Totland, when the effects of the drink took hold, making the last two hundred yards to Solent Serenity seem a long way.

I slept in the following morning and, feeling no ill-effects from the previous night when I got up at nine, decided to go down to the *Lily Jade* to get the paintbrush I needed to finish the kitchen. I dressed quickly, knowing the buses to Yarmouth were running only once an hour on New Year's Day.

As I went aboard I thought about the disturbed papers. Of the crew Jean Lubec was the only one I felt had secrets. He wasn't as open as Soo or Scotty – not that that in itself meant anything and the man was certainly entitled to his privacy. Anyone could've been to my cabin using the internal stairway or the door next to the funnel because the only time I locked them was on occasions like this when I was going to be away from the vessel. Looking for the paintbrush in the foc'sle locker I thought about Soo and Scotty and concluded none of my crew had any reason to want the information in those papers.

After a quick look around the *Lily Jade* to make sure everything was secure I went ashore to catch the bus back to Totland. I had forty minutes to kill and wandered around the deserted wharf area by the marina admiring some of the fine craft owned by the wealthy people in the area.

There beside the slipway, high and dry on the sand and tied to the stone quay by its painter, was the rowing-boat that belonged to Jean Lubec, the man who seemed to have secrets. Almost without thinking I untied the rope, dragged the boat down into the water and set off to look at his lobster-pot.

It was further than I thought and I nearly turned back when I realised I would miss the next bus; but even though I was sure I would only see an empty fishing cage, curiosity made me continue rowing across the bay towards Sconce Head. I knew it was more or less on the line between the point and the *Lily Jade,* and kept glancing over my shoulder to make sure I was on course. The slight chop on the water made the lobster-pot invisible until, fifty feet away towards the beach, I saw a wave break over the top of it.

When I hauled the pot up I thought it was empty; there certainly wasn't a crab in it, never mind anything bigger, but as it tilted I saw something fall to the side. It was a small oilskin package that obviously hadn't been there long as it wasn't slimy when I took it out. Inside the material I could feel something hard. I turned it over and undid the thronging as the boat rocked in the low swell.

The pale wintry sunlight reflected in the droplets of sea-water on the oilskin, reflections that became brighter when I unfolded the material to reveal more than half-a-dozen gem stones resting on my lap. They didn't exactly sparkle and I tried to think where I'd seen something similar before. Picking one up I remembered the two photos on the wall when Kathy and I had visited her Grandpa. These were uncut diamonds. I turned a stone in my palm over with a finger on my right hand and immediately wished I hadn't as a larger wave rocked the boat tipping the other diamonds off my lap. Frantically I scrabbled to pick them out of the two inches of water slopping around my feet in the bottom of the boat.

Each time I retrieved a diamond I wrapped it in the oilskin and placed it in my pocket for safe keeping. After recovering seven stones I couldn't find any more, despite going down on my hands and knees, oblivious off the cold water soaking into my trousers, to feel along the chines of the boat in case I'd missed any. Ten minutes later I'd found nothing and my fingers were numb. I tied up the oilskin and put it into the lobster-pot, which I lowered back into the water.

As I started the row back to the marina many questions came to mind. Although I had no answers I felt certain the diamonds had some connection with the visit of the police on Boxing Day and began to wonder what other secrets Jean Lubec might have.

Chapter Twenty

Over the weekend, as I finished the paintwork in the kitchen, I kept thinking about Lubec and the diamonds, Soo and, of course, Kathy. I wished she'd told me why she thought I needed to be careful – not for myself but for her, because to me it seemed she could be the one in danger; but what from exactly?

'Och, ye bloody wee Chinese monkey!'

'Chief no see. He no see.'

The voices drifted across the wharf on Sunday evening. I smiled. At least half the crew of the *Lily Jade* seemed back to normal. I crossed the brow as Soo emerged from the galley laughing, with a red-faced Scotty in pursuit.

'Captain Chris. Chief no see!'

'I'm telling ye, Chris, this upstart is goin' too far and I'll, I'll…'

'I don't want to know,' I said, heading up to my cabin.

Jean Lubec must've returned late, because I didn't hear him come aboard. The next day, as we loaded cargo for Shoreham I couldn't help but watch him, trying to understand the man beneath the tough seaman exterior who was connected to the diamonds. However, it was a very ordinary day at the start of 1954, with no-one doing anything unusual except saying Happy New Year at breakfast.

There was little cargo and we finished work at 1400, the last of it due to arrive on Tuesday morning. With a couple of hours of daylight left I wondered if Lubec would row out to the lobster-pot, and it became a bit of an anti-climax when he spent the afternoon in his cabin working on a model ship and sleeping.

We sailed to Shoreham and on Wednesday, after we'd shifted ship to the timber wharf and started to load cargo for Yarmouth, I told everyone I had to go to the shops and headed to Malcolm's house. I knew he'd be home as I'd rung him at work from Jim Middleton's office just before sailing yesterday.

'It took a bit of doing, but I managed to track down the specialist who wrote that report on Soo,' Malcolm said, as I hung my coat up and went into the kitchen.

He held up the kettle and I nodded. 'He'd left Guys and had set up his own private practice near Piccadilly while waiting for a place in Harley Street to become vacant.'

'What did he say?'

'He was astounded Soo was still alive and asked if I had the address of Doctor Chang in Southampton so he could investigate the powders he'd given him.'

'Did he say anything else about the illness?'

'Not in detail, just that it was an inoperable growth invading the stomach. He couldn't suggest anything more than Soo keeps using the powders, whatever they were, whenever necessary.'

He poured the tea and sat down. 'Now what's your news? You were quite secretive on the phone.'

I put the envelope containing the papers he'd wanted on the table. 'Two unrelated incidents, one of which concerns these.' I told him about the disturbed papers in the files, and that I'd first thought of Lubec. 'Then I realised everyone had been alone in my cabin, even Kathy, and probably you.'

'I'll have another look at the papers and see if I can spot anything that could be of interest to anyone.'

'It was papers concerning the early days of the *Lily Jade,* before I bought her, that were disturbed most.'

'In which case you'd better give me those as well, we don't want anything to mysteriously go missing. What about the other "incident", as you called it?'

Malcolm sat stony-faced and silent as I told him about the lobster-pot and the diamonds. 'What do you think?'

'Have you told anyone else?'

'No, I didn't know *who* to tell, except you.'

'Good,' he muttered, almost to himself, as he stared out of the window before turning back to face me. 'I don't like it, Chris. I sense a strong possibility of criminal activity, with you and the *Lily Jade* caught in the middle.'

'Should we go to the police?'

Malcolm shook his head. 'Not yet. There's nothing to connect the diamonds with anyone, and police activity could put you in danger from whoever's involved.'

'You're the third person to say that.'

'Say what?'

'That I'm in danger – remember Soo and Kathy said it as well.'

'I'd forgotten that, but you're right, Chris. Maybe, Kathy and Soo have found out something about what is going on, and if so, they could also be in danger.'

Kathy's words returned once more. 'There's something strange going on, that's what Kathy said, Malcolm.'

'And, Soo, what did he see?'

I looked at the clock on the wall and remembered that day in April 1952 when I'd come down for Easter, when I'd first seen the *Lily Jade*. My mind raced back over the past twenty months. The trip to Zeebrugge to see Jacques Kessel. Finding a crew and the fact Basil had gone back to New Zealand, an event that had brought Lubec onto the *Lily Jade*. Finding Solent Serenity and meeting Kathy – Kathy! I dwelled on our first times together. Discovering Jacques Kessel was her grandfather and our trip to Zeebrugge for his funeral, where we saw Simeon. Diamonds, the family's connection with them and the photos on the wall of the house in Canterbury, and then what I'd found in the lobster-pot.

A chill went down my back and I reached out to the hand in front of me. 'Malcolm!'

His eyes met mine, recognising the urgency in my voice.

'I don't think I ever told you, Kathy's Grandpa worked as a diamond cutter for De Beers, and her brother Simeon also works for the company, although I've no idea what his job is there.'

'Do you think he... and Kathy could be involved?'

'I don't know what to think; I can't imagine Kathy or her Grandpa being involved in anything criminal.'

'Unless they were under a threat of something else.'

'I'm worried they'll get hurt.'

'There's been no indication of a physical threat so far. Kathy didn't sound frightened when you spoke to her, did she?'

'No, she seemed more worried about me.'

'And providing we don't antagonise the situation, I think they'll remain safe. I'll make some further enquires in Holland, but, at the moment, I think you should just watch and listen without revealing what you know.'

'How about Scotty and Soo?'

'Difficult, especially as we don't know what Soo saw that night. I think you should only ask questions if something comes up in conversation, because Soo also said you were in danger and unless we get some idea of what he meant... well, who knows what might happen.'

I left Malcolm feeling confused and upset that I couldn't fully trust any of those people who had become such close friends. I felt like getting hold of Soo and Scotty and asking them outright about everything, but then I thought of Kathy and became determined to do as Malcolm had said, at least until I saw him in a couple of weeks.

I forced myself to make jokes and laugh with everyone, pretending everything was normal and it seemed to work, except for some odd looks from Soo. At first I put his reactions down to another stomach upset, but I caught that quizzical look in his eyes too many times in the next few days.

As it turned out it was Scotty who changed my mind and made me ignore Malcolm's advice. We'd left Shoreham with a full load of timber and I'd come down from the bridge for lunch leaving Lubec in charge. Soo put a plate of beef stew in front of Scotty as I arrived.

'Same for Captain Chris?'

'Yes please, Soo.'

When my plate arrived Scotty coughed as he tried to swallow a mouthful of food too quickly. 'Soo, would you go down and check the fuel in Agnes's daily tank? I can't remember if I pumped it up this morning.'

Soo nodded and then turned to me shaking his head. 'Chief getting too old, Captain Chris. He forgetting things like that.'

'I'll give you old, ye cheeky Chinese lantern!'

Soo laughed as he left to go down below, but looking at Scotty I knew the whole thing had been a ruse to leave us alone.

Looking thoughtful, he had another mouthful of food before he spoke. 'Is everything alright, Chris? I mean with the *Lily Jade* an' all.'

'Yes, everything's fine, Scotty. Why do you ask?'

'Oh, I don't know, you just seem…'

He went quiet as Soo returned, calling him a silly old fool and I laughed happily and loudly at the antics of two good friends appearing to abuse each other unmercifully.

In Yarmouth the following morning, when I took some papers over to Jim Middleton I gave a brief knock on his door and opened it.

'Oh, sorry, Jim, I didn't know you had company,' I said, hearing him speaking to someone. Then I realised the other person was Scotty. Momentarily the two looked at me strangely before Scotty broke the silence.

'Och, trust the skipper to interrupt us when we're planning our next decent booze-up.'

We all laughed, but as I put the papers on the desk and left I had the distinct feeling that I, or the *Lily Jade* had been the subject of discussion, rather than a drinking session and wondered why Scotty had felt unable to talk to me about whatever was on his mind – but then there was no proof they *had* been talking about me.

I forgot about it when, half-way along the wharf, I saw Lubec beckoning to me from the deck of the *Lily Jade*.

'The rope snotter on this pack of timber has jammed,' he called down as I neared the ship's side. 'I need you to come back on the winch slowly while I free it down in the hold.'

It took only a few minutes to correct the problem and we saw Soo return aboard with some stores, announcing to both of us that we were going to have a cup of tea or coffee in five minutes.

Lubec smiled. 'We've been told – can't argue with Soo.'

I laughed, and again I had mixed feelings about this ever-efficient seaman.

By the time Soo had brewed the tea Scotty had returned from ashore and as he sat down I knew that not only could I trust him with my life, but I now wanted desperately to talk to him, despite Malcolm's warning.

'Good cup of tea, Soo, but when are ye goin' to brew it cold with a foamy head?'

'Chief drink too much beer now. Soo stick to hot tea.'

I found myself turning an idea into reality almost before I'd thought of it. 'Scotty, he's deprived you again and that's not fair, is it? Never mind, I'll take you up to the pub at lunch-time.'

Scotty held his cup in mid-air. 'You will? On a working day?' he said, waiting to see if I meant it.

I realised what I'd said, but my need to talk to him seemed more pressing.

'Don't you believe the Captain when he tells you something important?'

Soo and Lubec looked at me curiously before watching Scotty's reaction as he stood up, came to attention and saluted. 'Chief Engineer, Scotty McBryde reporting for shore duty – **Sir!**'

'Very good,' I said, joining in the game. 'Shore party will muster on the brow with essential equipment at 1230 hours.'

'**Sir!**' Scotty rubbed his chin. 'What's the essential equipment, Chris?'

'Just your wallet, Scotty, I'm not buying all the drinks.'

Soo collected the empty cups chortling, 'Captain Chris caught Chief. Captain Chris caught Chief.' Even Lubec was laughing as he went back out onto the deck.

We went up to The Old Yawl and I bought both of us a pint while Scotty studied the menu.

'I fancy the Guinness pie, Chris.'

'Sounds good, I'll order two of them.'

When I returned Scotty had already emptied half his glass and was staring at a painting on the wall. 'Thirsty were you?'

'What? Oh sorry, Chris, I was miles away.'

'Thinking about what?'

Scotty hesitated, then put his glass down and stared at me. 'Like I said to you yesterday, Chris, I wondered if everything was alright because you've seemed a bit on edge and, what shall I say… remote, not talking to everyone as much as usual.'

'I'm worried about Kathy. Something's wrong but she won't tell me anything and I haven't been able to go and see her. I love that girl,

Scotty.'

'I know, Chris,' he said, getting up to buy another two pints. He didn't mention Kathy when he came back, but turned the conversation to the ship and Agnes who, apparently was in perfect health except, as Scotty put it, "having a slight wheeze at manoeuvring speed". What cure is available for a diesel engine with a "slight wheeze" I wasn't sure, but I knew "Doctor McBryde" would fix it.

The log fire was blazing and the small bar had become so warm I removed my jumper. Scotty stopped analysing Agnes's ailments and waved a finger across his neck. 'Ye no wearing Soo's good luck charm today, it's the first time I've seen you without it.'

My hand flew to my neck and then reached down into my shirt, but the necklet had gone. I was devastated. 'Scotty, I've lost it. I can't believe it. It was so special after all the effort Soo put into making it.'

'I'm sure it'll turn up, Chris. I expect it's in your cabin tangled up in a shirt or something.'

'I hope so, Scotty, I hope so.'

Lunch came and with it a third pint, which was more than my limit, and I put it in front of Scotty, whose glass emptied as fast as the pie disappeared from his plate.

'No more for me,' I said, as he started on the full glass. I was picking at my food, still dismayed by the loss of Soo's present.

'Ye know, Chris, I reckon something strange is goin' on.'

Kathy's exact words. I forgot about Soo's pendant, my mind fully focused on the effect of the beer that had loosened Scotty's tongue, as I'd hoped it would. However, all I said was, 'What do you mean, Scotty?'

'Well, I was with Jim Middleton the other day and he told me a stranger had come into the office wanting to know if you were still the captain and owner of the *Lily Jade*. When Jim said you were, the man asked if you ever took the ship across to the Continent. Jim said he didn't think so, but it was nothing to do with him where you took the *Lily Jade*. The guy pestered him for quite a while about our cargoes and ports of call.'

'Is that what you and Jim were talking about this morning?'

'Yeh, we weren't sure whether to tell you or not, but it's not the first time Jim's been asked that sort of question.'

'Who else has been snooping around?'

'He doesn't know. It was a while ago and he thought the woman might've had some cargo to send somewhere, and he told her to talk to you about it.'

'A woman?'

'Yes, but he doesn't remember anything about her; he didn't take any notice at the time.'

I got Scotty his fifth pint and decided I'd have another half myself. 'That's strange all right. I'd better have a chat to Jim about it.'

'There's something else, Chris,' Scotty said, lowering his voice and looking around before leaning towards me. 'It's Lubec. I'm not sure what to make of him.'

'Why?'

'One evening before Christmas, when I was fiddling with Agnes, he came down below wanting to borrow a hacksaw blade to cut something for his model. He'd had a few beers and we got talking about the *Lily Jade* and where she'd been built. Then he started poking around the engine room and when I asked if he was looking for something he said, did I think there were any hidden compartments behind a bulkhead or under the bottom plates.'

'What was he looking for?'

'I asked him that. He laughed and mumbled something about, "maybe things had been hidden on board during the war". I put it down to the beer until last week when he started asking if you kept in touch with the family of the man who owned the *Lily Jade*.'

'Jacques Kessel?'

'Yes, if you wrote to his sister or someone, but he got interrupted before I could say anything.'

'Thanks for telling me all this, Scotty. As you say, a lot of strange things have been happening. Last week I found the papers in my filing cabinet were all out of order.'

'Who would want…?'

Immediately my mind crossed Scotty off the list. 'I don't know,' I said. I decided not to mention the lobster-pot and the diamonds as Scotty seemed to have already pinpointed Lubec as the source of any trouble aboard the *Lily Jade*.

Back on board I met Jean Lubec with a towel around his waist heading for the shower, a tiny cubicle Scotty and Soo had built by the entrance to the engine room – a great improvement on the metal tub that used to hang on the bulkhead there.

'No more cargo until the morning, Chris. I'm going to get cleaned up and go over to stay with my brother in Newport for the night.'

'Fine, Jean. Have a good time.'

Up in my cabin I sat down to tackle the paperwork, but feeling full of pie and beer I went on deck beside and gazed across the marina. It wasn't even three o'clock but with the overcast sky it seemed the evening was already drawing in. A cold breeze swept up the Solent and I leant up against the warm funnel as I thought about what Scotty had said in the pub.

I heard, rather than saw, someone go across the brow. It was Lubec. He wandered along the wharf and then looked back at the *Lily Jade* before turning towards the slip-way and jumping down onto the beach. I stood motionless as he looked up again before dragging the row-boat down to the water.

Slipping inside my cabin I went to the bridge and got the binoculars as he started to row out to the lobster-pot, however, after five minutes I could hardly see him in the fading light.

That evening I used my key to enter Jim Middleton's office and tried to ring Kathy, but there was no answer.

Chapter Twenty-One

On the short voyage to Weymouth I didn't have enough time to search my cabin thoroughly, but Soo's charm certainly wasn't caught up in one of my shirts. I also wondered if a small oilskin package was somewhere in Lubec's cabin.

As usual, after we'd tied up and the derrick had been rigged for work, Jean Lubec got ready to go ashore on his regular day off. It was a small cargo we'd brought from the island and knowing we wouldn't load for Fowey until the following morning, I went and found Soo in the galley. 'I need to go ashore for a while, so I'm leaving Captain Soo in charge.'

The words "Captain Soo" made him laugh, but secretly I knew he felt proud at the confidence I'd shown in him.

'Soo make sure all cargo ok.'

'*Captain* Soo just needs to make sure all the cargo for Fowey stays on board.'

'Soo fix that good!'

'Thank you, *Captain*.'

He chuckled and went to his cabin, returning seconds later wearing the jacket.

I nodded and went up to my cabin, got changed and stood by the door leading out onto the deck. I didn't have to wait long before I heard someone cross the brow and Lubec came into sight.

Immediately I set off down the stairs to follow him, determined to try and solve at least one of the "strange things" that were going on aboard the *Lily Jade*.

I kept well behind Lubec to avoid any chance of being seen, to the extent I almost lost him as he took left and right turns through the streets of Weymouth. Then, near the railway station when I turned a corner he'd disappeared. I hurried towards the station entrance and glancing left as I crossed the road I saw him emerge from a tobacconist almost in front of me. A truck stopped outside the station and I hid behind it as the driver jumped out and opened the rear doors. Looking through the vacant cab I could see Lubec waiting at the bus-stop across the road. The driver of the truck took a couple of cartons into a shop behind me and, when he returned calling out he had another six boxes in the truck, I knew I could remain hidden a little longer.

A couple of minutes later a Southern Dorset bus arrived at the stop and I watched Lubec take a seat on board, instinctively ducking down as he looked in my direction. After it pulled out and disappeared around the corner, leaving a cloud of exhaust fumes behind, I went across to the stop and checked the timetable. The next number 29 wasn't due for almost half-an-hour and was heading to Bridport calling at several places along the coast. Although I had no idea where Lubec was going I decided to make the journey, even though the return trip would be in darkness.

The bus travelled close to the Chesil Beach, passing through the villages of Fleet, Langton Herring, Abbotsbury and Burton Bradstock before turning inland towards Bridport. I saw nothing that could have been a likely destination for a man possibly carrying diamonds, and certainly, I didn't see Lubec. I wasn't surprised, but didn't consider it a waste of time if, at some stage in the future, something happened that I could associate with a place I'd seen that afternoon.

Lubec returned the following morning. Although he acted normally and was his usual efficient self, when I spoke to him he seemed slightly agitated about something, but I didn't mention it.

As usual we sailed at noon, and as we turned south-west past the end of the Chesil Beach I was staring at that line of stones disappearing into the haze, thinking of the bus trip I'd made the previous day, when Lubec arrived to take over the bridge. He just grunted when I tried to make conversation and I left him to go down to lunch, the familiar "clack, clack, clack" of the pebbles in his pocket fading as I went down the stairs.

I ate quickly and returned to my cabin to make a thorough search for Soo's charm. Two hours later I'd turned the place upside down but had found only a letter from the solicitor in London that I'd lost weeks before. I vowed to cover every inch of the hold when it was empty in Fowey as I couldn't bear the thought of telling Soo I'd lost his present. He may have already noticed I wasn't wearing it, but he hadn't said anything.

When the search of the hold proved fruitless the next most likely place was Solent Serenity. By three o'clock Monday afternoon, when we were back in Yarmouth, there were only a few blocks of sandstone to discharge and I found Scotty and Soo having a cup of tea. Instinctively I pulled the collar of my shirt closer around my neck to hide the absence of the charm. 'I'm going up to Solent Serenity for a few hours, unless everyone needs to go ashore.'

'I'm goin' to meet Fiona at Jim's place at five.'

I looked at Soo, knowing Jean Lubec had gone to Newport after lunch.

He smiled. 'Captain Chris go to palace. Captain Soo look after *Lily Jade*. Make sure all Bristol.'

Scotty and I laughed at his shortened version of the nautical phrase. 'Thank you, Captain Soo, I know you will.'

For four hours I searched Solent Serenity looking for the love charm but only achieved sorting out cupboards and drawers that left me with a pile of rubbish. It seemed I would have to confess my loss to Soo, but decided not to do it just yet in the hope it would turn up when I was looking for something else.

It was just after 8 P.M. when I arrived back at the wharf and, although I was hungry I used my key to the Harbour Master's office to ring Kathy. As I waited for the connection I made up my mind to get the telephone connected to Solent Serenity during the next few weeks.

The sound of her soft voice startled me as I'd heard only half a ring of the phone. 'Kathy, my sweet girl, how are you?'

'Oh, Chris; so much better for hearing your voice. How are things on the *Lily Jade?*'

For the next few minutes, as we exchanged news I was trying to find the right moment to ask the important question that was on my mind. Eventually there was a slight pause. 'Kathy, I haven't seen you since the beginning of December. How and when can we be together again?'

'Chris, if it were possible I'd leave Canterbury now, even if I had to walk to Shoreham or the island. My wonderful man, I think about you and want to be with you all the time, so believe me, the first chance I have to get away I'll let you know.'

'Is everything alright with Grandpa now?'

'I'll tell you what I know when I see you, Chris.'

We talked for over half-an-hour about places we would go and things we would do together, creating a warm passionate world that was in stark contrast to the dark winter's night outside. I felt elated and was oblivious of the freezing temperature as I returned to the *Lily Jade*.

'Captain Chris sitting down. He hungry. Soo fix.'

I shook my head at his intuition, but did as I'd been told until Soo appeared with a plate of toast and eggs. Immediately I saw he was ill again. 'Don't worry about me; you need some of your magic powders.'

'Soo get now,' he said, going to his cabin.

I left my food and, from the cupboard where we kept a stock of tomato juice I took a small bottle and emptied it into a glass. Once again, within minutes of taking the powders he'd mixed in the drink Soo seemed out of pain and perfectly well, but I was worried as to how long this miracle cure could keep working. He went to lie down on his bunk and before I'd finished my meal I heard a soft but regular snoring coming from his cabin.

Two days later at Malcolm's house I told him how Lubec had rowed out to the lobster-pot and that I'd tried to follow him in Weymouth.

'A number twenty-nine bus isn't a lot to go on, and as far as the diamonds are concerned it won't mean anything to any of my contacts on the Continent as rumours of gems being stolen are rife and nobody mentions it.'

'Or they don't want to, for fear of reprisals?'

'Precisely. I think we should just watch and wait, unless you or the *Lily Jade* is involved again.'

I returned to the ship where everything seemed normal as we loaded timber for Yarmouth and during the next few weeks I forgot about the events concerning Christmas and Jean Lubec as our cargoes increased. We traded up and down the coast as regular as clockwork, except for one voyage from Fowey when Agnes overheated with a blockage in the cooling water intake. She wasn't the only one to get overheated as, with much animated talk, the Chief and Senior Second engineers sorted it out quickly, if not quietly.'

Chapter Twenty-Two

'Chris, have you got a minute?'
It was Monday morning, 15th February and we'd just arrived in Yarmouth after a voyage from Fowey. I looked down over the ship's side from the deck by the funnel, where I was red-leading bare steel after chipping away some light rust, to see the familiar face of the Harbour Master. 'What can I do for you, Jim?'

He glanced at the foc's'le where Lubec was operating the winch and then at Soo who was unhooking some bags of china clay on the wharf. 'Come over to the office when you get a chance,' he said, tugging at his grey whiskers.

I nodded and he turned to walk back down the wharf, leaving me wondering why he hadn't told me what he wanted; Jim Middleton was usually so outspoken.

'What's the secret?' I asked twenty minutes later as I entered his office.

'I've no idea, but Malcolm wants you to ring him without anyone else knowing about it.'

By the time Malcolm answered the ringing telephone I felt quite apprehensive about what it might be my best friend had to tell me. 'Malcolm?'

'Who else would answer this number?'

'You have something urgent to tell me?'

'Don't sound so worried, Chris, it's good news I've got for you.'

After the clandestine demeanour of Jim Middleton that morning, the last thing I'd expected to hear from anyone was good news and for a moment I was speechless.

'Chris? Are you there?'

'Yes, Malcolm; you just caught me unawares.'

'Can you get away from the *Lily Jade* for the night on Wednesday? It's 17th February.'

'That's your birthday isn't it? I suppose so, but why?'

'Yes it's my birthday and I want us to go out for a very special evening.'

'Why is this birthday so special?'

'It's not; it's where we're going and whose going to be there.'

'What've you lined up, seats at a London show?'

'Better than that. I had a phone call from a certain young lady who asked if I could arrange a secret meeting between you two that evening.'

'Kathy!'

'Who else? She's been sent to help set-up a new surgery at Rye on the Kent coast and wondered if we could go up there.'

'It doesn't sound like much of a birthday celebration for you.'

'You and Kathy getting together will be treat enough, Chris. The only question I needed to ask was would we be staying the night? If so, I'll book some accommodation.'

'I… I don't know; Kathy…'

'Enough said, I'll book a hotel.'

My mind was numb, but with happiness – in two days I'd see Kathy again. I thought about the ring in my drawer back on the *Lily Jade*, hoping this time I could find the right place and time to express my feelings, and then I remembered Malcolm and the fact it would be his birthday, but somehow I knew neither would come between

Kathy and I.

'Ring me when you get to Shoreham tomorrow and we'll organise a time to leave on Wednesday.'

In my cabin the devious side of my mind came up with a reason I had to be away from the *Lily Jade* for the night on Wednesday. I rehearsed it many times and by the time we were due to sail the following morning I'd convinced not only the crew, but almost myself, that I had an appointment with a solicitor in London the next day. The voyage to Shoreham was a blur, my ship-handling on arrival done more by instinct than anything else, knowing I would see Kathy tomorrow.

The Rover hugged the bends along the country roads passing through Lewes and Hastings on the way to Rye, where we arrived in the last sunlight of a fine winter's day. The town sat on a small hill and as we drove down the cobbled streets the noise from the car echoed off buildings that had a delicate, china-like quality. The Walland Hotel, near the tiny harbour and named after the nearby marshes, was almost two hundred years old and Georgian in appearance.

'Your name, sir?' asked the man behind the desk.

'Bowden, Christopher Bowden.'

'Thank you, sir.' He flicked through the pages of a register. 'Your wife left a message to say she will join you when she returns from business at Houghton Green.'

I looked at Malcolm, who was smiling, and was about to say something when he put a finger to his lips.

As I climbed the stairs and walked along the wood-panelled corridor towards room 217, paintings and sepia photos on the walls gave an insight into the history of Rye and its fishing fleets during the past 250 years. When I opened the door to the room another surprise awaited me. Quickly, I had a wash, got changed and went down to meet Malcolm in the lounge, leaving Kathy's Christmas present on the bed.

I got two drinks and stood by the bar waiting for him. 'That's not a room, it's a suite! And with a balcony overlooking the harbour,' I said, when he arrived ten minutes later.

'I thought you and Kathy might like something special, considering it's been a while since you've seen each other.'

Malcolm said something else, but I didn't hear him, as over his shoulder I saw Kathy enter the room wearing the moss-green outfit.

'I see you found your Christmas present.'

'It's beautiful, thank you, Chris.'

Her grey-green eyes sparkled as she approached, and then we were in each other's arms kissing passionately, almost obscenely, oblivious of the other patrons and the fact it was Malcolm's birthday we were supposed to be celebrating.

'Happy birthday, Malcolm,' Kathy said, raising the glass that had been put in front of her as we eventually sat down.

'Yes, happy birthday,' I echoed, reaching under my chair for the parcel I'd brought down with me from room 217 and placing it on the table next to the brightly wrapped present Kathy had taken from her bag.

'Thank you, both of you, but your happy faces would have been present enough.'

Kathy and I held hands, gazing into each other's eyes as Malcolm opened the packages. Kathy had given him a pair of leather driving gloves and a key-ring with a Rover badge on it.

'This feels heavy,' he said, picking up what was obviously a book.

'It might give you some answers to all those questions you keep asking me,' I said, as he unwrapped a large volume that explained coastal navigation and ships lights. I turned to Kathy. 'Speaking of answering questions, would you like to tell me about all the secrecy surrounding this evening?'

When the sparkle in Kathy's eyes faded I wished I hadn't mentioned it, but I squeezed her hand and the smile returned before she spoke. 'Maybe I'm silly; imagining things that aren't happening at all.'

'Do you want to tell us?' Malcolm asked.

'It's Grandpa. I think Aunt Vivian's holding something over him, especially since Marcos died. I've only seen her twice since then and both times she seemed aggressive; asking what I was doing and had I seen Chris or visited the *Lily Jade* since December – she knew about that.'

'Asking about me?'

'Yes, that was before, in late November. She asked about the ship and its history before you bought her.'

'What did you say?'

'I said I didn't know anything except you bought her from my grandfather, Jacques Kessel. She went on to say something about not putting Grandpa under too much pressure and it would be easier for him if I found out some of that information.'

'What did you do?'

'I didn't know what to do. I nearly told you everything, Chris, but… but I was frightened it would put more strain on Grandpa if you tried to help by confronting her. He's not a young man, Chris.'

Her eyes went misty for a moment and I kissed her gently on the cheek. 'It's all right, Kathy, I understand.'

She shook her head. 'No you don't, Chris. I did something for which I'll never forgive myself. I went behind your back instead of trusting you and asking for your help, and I wouldn't blame you if you asked me to leave right now, but I have to tell you. I went looking for that information.'

I realised what she meant. 'It was *you* who looked through the papers in the filing cabinet. It must have been when I went over to the timber yard.'

'I'm so sorry, Chris – what must you think of me?'

I remembered Soo's story, and his sixth-sense that I would never understand. 'I think you are a very brave and caring girl, Kathy Wembourne, and I love you.'

She flung her arms around my neck and buried her head into my shoulder. 'Oh, Chris!'

As we took a sip of our wine, I wasn't prepared for the next part of her story.

'There wasn't much I could tell them, but it seemed to be sufficient at the time.'

'You said "them",' Malcolm interrupted. 'Do you know who "they" were?'

'No, just a couple of men with Vivian.'

'When did you meet them,' I asked, still thinking about the papers in the filing cabinet and what possible information these people could've wanted.

'At Christmas; that's why I said I couldn't see you. Grandpa wasn't feeling too good and he asked me if I'd go with him to see Vivian, although at the time I had no idea they were going to the Isle of Wight.'

'You were on the island? At Christmas?'

She nodded, those grey-green eyes widened and a tear rolled slowly down her cheek. 'I was so close, Chris,' she said, fumbling for a hankie in her bag. 'When we spent Christmas Eve in a pub in Freshwater I was determined to see you either Christmas Day or Boxing Day.'

'On Boxing Day we were down at the *Lily Jade* with Soo and the police.'

'I knew that before you told me.'

'How would you've…? I thought you were in Freshwater?'

'No, on Christmas morning we went down to the boat, the one that'd belonged to Marcos. It was tied up at Totland pier.'

'You were there? Just down at the pier?'

'I almost managed to slip ashore to see you on Christmas afternoon, but Vivian stopped me, insisting I look after Grandpa, saying he wasn't well after all the time he'd spent talking with her friends. We were there until late Boxing Day morning, when Jean Lubec arrived, saying something about police in Yarmouth, but Vivian shut him up until I was out of hearing, leaving me with Grandpa while they had a heated discussion about something. Then the engine started and we sailed up the Solent to a pier near Southsea where Grandpa and I, plus Vivian and one of the men got off before the boat disappeared into the Channel.'

'What about Lubec?'

'He got off before we left the island. I don't trust that man, Chris. I have a bad feeling about him – that's the real reason for the secrecy and why I organised tonight with Malcolm. Of course I trust Scotty and Soo, but I didn't want a forgetful word letting Lubec know I'd seen you again. I love you, Chris, and I don't want anyone to hurt you.'

I kissed her and dried the tears that had formed in her eyes once more. 'As I said, Kathy Wembourne, you are a brave and caring girl.'

I'd almost forgotten Malcolm was there until he spoke. 'What happened after the boat had gone, Kathy?'

'Vivian disappeared with the man and I took Grandpa home on the train.'

'Chris, I think I know what Soo saw on the cliff top that upset him so much on Christmas Day.'

'The boat!'

'And possibly the beautiful young lady sitting next to you.'

I remembered that afternoon and turned to Kathy. 'Soo gave me a love charm that I should be wearing for you now,' I said, stroking her auburn hair, 'but I've lost it. I've searched everywhere.'

Kathy raised her head and kissed my cheek. 'It'll turn up.'

I hoped she was right. 'Kathy, have you any idea what threat Vivian might be making to Grandpa?'

'No, unless it has something to do with his work before he retired.'

'That could be why Lubec came to warn them about the police,'

Malcolm said. 'Maybe they've been using the boat to bring the stuff over from the Continent.'

'But you said there were no reports of major theft in Holland.'

'None that they've found out about, or are prepared to talk...'

'Chris? Malcolm? What are you talking about? What's all this about Lubec and the boat?'

I looked at Malcolm, who nodded, and I told Kathy about rowing out to the lobster-pot and what I'd found.

'You think Vivian has Grandpa working on stolen diamonds?'

'It's a possibility,' Malcolm replied, 'but we have no proof of anything illegal and the police who came to the *Lily Jade* never mentioned diamonds.'

'What should we do?'

'Kathy, I think you and Chris should forget all about it and enjoy my birthday, because this evening won't last forever.'

* * * * * * *

Our table was in an alcove alongside a balcony overlooking the harbour, a perfect setting for the meal that was extraordinarily good. The third bottle of wine was probably unnecessary, however, when Malcolm excused himself I was glad there was enough left for Kathy and I to share a drink on our own. The open fire had worked well, too well, as now the room felt somewhat stuffy and the heat overpowering.

'Shall we go outside, Chris?'

'Why not, but put your coat on, it'll be cold.'

When I opened one of the tall, stained-glass French windows the cold air felt crisp and fresh on our faces. There was no wind, the night so still we could hear each wave breaking as we stood on the balcony. Reflection from a sliver of new moon on the horizon appeared almost crystallised in the water, matching the stars above and the frost appearing on the lawn in the rapidly falling temperature.

'It's as if time stopped for a moment,' Kathy said, putting her arm around my waist. 'A frozen memory to be kept forever.'

'I took her other hand off the metal railing; it was cold and I pressed it against my body as she turned towards me. 'I may have something to help you remember this moment stopped in time.'

She smiled and put her head on one side questioningly, the twinkle in those grey-green eyes as bright as the frost on the street-lamp below.

There wasn't enough room on the tiny balcony for me to go down on one knee and I hoped Kathy would forgive me. Instead, with my right hand, I took the small box from my pocket and flipped it open.

'Kathy, my sweet girl, would you share this moment in time, and every other moment of our lives with me?... Kathy; will you marry me?'

A small tear, like a miniature icicle, ran down her cheek and then she looked up and nodded before throwing her arms around my neck. 'Yes, yes my darling, Chris. You and I forever – thank you, my wonderful man.'

I put the ring on her finger and for several minutes, oblivious of the cold, we stood with an arm around each other's waist as Kathy held her left hand out in front of us, the diamond and sapphire ring sparkling like the stars above. We said not a word, letting the silence of the night envelop us as we kissed on that balcony until a breeze sprang up, making the freezing temperature uncomfortable.

'We'd best go back inside; I don't want my fiancé to catch a chill, and Malcolm will be wondering where we are.'

'And have I got something to show him,' Kathy said, still looking at her ring.

He wasn't at our table, which had been set with a fresh tablecloth and it was several seconds before I saw him waving from a small lounge area next to the bar. Hand-in-hand we went over.

'What've you been up to outside? You look like two excited

children who have been playing in the snow!'

'Malcolm... We...' Kathy stammered, holding out her left hand.

'Congratulations!' he said, standing up and giving Kathy a big kiss before shaking my hand. 'That's the best birthday present I could've had.'

A bottle of champagne appeared and was consumed with much laughter, about what, none of us could remember the following morning.

Kathy and I floated up the stairs to room 217. Inside I kicked the door shut, refusing to let go of her sweet kisses. There was a gentle thump as Kathy dropped her handbag on the floor.

I squeezed her shoulders and she buried her head into my neck. 'I can't believe the most wonderful girl in the world said she would marry me,' I whispered.

Kathy looked up and stroked my face. 'How could *I* be so lucky?'

We stood in silence for several seconds; the closeness of our bodies creating a desire that couldn't be ignored.

Gently, I undid the buttons on the back of the green dress and it slid to the floor without a murmur of protest from Kathy, whose fingers started to undo my shirt. One button proved stubborn and then I heard it bounce on the coffee table. My arms reached around her back and unhooked the lace bra, releasing those tanned breasts, which she pressed against my bare chest.

'Kathy, my most precious girl,' I murmured, stroking her hair.

'Oh Chris, Chris...'

She said no more as our lips met briefly before the rest of our clothing was discarded onto the floor.

I picked her up in my arms, and again we kissed as I carried her to the other room with its huge bed. She laid back, her auburn hair spread across the turned-down sheets as, gently, I kissed her firm nipples while our hands explored each other's naked body.

'Oh, Chris; yes, Chris...' Her hands took my head and lifted it, an urgency emanating from those grey-green eyes. 'Now, Chris; come into me now.'

We rolled from one side to the other, each pausing on top of the other to smile at the face below before attempting to push our bodies closer together than was physically possible. For hours there was no insanity that night; just the true feelings of two people who had found their soul mate.

Chapter Twenty-Three

I awoke to find Kathy's hand resting on my chest with the diamond and sapphire ring, the only thing she was wearing, reflecting the first light of the morning. She stirred and I knew in less than two hours we must part. As she opened her eyes and smiled, first at me and then at the ring, I knew we would spend some of that time to continue the passion that had consumed us into the early hours of the morning.

Houghton Green was just a couple of miles north of Rye and we took Kathy to the new surgery in the Rover as she'd missed the bus when we'd lost track of time. The still of the previous evening had been replaced with a cool wind and light drizzle as we held each other close for the last time.

'Somehow, my darling, I have to see you again soon, very soon.'

'Oh yes, Chris – no more weeks apart, regardless of diamonds or whatever else.'

The car was warm and I'd fallen asleep before we approached Brighton, only waking when Malcolm nudged me as he drove up alongside the *Lily Jade*.

'Get everything sorted out with ye solicitor?'

Scotty was standing by the brow as I went aboard, a large spanner in one hand, a mug of tea in the other and a thick line of grease across his face.

'Er, yes. Everything's sorted out,' I said, having forgotten about my cover story. 'Is everything all right down below? You look as if you've had a fight with Agnes.'

'Och, she's bin a wee bit temperamental. If she no behaves herself I'll have to take the big hammer to her.'

Soo appeared wearing his jacket, a mug of steaming liquid in his hand. 'Tea for Captain Chris. Captain Soo speak with wood man Dawson. He say bring *Lily Jade* to wharf for wood at eleven o'clock. It good job you come back Captain Chris. Captain Soo not know how to drive *Lily Jade*.'

'In which case Captain Soo should learn. Captain Chris will teach you.'

'Captain Chris make joke,' Soo chuckled.

'No joke,' I said, shaking my head.

'Oh, so ye no satisfied with being the Senior Second engineer now, ye want to take over the whole ship?' Scotty waved the spanner in the air. 'Agnes'll be fearful when I tell her, us stuck down there with you in charge.'

'Chief let Soo know what Agnes say except hiss and thump.'

'I'd like to know that as well, Scotty.'

'Och, ye all getting as daft as me,' Scotty said, heading back towards the engine room.

The last pack of timber landed in the hold just after eleven on Friday morning and I went over to finalise the paperwork with Peter Dawson. 'Could you do me a favour?' I asked.

'Sure, Chris, what is it?'

'I know we always let go the lines ourselves, but today could you be on the wharf and toss the stern-line aboard?'

Just before sailing time I went aft and slackened off one of the stern-lines so a small bight hung down towards the water to make it easy for Peter to throw it off the bollard.

At noon Scotty had gone below and Lubec had gone for'd for departure as usual, taking in the other head lines except the one on a bight that could be slipped from on board. Soo did the same with the stern-lines and I waved to Peter Dawson who was standing by a pack of timber.

'Soo,' I called over the bridge wing. 'Come up here.'

'Still have stern-line, Captain Chris.'

'Never mind that, come up here.' He looked at me hesitantly. 'Yes, come up now.'

He arrived glancing over his shoulder as if he felt guilty leaving the stern-line.

'Right, Captain Soo, with my help you are going to take the *Lily Jade* to sea.' I laughed. 'Close your mouth until you're ready to give orders.' I explained what I did and he understood as he'd seen it happen countless times. 'Take her away, Captain Soo!'

He leant over the bridge wing. 'Let go aft, please, Mr Dawson.'

Peter lifted the bight of rope off the bollard and threw it aboard before standing back to watch with a smile on his face.

Soo went behind the wheel and put his mouth to the voice-pipe. 'Dead-slow ahead, chief.'

There was no response from below. 'Try again,' I said grinning, trying to picture Scotty's face.

'Dead-slow ahead, Chief.'

'Are you playing games, ye Chinese monkey?'

'No, chief. This Captain Soo learning from Captain Chris. Dead-slow ahead, chief.'

'Ooh, Agnes… I mean… *Yes sir. Dead-slow ahead, sir!*'

The engine thumped into life. The *Lily Jade* moved forward, the stern swinging off the wharf as the weight came on the for'd line.

'Stop engine, Chief.'

'Stop engine, Captain, sir!' floated back up the voice-pipe.

The weight eased on the for'd line and Lubec let it go without waiting for an order from either Soo or I.

'Dead-slow astern, Chief.'

'Dead-slow astern, Commodore.'

'Who Commodore?'

'You are, ye cheeky monkey!'

The *Lily Jade* drifted off the wharf into the middle of the dock, where we swung round and headed out to sea. Soo gave his last order to Scotty as we cleared the buoys and set course along the coast. 'Full-away, Chief.'

'Full-away, Admiral, Your Lordship.'

Soo stayed on the bridge for nearly an hour, learning how to take bearings and apply the errors of the compass until Jean Lubec came up after having his lunch, which he'd found cooking in the oven. He took over the watch from Soo, but didn't join in the fun of it, giving me a look of disapproval.

'Thank you, Captain Chris,' Soo said, as we went down for our meal, the clacking of stones fading behind us.

'You can come and learn any time if you're interested. It's not…'

'Ah, 'tis the Admiral and his First Lieutenant. Pray be seated, gentlemen, luncheon is served.'

Scotty stood with one tea-towel over his arm and a second wrapped around his head as a chef's hat. The table had been set with a cloth and cutlery and in his hands he held a can of tomato juice and a glass.

I guided the surprised Soo to the table.

Scotty presented the can to Soo. 'This is a 1953 vintage juice brewed in…' He looked at the can. 'Er, somewhere where they have good tomatoes, sir.' He opened it and poured the contents into the glass. 'Would the Admiral care to taste the brew?'

Soo was confused and both Scotty and I couldn't hold back the laughter any longer. 'He'll make a good deck officer quicker than you think, Scotty.'

'Well done, Soo. I'm nae surprised, you're a cluey chap.'

'Cluey chap? Captain Soo a cluey chap?'

'He means you're clever, Soo,' I said, wiping tears of laughter from my eyes. Soo smiled and I felt content as the *Lily Jade* headed towards Yarmouth.

I felt content for the next three weeks as we steamed up and down the coast without any hiccups. Soo came to the bridge several times when I was there to learn about buoyage and other aspects of coastal navigation. Spring seemed to have come early as we encountered no more gales, the better weather allowing some essential maintenance to be done around the ship.

I'd rung Kathy twice each week and we'd managed to see each other twice, although both times we'd kept our meeting a secret from everyone except Malcolm.

The first time was to have been an afternoon in Brighton when Kathy had been sent back to Houghton Green for three days. It was going to be just a couple of hours because although she had the day off, Kathy had an early start the following morning and I had a surveyor coming down to the *Lily Jade* to issue a new certificate for the derrick, but we both felt it was worth the effort.

As it turned out we had half a day together because Malcolm surprised me, and in turn I was able to surprise Kathy. Malcolm had been giving me driving lessons in the Rover and on the previous visit to Shoreham I'd passed the test.

'Take the car, Chris,' he'd said, when I'd told him I was meeting Kathy in Brighton.

'But I've only just got my licence.'

'You trusted me to handle the *Lily Jade*, so I'm sure I can trust you with the Rover.'

I rang Kathy, saying I would be able to get to Brighton earlier, but didn't say how, as she knew nothing about my taking the driving test.

I saw her standing beside the entrance to the Palace Pier, where we'd agreed to meet, but she was looking at the bus behind me and didn't notice the Rover until I'd circled the roundabout and pulled up beside her. 'Could I give the beautiful Kathy Wembourne a lift?' I called through the open window.

'Chris! What are you…? That's Malcolm's car.'

She got in and I stopped the questions by kissing her until the horn of another vehicle made me realise I couldn't stop there.

Laughing, we'd driven east along the coast a few miles to Rottingdean and parked on the sea-front. The breeze off the water was cold, so we walked through the village with its quaint old buildings until we found a sheltered spot in the sunshine on the village green beside the duck-pond. The hours had passed too quickly. Kathy's bus back to Rye had left and so, after a meal in the pub, I had my first experience of night-driving as I took her back to the new surgery in Houghton Green, where we'd cuddled and said our farewells in the back seat of the Rover.

The second time was over a weekend when Kathy came to the island and we'd had almost two days together at Solent Serenity. The weather had been cold and wet, but we'd never noticed it.

Chapter Twenty-Four

I was surprised to see Peter Dawson at our discharge berth in Shoreham on the Tuesday afternoon at the beginning of March. Normally he didn't come down until Wednesday to discuss the timber load and when the *Lily Jade* would shift down to the berth by the yard.

'Do we have something special this trip?' I asked, as he entered my cabin.

'No, Chris, just a normal load, but I had a call from Malcolm Chatwin; he wanted you to ring him when you arrived. You can use the phone in my office.'

I wondered what it was that Malcolm considered so urgent.

'I'm sorry, sir, Mr Chatwin is out of the office. May I ask who is calling?'

'Captain Bowden.'

'Oh, Captain Bowden,' the female voice replied. 'Mr Chatwin asked me to give you another number to ring should you call while he was out.'

The number she gave me turned out to be a solicitor's office in Lewes. The lady who answered said Mr Chatwin was in a meeting, but asked me to wait a few moments. Less than a minute later the familiar voice came on the line. 'Chris, I can't talk now but I need to see you. Can you come to the house tonight, say about eight o'clock?'

'Yes, not a problem, but what's…?'

'I'll explain tonight.'

I approached Malcolm's house that evening thinking he must've heard something from his contact in Holland. He led me into his lounge room and poured me a glass of wine to compliment the cheese and biscuits laid out on the coffee table.

'Sit down, Chris.'

From the tone of his voice I began to think it wasn't good news he had to tell me.

He passed me a newspaper. 'I doubt you'll be able to read the article, but look at the photo at the bottom of the page.'

I scanned down the columns of print, without trying to read a word of the strange language until I came to a picture of two elderly ladies, immediately recognising the smiling face of one of them. It seemed only yesterday Kathy and I had been talking to her. 'That's Fleur,' I said. 'Jacques Kessel's sister.'

'I was afraid you'd say that.'

I looked at Malcolm.

'Fleur and her sister, Yvette, have been found murdered in a house at Vianden, in Luxembourg.'

My eyes returned to the paper and the photo of the intelligent woman I'd met in Zeebrugge. 'But why…?'

'Why would someone murder two old ladies? The police in Luxembourg certainly don't know yet, but what makes the article interesting is the last sentence that says the Dutch police are assisting them in their enquires.'

'Because she was Laurens Oostermeer's wife?'

Malcolm nodded. 'And from that, an association with the *Lily Jade*, and therefore, you. It appears the murderers were after something in particular as none of their jewellery was taken.'

'That's the same as when Laurens was murdered. Jacques told me no money, jewellery or silverware was touched.'

'That *is* interesting. I'll talk to my contact in Holland to see what he can find out from Luxembourg.'

'I must tell Kathy – they were family.'

'Warn Kathy to be careful. Tell her to look after her Grandpa, but not to say anything that could cause anyone to suspect she might be involved in any way. And you be careful too, Chris.'

'What about Lubec? Should I sack him?'

'If you do that at the moment, for no good reason, it may put you and everyone connected with the *Lily Jade* under suspicion or in danger.'

I sat in silence wondering where all this would end.

'Go and ring Kathy, it'll be easier to talk from here.'

I heard the phone in Canterbury start to ring and immediately Kathy answered. 'Chris! You must've known, I was just about to ring Malcolm and ask him to pass on the news.'

'What news?' I asked, thankful it was obviously something good she had to tell me.

'The surgery is being re-painted and I've got the whole weekend to come down to Solent Serenity.'

'That's wonderful my dearest girl, we'll have two whole days together!'

'Don't forget you've got a ship to run.'

'I'll have a word with Captain Soo.'

We laughed as we discussed plans for the weekend and I decided to wait until then to tell her about Fleur and Yvette.

Any plans Kathy and I had made for our time at Solent Serenity were to be thrown into disarray the following morning.

'Ah, Malcolm, just the chap I wanted to see.'

Malcolm, who had come to tell me he'd managed to contact his friend in Holland, turned and smiled at the stocky man with a mug of tea occupying the doorway to my cabin. 'What can I do for you,

Scotty?'

'Well, you've no made a trip with us for a while and, seeing as how you've learned all that navigation thing, I wondered if you'd like to help me down below for a voyage?'

'What would Senior Second engineer Soo say about that?'

'Och, that rascal reckons he's ready to take command of the Queen Mary, he hasn't spoken nicely to Agnes for weeks.'

It was obvious Scotty had an ulterior motive, but it *had* been a long time since Malcolm had made a trip to the island. 'What about it, Malcolm, are you busy this week?'

Malcolm looked at me as if to ask, what's going on? and, as Scotty sipped his tea I shrugged my shoulders.

'No, I've no appointments until next Monday; so why not.'

'Och, that's great. I'll tell Agnes to expect a new face.'

'Don't ask, because I don't know,' I said, after Scotty had disappeared.

Soo arrived with cups of tea for us. 'I need to make extra food this voyage, but now Soo go to fix timber for Mr Malcolm's car.'

'Once again, don't ask,' I said, after Soo had gone, 'but you're going to find Scotty and Agnes a different experience to being on the bridge.'

'I'll bring some old clothes.'

'And a Scottish dictionary, if there is such a thing!'

* * * * * * *

'Could I have the weekend off to see my brother in Newport?'

I'd just taken over from Jean Lubec and he was standing in the corner of the bridge, the familiar "clack, clack, clack" emanating from his pocket as he fingered the stones. 'That'll be fine, Jean. I don't know of anything special happening.' Secretly I hoped that odd events during the past two days weren't conspiring to upset my time with Kathy.

He nodded his thanks and went down below.

The *Lily Jade* rolled gently in the low swell coming up the Channel and I wondered if Malcolm was feeling queasy being down below with Scotty and Agnes instead of up in the fresh air, although I knew the motion would ease as soon as we got into the lee of the island.

Twenty minutes later Soo arrived and I explained to him about the buoyage system we were passing.

'Soo make pictures to remember,' he said, trying to scribble on a piece of paper and steer the *Lily Jade* at the same time.

'Captain Soo should concentrate on steering at the moment, while Captain Chris finds him some pictures.'

The door slid open and Malcolm stood there wiping greasy hands on an old rag.

'You'd best wipe the black blob off your nose as well,' I said.

He smiled and I knew he didn't have a problem with seasickness. 'It's a different world down there: it's fascinating, but I wouldn't take it on as a job.'

'Mr Malcolm take the wheel, please. Soo go talk to Agnes or Chief be upset.'

'Did Scotty say why he wanted you to make this trip?' I asked, after Soo had gone.

'No, but he did ask if I was busy on Saturday evening, so he's got something planned.'

'He doesn't know Kathy's coming down.'

'And no-one knows you're engaged?'

I shook my head. 'No-one except you knows that at the moment; after what happened in Luxembourg.'

On Saturday morning I saw Jim Middleton come aboard with a pile of envelopes. 'I hope they're not all bills?'

'No, and they're not for you, they're for Scotty.'

'Good luck, he hates paperwork!'

By 10 A.M. two-thirds of the timber had been discharged and Jean Lubec had already gone to Newport as Soo, Malcolm and I took a short break. I was trying to finish cargo as soon as possible as I knew Kathy would be arriving at Solent Serenity about one o'clock.

'Och, I knew I'd find the deck department sitting around drinking tea.' Scotty had a huge grin on his face and, in his hand some of the envelopes Jim Middleton had brought aboard. 'Here ye are,' he said, passing one to each of us. 'Where's Jean?'

'He's gone to see his brother in Newport for the weekend.'

'Oh, well, I suppose he won't be coming,' he said, putting the last envelope back in his pocket.

'Coming where?' I asked.

'Ye'd find out if ye'd open the envelope!'

As one the three of us slit open our envelopes and took out the card inside. Mine read:

> **Captain Christopher Bowden**
> *is warmly invited to help celebrate*
> *a momentous event taking place*
> *at The Dovecote Tavern in Freshwater*
> *on Saturday 6th March 1954 at 7:30 p.m.*

'What's all this about?' I asked, thinking of Kathy.

'You'll find out tonight.'

'I bet Soo knows,' Malcolm said, looking at the smiling Chinaman.

'Soo say nothing.'

Scotty glared at him. 'Soo better bloody not!'

I decided not to mention Kathy, as I knew with Jean Lubec away in Newport she would feel comfortable and, except for Malcolm, her presence would be a surprise for everyone.

Malcolm parked the Rover in front of the now-defunct railway station in Freshwater, the train service axed by the Government the previous September. Already, after just one winter the building was starting to look neglected: accumulated dirt gathered in the corners and the paintwork was starting to peel.

Kathy saw me and waved as she got off the bus from Newport when it pulled into the station forecourt. 'Chris, my darling, what a wonderful surprise!'

We kissed and then I turned towards the Rover. 'Transport awaits you, fair lady, to the finest hotel on the island.'

'Malcolm! Did you know I was coming?'

'He's the only person who knows you're here.'

'Until tonight,' added Malcolm.

'I'll explain in the car,' I said, in reply to Kathy's puzzled look.

As Malcolm drove through the lanes to Totland I told Kathy of the mysterious evening Scotty had planned. 'I know we were going to have a special weekend together, but Lubec won't be there and Scotty would never forgive us if we didn't go.'

The Dovecote Tavern was a blaze of light as Malcolm, Kathy and I approached it that evening, and before we reached the door we could hear Scotty's voice above the noise of the other patrons.

'Kathy! My dear girl, this is a wonderful surprise. I'm so glad to see you.'

'I hope it's alright, Scotty, I didn't have an invitation.'

'Och, only because I didn't know ye were coming to the island. Why didn't ye tell me, Chris?'

'I'll explain later, Scotty, after we've enjoyed your "momentous event".'

'Oh, aye, well you'll have to wait a wee while, meantime have some nibbles and a drink.'

Scotty had booked the small bar at the back of the pub where a blazing fire in the corner kept the chill of the evening at bay. There were many people I didn't know but Jim Middleton and Soo came over to greet us.

'Miss Kathy! Soo not know you come. You put wool on Soo's eyes.'

'That would be the first time, Soo,' she said, giving him a peck on the cheek, 'and probably the last.'

'What's the momentous event, Jim?'

'I don't know, Chris. I've asked Soo, but he's sworn to secrecy and when I asked Fiona about tonight she just said she had something on.'

At eight o'clock Scotty was standing by the bar when, from behind the curtains, somebody rapped on the doors that lead out into the garden. There was silence as Scotty strode across the room, pushed the curtains aside and flung open the doors. A rush of cold air came in from the darkness, followed by Fiona in a full-length, plum-coloured satin gown with a string of pearls around her neck and a stole across her shoulders.

Scotty shut the doors and led her towards the fireplace before turning to face us. 'I'd like to thank ye's all for coming this evening because…'

Turning to Fiona, who had removed her gloves, he took her left hand, which wore a sparkling diamond ring. '… Because this wonderful lady has agreed to marry this silly old Scot. So welcome to our engagement party.'

Jim Middleton stood with his mouth open. His hand dropped and malt whiskey spilt into his beard. 'You obviously didn't know, Jim?'

'Chris, she's a cunning lass, my cousin.'

Kathy squeezed my arm and then turned the engagement ring she'd put on her right hand and smiled at me as we moved towards the throng of people congratulating Scotty and Fiona.

Music started to play and the floor cleared to allow Scotty and Fiona the first dance before everyone joined them. As we danced I held Kathy close, but even then, it was hard to hear her voice above the music as she whispered in my ear.

'I wish *we* could tell everyone, Chris.'

'We shall, but not tonight – tonight belongs to Scotty and Fiona.'

'Can we do it soon, Chris? I don't even wear my ring at home in case Grandpa asks questions. I keep it on a chain around my neck.' She squeezed me tightly and we almost stopped dancing in the middle of the floor. 'I love you, Chris, and I want to tell the world.'

I returned her squeeze, together with a kiss. 'Tomorrow, at Solent Serenity. At least we can tell our close friends.'

Immediately that decision gave us sense of freedom as we whirled around the floor, becoming intoxicated by the music and the drinks that followed until, eventually, the landlord, fearful of being caught open after-hours, escorted everyone from the premises at midnight.

Laughing and joking, the three of us ambled back to Solent Serenity. 'Goodnight Malcolm,' Kathy said, as I led her upstairs to our bedroom.

I opened a window and we lay naked in each other's arms listening to the breaking waves before drifting off to sleep sometime in the early hours.

Chapter Twenty-Five

We were busy the next morning as I'd invited Jim, Scotty and Fiona for lunch. It was almost noon when Malcolm looked at his watch and said he would go down to the ship to collect Soo.

As the sound of the Rover faded, I went and found Kathy in the kitchen.

Her eyes sparkled as she held up her left hand. 'Look, Chris. My ring's in its proper place – forever!'

'I agree. No more secrets.' I took her in my arms and we kissed before she turned to continue peeling vegetables.

'Forget lunch for a moment, I need to talk to you.'

'Is something wrong, Chris?'

'Bad news I'm afraid.'

Outside it was a warm spring morning; the first blossoms were starting to show and a buzzing of insects invaded the air. We sat on the bench beside the half-finished pond and I told her about Fleur and Yvette.

Tears filled her eyes. 'Why?'

'I wish I could tell you, my darling,' I said, resting her head on my chest, 'but I don't know. All I can say is there seems a possibility of some connection to Laurens Oostermeer's death.'

'What are you trying to tell me?'

'Just be very careful, Kathy. There are similarities to Laurens murder, mainly the fact no money or personal items were taken. It seems the murderer was looking for some particular item and, unfortunately, we're linked to the situation by Jacques and the *Lily Jade*.'

'Do you think this is all to do with the diamonds you told me about in Rye?'

'It could be, or there may be no connection at all.'

I took her in my arms, our lips met and the press of her body made my skin tingle. 'I wish I could be with you all the time to keep you safe.'

'I'm a big girl, Chris and I think it's *you* who should be careful, especially with Lubec around – he scares me.'

We heard the Rover pull up, followed by another car and the chatter of voices.

'Captain Soo, I'm so pleased to meet such an important man.' Soo stood resplendent in his jacket and giggled at Kathy. 'I think,' she continued, 'you should use your authority to quell this rabble.'

Kathy pointed to Scotty, Fiona, Jim and Malcolm, who were having a noisy debate about car engines. They must've heard her as they went quiet and bowed to Soo.

He ignored them, staring at Kathy until, yelling something in Chinese, he ran over to us, pointing to the ring and glancing towards me.

I nodded.

'What's that Chinese chop-stick up to now?'

Soo turned to Scotty, holding up Kathy's hand. 'Chief not only one with big secret. Captain Chris and Miss Kathy also engaged! So good for Captain Chris.'

Malcolm laughed as Scotty, Fiona and Jim stood silent.

'Miss Kathy wonderful girl, but naughty,' Soo continued, turning towards her. 'Miss Kathy putting wool on Soo's eyes every day. Soo must be losing think power.'

'Never again, Soo.' She took the Chinaman in her arms and gave him a long kiss on the lips. His eyes widened and he backed away laughing.

Suddenly we were surrounded by the others.

'So, my cousin's not the only cunning person around here.'

Before I could reply to Jim, Scotty had grabbed me by the shoulders and Fiona was embracing Kathy. 'Chris, congratulations, but ye'r worse than me, keeping a secret like that.'

'There is a reason, Scotty. It's nothing personal, but we would like you all,' I said, looking at Soo and Jim, 'to keep quiet about our engagement for a while. I'll tell you all about it soon; but now it's lunch time.'

The episode set the mood for the day; Kathy and I forgetting all about diamonds or danger.

However, the laughter and celebrations faded after lunch when Soo had another stomach pain. 'Not Captain Chris's food. Last night too much. Soo ok soon,' he said, sipping on his tomato juice and powders.

An hour later he was fine and I began to wonder if a different specialist might consider surgery possible.

During lunch Malcolm had offered to drive Kathy home to Canterbury. It was a long way from Shoreham and although we both protested, he insisted on taking her. Later that afternoon we all went down to the ship as I didn't expect Lubec back until that evening or the next morning, which meant Kathy could enjoy looking around the *Lily Jade* again.

Soo made early afternoon tea and produced scones, jam and cream, which he'd prepared that morning, and we took them up to the deck outside my cabin and sat in the sunshine.

Fiona almost fell over the door-step laughing when Soo gave Scotty a scone filled with shaving cream. 'Oh, Soo, you're priceless,' she cried, holding onto the Chinaman. 'Just look at the man I'm going to marry!'

Scotty stood covered in food as he tried to spit out the remains of the soap. 'You, ye Chinese...!' he spluttered, and then burst out laughing.

All too soon the sun was getting low in the sky. Jim, Fiona and Scotty had left and in my cabin Kathy and I said goodbye. 'Have a safe trip home, my darling. I know Malcolm will look after you.'

'You take care of *yourself* Christopher Bowden. I don't want my fiancé being hurt by diamonds, murders or anything else. I just want all that to be over so we can live our lives together.' We kissed long and passionately. 'Whatever happens, I'll always love you, Chris.'

We crossed the brow to where Malcolm was waiting with the Rover. 'Thanks for coming,' I said to him.

'A double engagement party? I wouldn't have missed it for the world.'

It was almost five o'clock when I stepped outside my cabin and gazed up at the cumulus cloud that promised fair weather for the next couple of days. The late afternoon sun hit the water and there, almost silhouetted, was Lubec rowing out to the lobster-pot. I didn't want to know about it today and went back inside to correct the charts from the latest Notices to Mariners.

Engrossed in the paperwork, I didn't hear him come up the stairs. The knock on my door was cursory and before I could say "come in" the big man was standing in the doorway.

His eyes were narrowed and there was spittle in the corner of his mouth as he stood there staring at me. 'Listen, Bowden, I don't interfere with your ship, I just do my job and if you don't want any hassles, keep your hands off my personal belongings.'

He came over to the desk. 'I thought I'd lost something until this afternoon,' he continued, 'but then I found it in the bottom of my boat.' He opened his hand to reveal a solitary uncut diamond. 'I also found this!' He opened the other hand and there on his large palm lay the love charm Soo had made for me, its gold chain tangled up in the intricate carving.

I almost said this was *my* ship and that he had ten minutes to get off the *Lily Jade*. Instead, remembering Malcolm's words I tried to put the onus back on him. 'Maybe you don't want to work on the *Lily Jade* any more?'

He dropped the charm in front of me and hit the desk with his fist 'You don't get out of it that easy, Bowden. I'll be here a while yet, until everything's sorted. For your own good don't talk about this.' He waved the diamond under my nose. 'And maybe you should co-operate with me about other matters.'

'What other matters?'

He looked at me, uncertain if I really didn't know anything, or was just trying to bluff him.

'We'll discuss that later.'

The door slammed and I was left staring at the charm and thinking of Kathy, our future and the *Lily Jade*. The aura of the weekend had evaporated.

The next morning, as we loaded the last of the cargo and prepared to sail for Weymouth, Jean Lubec avoided conversation by keeping out of my way. Soo realised something was wrong and looked worried. Scotty made his usual jocular remarks, except today nobody laughed and by ten o'clock he became sulky and disappeared below, muttering that Agnes would listen to him.

On the short run to Weymouth I always stayed on the bridge for the whole trip if there was work to be done on deck. Today there was nothing to be done, but Jean didn't come up to take over.

It was late afternoon as we tied up. On the wharf was the black Austin Sheerline I knew belonged to Vivian and standing beside it were two men, watching the *Lily Jade* approach the berth. One was wearing patched corduroy trousers and a flannelette shirt, a cigarette bobbing up and down in the corner of his mouth as he spoke to a tall man dressed in a suit, who had a moustache and neatly combed dark hair.

Without a word Lubec came down from the focs'le, and before

Soo could put out the brow, jumped over the side onto the wharf. The driver's door of the Sheerline opened and the mousey woman emerged. The three spoke briefly, with Lubec doing most of the talking before Vivian glared up at me on the bridge of the *Lily Jade*. Even at that distance I could see a menace in her eyes that made me feel uncomfortable. Suddenly they were gone and moments later the silence was interrupted by Scotty ranting at Soo about what was for tea. I knew it was all in jest, but today no-one was laughing.

The events of the past twenty-four hours faded and life almost returned to normal on the voyage to Fowey. Lubec spoke to me without mentioning his boat and Soo had a big smile on his face, which I knew was because he'd noticed I was wearing his charm again. I tried to ring Kathy from Fowey, but there was no answer.

In the distance at first light on Saturday 13th March I could see the white rocks that formed The Needles in Alum Bay at the western end of the island. Close to the rocks, in the dark shadows created by the cliffs behind them, I saw another white speck that, through the binoculars, seemed to be the wake of a small boat travelling at speed. Within a few minutes it had rounded the point and disappeared into the low swell moving up the Channel.

'Are you seeing Fiona today?' I asked Scotty at lunchtime. Half the cargo had been discharged and the rest would wait until Monday.

'Nae, more's the pity, she had to go back up north until the end of next week at least. Maybe it's a good thing, as I've got work to do on Agnes. How about yourself?'

'I'm going to try and lay some paving at the back of Solent Serenity now the ground has dried out a bit.'

I got off the bus at the Totland roundabout and sauntered down the road towards the pier and the cliff-top. Leaves were beginning to appear on most of the trees and there was a feeling that winter had finally finished. For some reason the gate was open when I arrived, but I thought nothing of it as I walked round to the back of the house, my mind intent on creating a path both practical and aesthetically pleasant for the cottage garden Kathy and I were developing. For almost twenty minutes I walked around considering curves and even a small central square with two paths radiating from a statue or fountain. I decided I'd better go inside and get a pad to make a sketch of my ideas.

As I approached the side of the house a gust of wind blew and I heard the back door slam shut and then, a second later, a slight squeak of the hinges as it swung open again. A piece of paper fluttered down the sideway to my feet. I picked it up and saw it was the electricity bill that had been sitting on the kitchen bench.

Inside everything seemed normal in the kitchen except for two more pieces of paper on the floor. I was trying to work out how the back door had come to be open as I went towards the lounge room to get a pencil and paper from my desk.

I stopped in the doorway, my mind trying to take in the scene before me. The chairs were turned upside down; every drawer in the desk had been emptied onto the floor, as had the shelves of the bookcase. Dazed I went to the dining-room, where a similar scene greeted me. The contents of the bottom cupboards in the sideboard were strewn across the floor and one glass shelf had been pulled from the top. It and several champagne flutes lay broken amongst the debris. With trepidation I went upstairs, only to find a situation that was, if anything, worse. Drawers had been emptied on the floor and all my clothing was scattered around the bedroom. In the bathroom there was a sickly smell of aftershave and shampoo mixed in a sticky mess on the tiles.

Slowly I went back down to the hall and the telephone that had been installed two weeks earlier. I lifted the receiver and, to my relief, heard the click indicating it was still working and dialled 999.

'Police please,' I said to the operator enquiring which emergency service I required. The call was put through to Newport, the main police station on the Isle of Wight.

'Where are you calling from, sir?'

'Totland.'

'And the nature of the emergency?'

'My house has been burgled, but I've no idea when it happened as I haven't been here for a week.'

'The local station in Freshwater is closed over the weekend, but I'll try to get the sergeant at home. Could I have your number, please?'

Twenty minutes later the sergeant called, asking if I could wait until the morning before he came round as he was about to go to a wedding. It seemed a reasonable request as he added nothing could be done until the forensic people came out from Newport on Monday.

I felt the need to talk to someone and nearly rang Kathy, until I realised she would just worry about me and the house. Instead I called Malcolm, but there was no answer. Finally, I decided to call Kathy, vowing not to mention the burglary, but again there was no answer, so I locked everything up and went back to the ship.

'I canna' believe it!'

'You'd believe it if you saw the mess, Scotty.'

'Not good for Captain Chris. Maybe we go to fix palace?'

'Thank you, Soo, but nothing can be done until the police have been on Monday.'

'Sorry to hear about the house, Chris. It's no good when someone else mucks about with your things.'

I looked at him. 'No Jean, it's not.' His impassive face gave no clue, but the lack of sincerity in the voice suggested there was just a sly reference to his rowing boat.

That evening I used my key to Jim Middleton's office and tried to ring Kathy again, but still there was no answer. I was, therefore, pleased to hear Malcolm's voice after the phone had only rung twice.

'Don't touch anything,' he said, after I'd told him what I'd found. 'I'll be down first thing tomorrow.'

The next morning Scotty and I saw the Rover drive off the first ferry and swing round to the brow of the *Lily Jade*. 'Something smells good,' Malcolm said, as he came aboard.

Soo appeared from the galley, a plate of steaming food in each hand. 'Mr Malcolm make big drive early. Must come and have breakfast.' Lubec was nowhere to be seen as the four of us sat down to Soo's cooking.

Scotty was telling us about a time when some hooligans had got down the engine room of a ferry one night and did a lot of damage, when Malcolm noticed I was wearing Soo's love charm and was about to say something, until I gently waved my hand. Later that morning we went out to the Rover to go up to Solent Serenity and I fingered the charm as I got into the car beside him. 'I'll tell you afterwards,' I said.

'Have you any idea what's been taken?' Malcolm asked, as we all stood staring at the mess in the lounge room.

'I think I was still in shock; I didn't really take much notice.'

We went from room to room, but I realised I would find it impossible to work out what was missing until everything was tided up.

'Look, they missed my new camera,' I said, pointing to the hall table as we came back down the stairs.

'They also left an antique clock on the mantle-piece in the dining room; the mint coin collection on the coffee table and your gold cuff-links and tie-clip in the glass dish on your dressing-table upstairs.'

The three of us looked at Malcolm.

'Does anything strike you as familiar, Chris?'

I hesitated.

'It's the same as Fleur and Yvette's murders and, come to that, Laurens Oostermeer's as well. No valuables taken, as if they were looking for something in particular.'

'Murder?' spluttered Scotty. 'What's all this about murder?'

I realised Scotty and Soo had no idea of what had happened to people connected with the history of the *Lily Jade* – they also didn't know about Lubec and the diamonds. 'How about I take you all to lunch. I need something pleasant after seeing all this again and, yes Scotty; I'll tell you about the murders.'

Chapter Twenty-Seven

In the Dovecote we sat in the back bar next to the fire where we'd celebrated Scotty and Fiona's engagement. While we waited for our lunch I explained to Scotty and Soo about Laurens Oostermeer and his connection with Jacques Kessel and Fleur, plus the fact Kathy was Jacques granddaughter.

'Och, well, that starts to explain why those police came tramping all over the ship, but I nae understand what they were looking for at the time?'

'Neither do I, Scotty but it may have something to do with the diamonds.'

'Diamonds! Bloody hell, Christopher Bowden, what'll you tell me about next?'

I told them about the lobster-pot and the fact Kathy's Grandpa and brother worked in the industry. 'So that's why we asked you not to mention to Lubec about Kathy and I being engaged.'

'Soo think Captain Chris should watch closely after Miss Kathy. Make sure she ok.'

When Scotty and Soo went to fetch our food I told Malcolm about the charm and Lubec's threatening manner. 'I've no idea what he meant by "other matters" but I think he thought I was bluffing when I said so.'

'Don't mention this to the others, Chris. They've enough to consider without creating a potentially hostile situation aboard the

Lily Jade.' He didn't elaborate as Soo and Scotty returned with the meal.

'An' all this goin' on under me nose with me havin' no idea.' Scotty waved his fork at Soo. 'It's your fault, ye little Chinese monkey – you know everything that's happin' on the ship, but ye didn't tell Chief, did ye?' he spluttered, spraying potato across the table.

Back aboard the *Lily Jade* Malcolm and I discussed the burglary in my cabin.

'As I said, Chris, it seems whoever broke in was looking for something in particular.'

'I just have the feeling that Lubec is somehow connected with it.'

'If he was, he has the perfect alibi, being at sea with you on the *Lily Jade*. Let's see if the police find anything tomorrow; meanwhile try to remember anything else that might help, and be wary of Lubec. I'll take a quick trip to Holland to see if there's been any progress with the investigations into the murders.'

On Monday morning I went up to Solent Serenity and watched as the police went through the house. 'Nothing out of the ordinary, sir,' they announced after an hour, 'so you can start cleaning it up and then let us know what is missing.'

I started with the second bedroom as it had been the least disturbed and then went upstairs where most of the mess was my clothing that had been tipped out of drawers and thrown from the wardrobe. The worst part was cleaning up the dirt that had been traipsed in from the loft area adjacent to the bedroom, staining the grey carpet and I decided the rest of the clean-up would have to wait until the following weekend. Maybe Scotty and Soo would help me.

The next morning we sailed to Shoreham, and at lunch-time I went up to relieve Lubec on the bridge. He hung around for a few minutes rattling the stones in his pocket, the "clack, clack, clack" starting to get on my nerves until suddenly, it stopped and he turned to me.

'I suppose it was the Wembourne girl who told you about the

diamonds. I didn't think her grandfather had mentioned them to her.'

'No, Jean, no-one told me. I was all alone aboard the ship at Christmas and it was on an impulse I decided to row out and see if you'd caught anything. Why do you think Kathy's Grandpa would have said something to her?'

'Maybe he didn't. Maybe I was wrong.'

Maybe that's what Kathy had been worried about, I thought, that Grandpa was involved with, what she now knew to be diamonds, stolen or otherwise. I also remembered what Scotty had said about Lubec asking if I'd kept in contact with the Kessel family, but I said nothing and just watched the man. He seemed thoughtful for several seconds, looking at me as if trying to decide what to do next. Once more I heard the "clack, clack, clack" of the stones above the rhythmic note of Agnes down below.

'Did Kessel tell you about the history of this ship when you bought it?'

'Do you mean the fact it belonged to a shipowner called Oostermeer?'

'Yeh, what did he say?'

'Why are you so interested, Jean?'

A thin smile appeared on his lips. 'Something like the curiosity you had when you rowed out to my lobster-pot.'

I wasn't sure where this conversation was heading, but I became guarded about what I said, especially about Jacques' family and his comments about Laurens' murder. 'He told me he'd acquired the ship after the war when it was too small for Oostermeer's operations'

'Did he say anything else about Oostermeer?'

'Like what?'

'His life, hobbies, where he went for holidays – things like that.'

'No,' I said in all honesty, 'he never talked about Laurens except to tell me he'd been murdered, which I'd already seen in the papers.'

'Laurens? Was that Oostermeer's name?'

'Yes, it was, but why all this interest in a man who's been dead for more than two years?'

'Like I said, curiosity. If he talked to you about Oostermeer using his Christian name he must've known the man well, or you two were good friends. Have a good think, Bowden. Try to remember if old man Kessel told you anything else.'

Suddenly he was gone and, as the *Lily Jade* made a steady seven knots up the Channel past Hayling Island, I became angry Lubec had referred to such a fine man as Jacques as "old man Kessel".

That evening, in Shoreham, Malcolm wasn't home of course, so I couldn't tell him about Lubec's latest interest in Laurens Oostermeer and I wondered what he might be finding out from his friends in Holland. I tried to ring Kathy, but again there was no answer. I hoped Grandpa wasn't ill.

Back in Yarmouth, Soo and Scotty came with me to clean up Solent Serenity on Sunday. Scotty ranted on about hooligans as he went from room to room, not achieving much until I took him up to the bathroom and the sticky mess on the tiles.

'Try that, Scotty; it's like cleaning oil off Agnes, except it smells better.'

Downstairs Soo had the lounge and dining rooms back to normal in less than an hour before coming to see me. 'Sorry Captain Chris. I find this broken.'

It was a small glass ornament, a blue wheelbarrow that had belonged to my grandmother, who had kept it on the hall table in her country cottage at Reigate. It was a shame, but if that was the only casualty apart from the champagne glasses, I would be very lucky.

'Also rip on side of chair.'

'Don't worry, Soo, that happened during the move from London; and I'll take the glass wheelbarrow back to the ship, where I can glue it back together.'

I spent some time trying to note down what was missing. I thought of a few items, but crossed them out when I remembered most were on the *Lily Jade* and there were a couple of other things I'd thrown away. With the mess cleaned up I felt relieved until Monday evening when I tried to ring Kathy, and still there was no answer.

On the wharf in Weymouth the following afternoon, Vivian was waiting for Lubec with the Sheerline again. She seemed impatient, waving to him to get in the car and then disappearing with a squeal of tyres.

Two days later I'd piloted the *Lily Jade* out of Weymouth and down past Portland Bill at the end of the Chesil Beach before Lubec came up to take over the bridge. It was hard to judge his mood; the impassive look always left me wondering what the big man was thinking, although, I knew no-one could influence him once he'd made up his mind about something.

The "clack, clack, clack" of the stones reverberated around the bridge as he stood in the corner, apparently unwilling to take over and let me go down for lunch. The sound of the stones intensified and then faded as he stared at me, his head nodding in time with the rhythmic beat of Agnes down below.

'Did Kessel give you any extra bits and pieces when he sold you the ship?'

'What sort of "bits and pieces?" Spare parts?'

'No, family items he may have felt belonged with the ship rather than in his home.'

'He gave me nothing, but why are you interested in what Jacques Kessel did or didn't give me?'

'Like I said before, I'm just curious – like you were poking around at my lobster-pot.'

'Vivian put you up to all these questions, didn't she?'

'You know her name?'

'You introduced me to her,' I said, relieved I didn't have to mention

Kathy's connection with the woman.

'So I did. That doesn't matter; we just want to know about Kessel.'

'We?'

'Er, Vivian and I.'

'Why?'

'Private business.'

'If it's your "private business", why are you asking me about it?'

The *Lily Jade* rolled as I altered course for another vessel coming up the Channel, but Lubec didn't notice it.

'Because, somehow, you seem to be tied up with everything concerning that family.'

'I bought this ship from Jacques Kessel, that's all.'

'Who happened to be the grandfather of the Wembourne girl.'

'I didn't meet Kathy until after I'd bought the *Lily Jade,* and even then I had no idea they were related until Jacques died.' Why, I thought, did I feel it necessary to explain such things to him?

'You also know Kessel's sister, don't you?'

'Fleur?'

'Yes, and what about the other one?'

'I never met Yvette.'

'As I said, Bowden, you seem to know all the family so well I wouldn't be surprised if Fleur had given you something when you went over to Zeebrugge.'

How, I wondered, did he know I'd been in Zeebrugge for Jacques' funeral? I thought back to that day and remembered Kathy had spoken to her brother Simeon, who had told her not to contact him, using Lubec's words that he had private business with Vivian.

'All Fleur gave me was a photo of the *Lily Jade,* the *Caillou* as she was called then, the one that's been on the bulkhead in my cabin ever since. Anyway, what do you know about Fleur and Yvette?'

'Nothing, except I believe they live together, somewhere in Europe.'

I realised Lubec didn't know as much as he was trying to make out if he thought Fleur and Yvette were still alive, and that he was just hunting information, presumably on instructions from Vivian.

'What is it you, or is it Vivian, want from Fleur?'

'As I said, it's private business.'

'In which case don't ask me about it, and take over the wheel so I can go down for lunch.'

As I left him, wondering where I could find a replacement crew member, the "clack, clack, clack" of the stones started again.

After that conversation Lubec stayed out of my way during the voyage to Fowey and back to the island, speaking only when necessary as he handed over the bridge with basic navigation information and Scotty reinforced my thoughts about making a crew change.

'Somethin' odd has got into Lubec, Chris. He's still pesterin' me about somethin' that may be hidden in the engine room. Do you know what he's on about?'

'No, Scotty, I don't, and it may well be he's not sure either. But I do know I'm going to start looking for a new crew member.'

'Aye, well that's good, because I was about to suggest the same thing – not that he's done anythin' personal to me, but I don't like the nosey attitude he's got now.'

'I'll ask Jim Middleton if he knows anyone when we get into Yarmouth.'

Chapter Twenty-Eight

We were heading up the Channel towards Shoreham at lunch time on Tuesday 30th March, when Soo brought out one of his Chinese specials, which Scotty had recently stated were better than any English food. The Scot began devouring the mixture of steamed pork and greens with boiled potatoes covered in a toffee-like mixture, oblivious of the fact Soo and I were standing there watching him. Usually Soo would laugh when Scotty ate his food as if it was his first meal in a week, but today he looked serious.

'Is something wrong, Soo?'

'I hear you and Chief. Soo should not talk, but he agree with Captain Chris. Soo think it good if Lubec leave *Lily Jade*. He going to make trouble, Captain Chris.'

'Thank you, Soo, I'm glad you told me.'

If ever there was a confirmation of what I should do, the instinct of the astute Chinaman was it. I hoped his prophecy would not become reality before I'd found a replacement deck-hand.

The driver's door of the Rover opened as we approached the berth and Malcolm got out to take the mooring lines, waving to everyone.

'Mr Malcolm must stay for tea. Soo making English roast dinner.'

'How could I refuse, Soo?'

Impatiently, I didn't let Malcolm get into a conversation, but took him up to my cabin before Scotty appeared as I knew he must've had some news to be waiting on the wharf when we arrived.'

'News, yes – exactly what it means I'm not sure. I've been to Luxembourg, to the house where Fleur and Yvette lived. The authorities were reluctant to let me near the place at first, but then I had a bit of luck. One of the local detectives was a chap who had come to London for an exchange of ideas between the forces a couple of years ago and I was the lawyer who gave some lectures to the group. He remembered me and after I explained about you and your connection with the *Lily Jade,* he did everything he could to help.'

'So what did you find out?'

'They've found a letter, or a note, inside a Christmas card written to Yvette in 1951 from Peter Van Maarden.'

'Van Maarden?'

'It appears he and Yvette had been lovers towards the end of the war and may have even been engaged.'

'That could be the reason Laurens Oosteermeer was considered favourably when it came to funds for re-building his fleet.'

'Almost certainly, but remember he didn't get all of the money, a lot went missing. At some stage, and this is all supposition, Van Maarden may have given Yvette something valuable to look after until they were married.'

'Did they get married?'

'No. Yvette was knocked down by a German fleeing the allies on a motor-bike during the last days of the war and her head injuries caused her to forget everything that had happened since the death of her first husband in 1938. She didn't recognise Van Maarden, much less like him, after she came out of hospital and a family friend from Austria, then living in Luxembourg, took her in. She's lived there ever since, inheriting the house when the Austrian died.'

'So that was the connection with Austria?'

'Yes.'

'But if Van Maarden kept in touch with Yvette, he must've still had feelings for her?'

'I don't think so, because in the note he asked Yvette to return the government property she'd been looking after for him.'

'What government property?'

'That's one piece of the puzzle no-one knows at the moment. The police think it may go back to the missing funds originally allocated to Laurens Oosteermeer to re-build his fleet. Whether Van Maarden *did* give Yvette some genuine government property for safe keeping after the war, or if he was trying to hide something he obtained with the missing funds, no-one can say as yet.'

'Do you think Laurens found out about this "government property"?'

'Possibly he did, and maybe he decided to look after it in lieu of the funds he didn't get.'

'Which could have led to his murder. What do you think it could be?'

'I've no idea, but so many valuable items such as gold and national treasures from countries across Europe got moved or destroyed during the Nazi occupation, it's possible some became available on the black market. Whatever happened, there's now a definite link between Van Maarden, Yvette and the Oosteermeer family. Of course, that doesn't prove he's done anything illegal and he was in a meeting in Rotterdam at the time Fleur and Yvette were killed.'

'So it's just a routine police enquiry?'

'At the moment, and now it's been left to the Luxembourg police.'

'They're not the only ones who have been asking questions.' I told Malcolm about the conversation I'd had with Lubec on the bridge and how Scotty and Soo had helped me make up my mind to look for a new crew member.

'That's odd, especially the fact he mentioned Fleur and Yvette even if he didn't know their names, but it doesn't have any direct connection to Van Maarden.'

There was a knock on my door. 'How about a wee drink over at the Lord Nelson before we tuck into Soo's roast dinner? I'll buy the first round.'

'My word, Fiona's changed your ways, Scotty. You taking others to the pub!'

'Now then, Malcolm, I thought we were friends.'

'What would Fiona say about you going up to the pub?' I asked.

'Fiona knows full well I still go to the pub; so are you coming or not?'

'We'll take Soo with us. The roast dinner will be in the oven and he'll make sure we come back in time.'

That evening, to make time for an extra pint, Scotty conned Malcolm into taking us in the Rover. At the pub I went to ring Kathy, but the phone was busy.

'Only time for one more drink. Chief not be late by drinking with big glass. Captain Chris and Mr Malcolm ok. They have half glasses.'

'You've been told, Scotty,' I said getting up to go to the bar.

'Just a minute, Chris. I clean forgot, I've got a present for each of you in the car.' Malcolm went out and brought back a bag from which he took three parcels wrapped in newspaper and handed one to each of us. For Scotty and I there was a beer stein with an engraving of a castle overlooking a town and Soo had a smaller stem glass with the castle etched on one side.

'That's the castle perched on the hill above the town at Vianden. One of the prettiest places I've ever seen. Maybe the barman will christen them for you.'

'It's a pity you've only got an ordinary glass,' I said, when I returned with the drinks, 'but cheers and thank you, Malcolm.' I'd taken one sip when I noticed a photo in one of the newspapers that Malcolm had folded up. Somehow the man in the picture looked familiar – I knew I'd seen him recently. 'Who's that?' I asked, unable to read the foreign language.

Malcolm picked up the paper and passed it to me. 'That's our friend Peter Van Maarden. It's an article reporting how he was friends with Yvette.'

I was looking at the picture, trying to place the face when Soo touched my arm. 'That man on wharf in black car few weeks ago.'

'Malcolm – Van Maarden! He was on the wharf with Vivian a couple of weeks ago.'

Malcolm slowly put his glass down. 'Are you sure?'

'It was in Weymouth the week before the burglary.'

'Think carefully, Chris; can you remember anything else that happened about that time?'

I tried to recall events of that week day by day. I remembered the cargo we'd taken to Fowey and the good voyage back. The Needles lighthouse at dawn and... 'I remember seeing the wake of a small boat near Alum Bay that was in the shade of the cliffs and travelling fast. I reckon it was similar to the type of boat Marcos had.'

'Are you suggesting Vivian and Van Maarden were just leaving Totland after breaking into Solent Serenity?'

'I'm not suggesting anything; it's just what I remember.'

'Please, Captain Chris. We go soon before dinner burnt.'

With all the talking I'd forgotten to try and ring Kathy again. It had been three weeks since she'd returned home with Malcolm and, although I could understand her being out when I called, I thought she would've left a message with Malcolm or Jim Middleton. 'Give me a couple of minutes, Soo, I want to try and ring Kathy. I promise not to be long I just want to make sure she's all right.' As it had done during the past two weeks the number rang and rang, but there was no answer.

'I'm worried, Malcolm,' I said, as we drove back to the *Lily Jade*. 'I can't understand why she hasn't left a message with someone.'

'Come to the house in the morning and call the surgery. Maybe the vet sent her somewhere like the time she went to Rye.'

The dinner was magnificent and the antics of Soo and Scotty made us laugh all evening, but I couldn't stop worrying about Kathy.

Everyone went quiet when we heard Lubec stumble across the brow. He came to the doorway and leant against it holding a half-empty bottle of beer, his glazed eyes surveying the four of us. In one gulp he emptied the bottle and threw it over his shoulder, muttering something in a foreign language. There was a splash as it landed in the dock and a smile appeared on the big man's face before he swung on the door-frame and lurched down the passage to his cabin.

The next morning Gerald Griffiths sounded relieved I'd called. 'I've been wondering how to contact you, Captain Bowden; I thought you might know where Kathy had gone.'

She's not there?'

'No. A week after she came back from your engagement party...; oh, congratulations by the way.'

'What happened?'

'She asked to have some of her annual leave for some reason, but she was due back at the surgery on the twenty-second. That was ten days ago and it's not like her, Kathy is always so reliable.'

'Have you been round to her house?'

'Yes, both Kathy's and her Grandpa's. Both were locked up.'

'I'll let you know if I hear from her, Gerald.' I gave him Malcolm's number and he promised to leave a message if he had any news.

'I've no idea where Kathy could've gone for a week, Malcolm, or why she didn't tell me about it.'

Malcolm picked up the phone, made a call and passed the receiver to me. 'It's Ian Rathdowne; a friend of mine in the local police. Tell him about Kathy; he'll do all he can to find her.'

I felt happier after speaking to Ian Rathdowne. He sounded calm and efficient, asking several pertinent questions that hadn't crossed my mind as vital information to find a missing person.

When I returned to the ship later in the morning I found Soo had had another stomach attack. 'I've given him his powders an' two bottles of tomato juice, but it nae seems to be working as quick as usual.'

'Well done, Scotty, I'll go and see him.'

Soo lay on his bunk, seemingly asleep until I realised his eyes were open, staring at the porthole. There was no colour in his face, the skin an almost deathly white and his left hand clenched the bunk board, the fingers twitching against its varnished surface.

'How are you, Soo?'

He looked at me, and for a moment I thought he didn't recognise who was talking to him. Then he smiled.

'Captain Chris, good you back. Soo must get lunch for you,' he said, but from the expression on his face he knew he couldn't move.

'You'll do no such thing. Captain Chris will get lunch for Soo, if he tells me what he would like.'

Relief filled his face and a touch of colour returned to his cheeks. 'First more powders and juice. Then vegetables, just vegetables. Thank you, Captain Chris. You special person.'

'So is Soo.'

I gave him the powders and juice and went to cook a pot of vegetable soup. Outside I could hear timber being loaded into the hold and knew, whatever I thought of Lubec, he would look after the cargo in the manner of the true professional seaman that he was.

When I took Soo the soup his eyes were brighter, but it was obvious the attack had knocked the stuffing out of him. 'Captain Chris very good cook. Soon Soo have no job.'

'All right, I'll cook and Soo can be Captain. Soo will always have a job on the *Lily Jade*.'

Tears appeared in his eyes as he nodded. 'Thank you, Captain

Chris.'

By the time we sailed for Yarmouth the following day Soo seemed his normal happy self and Scotty was obviously happy to take the cheek being dished out to him, but I did notice Soo's movement around the ship still lacked its usual bounce.

'Good morning, Chris,' Jim Middleton said, as I entered his office on Friday, 'what can I do for you?'

'I wondered if you knew a seaman who would take a job on the *Lily Jade*?'

'Is someone leaving?'

'He will be if I can find a replacement. Jean Lubec is becoming aggressive and disruptive, which is a shame as he's the best seaman I've ever met.'

'I don't know of anyone, but I'll ask around.'

The telephone rang and I was about to leave as Jim answered it. 'He's right here, I'll put him on,' he said, holding the receiver out towards me.

'Chris, I've just had a phone call…'

'Malcolm! Have you heard from Kathy?'

'No, Chris, I'm afraid not, but I know Ian Rathdowne will contact me as soon as he hears anything.'

'Oh, sorry Malcolm, what were you saying?'

'I've just had a call from my contact in Holland. The police have been talking to people in Luxembourg who knew the Austrian lady, Yvette and, during the past few months, Fleur. There were two old ladies who had been close friends of the Austrian lady. All three had lost their husbands during the war and when they were shown through the house one of them remarked that some paintings that had belonged to Yvette used to hang in the dining room, but they had disappeared about three or four years ago. She couldn't remember what they looked like, except they had big ornate frames and seemed very old.'

'Do you think that was the government property Van Maarden mentioned in the note?'

'It could be, but of course there is no proof. The old lady thought there were three paintings and maybe one was smaller than the others, but that doesn't help the police much because so many art works went missing during the war. I do think though, it's possible that whoever murdered Fleur and Yvette were after those paintings.'

'Is that why the Dutch police and Van Maarden are interested in the *Lily Jade*? Do they think I've got those paintings?'

'I think the Dutch police may have got a tip-off from somewhere and are exploring all avenues, while Van Maarden, if he did hide them, hopes to find them first. That way he'll be a very rich man and there'll be no evidence against him after he's sold them abroad.'

'Well, I know I haven't got them, I wonder where they went?'

'They disappeared from the house before Laurens Oostermeer's murder. Maybe someone thought she'd given them to him.'

'But that was years ago; why would they go back to Yvette now?'

'Not Yvette. Remember when Laurens was murdered you told me Fleur was in Zeebrugge with Jacques Kessel and she only went to live with Yvette after her brother died.'

'Did they think Fleur had been given the paintings?'

'Either by Laurens or Jacques Kessel. It's all supposition of course, and now we may never know.'

'Jacques also told me Laurens had said he'd provided for Fleur, but they never found anything after his death; in fact he was deeply in debt. Jacques certainly never knew anything about any paintings, if they were ever there.'

'The police have no evidence as yet, but they are questioning Van Maarden, who will be getting quite desperate if he is involved, especially now a reward has been offered for information leading to the recovery of any of ten paintings that went missing towards the end of the war. Just be careful, Chris and let me know if you see or hear anything.'

'I'd rather hear from Kathy.'

'I'll ring Ian Rathdowne this afternoon to see if he's got any news.'

I put the phone down and hoped, considering she was Jacques Kessel's granddaughter, Kathy wasn't in some way caught up in all this business.

Jim Middleton tugged at his grey beard. 'Sorry Chris, but I couldn't help overhearing what you said about some paintings. Is that connected with the visit from the police at Christmas?'

'Yes Jim, but if you want to hear the whole story you'd best make another pot of tea, it'll take a while to tell.'

During the weekend I rang Malcolm three times; once from Jim's office and twice from Solent Serenity hoping he had some news about Kathy, but he didn't. I couldn't settle into any work around the house, and spent a lot of time on the balcony gazing over the Solent, remembering the first time Kathy and I had stood there while the estate agent waited by his car. It had rained that day, and rain, or fine spring weather as it was today, I wanted nothing more than Kathy to be with me. Even the *Lily Jade* seemed almost unimportant.

Late on Sunday afternoon I returned to the ship and as I walked along the wharf I could see Lubec in the distance rowing out to the lobster-pot. I wondered if Van Maarden was looking for the missing paintings and whether Lubec knew about them; or perhaps Vivian didn't trust him with such information.

Soo met me with a mug of tea, but I was still thinking of Kathy and took it to my cabin as I was in no mood for conversation. I couldn't concentrate on the small amount of paperwork needing attention before we sailed and went out on the deck beside the funnel.

I noticed Lubec return as I swallowed the last of the tea and was about to go inside when I saw someone approach him from the bus stop. He looked vaguely familiar and when he lit a cigarette that dangled from the corner of his mouth, I realised it was the man who had been on the wharf with Vivian and Van Maarden that day in Weymouth. Although he wasn't as big as Jean, I got the impression this might be his brother from Newport.

    The two talked briefly before Jean looked up at the *Lily Jade* as if he knew I was watching them. I felt exposed and pushed myself closer to the funnel. They spoke for several more minutes before the man threw his cigarette stub on the ground and headed back to the bus stop. When Jean turned and walked towards the *Lily Jade* his movements suggested he was upset and angry. I went inside. Lubec in that frame of mind wasn't something I wanted to confront just at that moment.

Chapter Twenty-Nine

'Scotty! What happened?'

It was ten o'clock on Monday morning and Soo had just put mugs of tea on the table when Scotty appeared from the engine room sporting a bruised cheek which, together with the left side of his mouth, had turned purple.

'Och, it's nae anything to worry about,' he said, gingerly touching the cheek. 'I had a wee argument with Agnes; forgot about a valve wheel near the fuel inlet.'

'Good morning, Jean,' I said, hoping the big man was in a better mood than I'd seen the previous evening.

'Morning,' he grunted, picking up his coffee. 'Last of the cargo will be here in half an hour.'

Scotty got up. 'In which case, I'll take my tea down below. I've a few wee things to sort out before we sail,' he said, his voice fading as he hurried down the alleyway.

Lubec swallowed the rest of his coffee and left without another word.

I sat there alone. Something was very wrong aboard the *Lily Jade*.

'Captain Chris?'

I smiled to myself. Not everything was wrong aboard the ship, I thought. 'Yes, Soo,' I said, turning around. I could not have been more mistaken. Again I was shocked. Soo wasn't smiling and I could see that, even though he wasn't having a stomach attack, he wasn't feeling well. 'Are you alright, Soo?'

A faint smile crossed his face. 'Yes, Soo always ok. But he worried, Captain Chris.'

'What about, Soo?'

'Soo feel bad things.'

'What sort of bad things?'

'Soo not sure, but worried about Captain Chris and Miss Kathy.'

Kathy! His words sent a shiver down my spine. 'What do you know about Kathy?'

'Soo know nothing, Captain Chris. Soo sorry. He just feel bad things.'

'Captain Chris is worried about Soo,' I said, poking him in the chest. Usually he would've laughed, but today there wasn't even a smile.

'Not worry about Soo. Soo happy. He on *Lily Jade*. You be extra careful, Captain Chris. Soo not happy with Lubec on *Lily Jade*. Soo feel bad things about him.'

I went to my cabin, now feeling distinctly uneasy about the situation aboard the ship and even more so about Kathy. I trusted Soo's intuition implicitly and knew I had to do something immediately.

'Morning, Chris. What's the matter? You look worried.'

'Two things, Jim. First, can I use your phone to call Malcolm, and secondly I want you to find me that replacement for Lubec as soon as possible. Anyone who knows the slightest thing about seamanship will do.'

'Help yourself to the phone, but what's the rush to replace Lubec?'

'Soo has bad feelings and I trust Soo completely. If he told me not to sail, I probably wouldn't.'

I told Malcolm about Soo and the general atmosphere aboard.

'He's right, Chris, take care and meanwhile I'm going to try and get the police to intensify the hunt for Kathy.'

We sailed at 1400. Clear of the wharf I swung the bow of the *Lily Jade* to port and headed out into the Solent. Fort Albert and Colwell Bay were on the port quarter and Hurst castle, with its white lighthouse, was abeam to starboard when Lubec came up to take over the bridge.

As he had done the previous time, he stood in the corner, the right hand in his pocket fingering the stones. The "clack, clack, clack" sounded louder today, or perhaps I sensed he was about to become unpleasant. If he did I vowed to sack him on the spot, instead of waiting to see if Jim Middleton could find a replacement in Yarmouth.

His eyes narrowed as he stared at me.

'Do you want to take over the wheel?' I asked.

'First I want to know what Jacques Kessel told, or gave you, with the ship.'

'Told me about what?'

'Laurens Oostermeer for a start.'

'He told me Laurens owned the *Lily Jade* before it was given to him, but you know that.'

The sound of the stones stopped as he took a couple of paces towards me. A huge fist with a stubby finger that was quivering slightly was held just inches from my face. 'Listen, Captain, bloody, Bowden, I reckon you know more about the Kessel family than you're letting on and you'd better have another think about that.'

'That's it, Lubec! It's time you left the *Lily Jade!*'

'I'll be glad to, just as soon as you've told me what I need to know.'

'You don't need to know anything. You're just a messenger for Vivian and Van Maarden.'

He looked at me in silence for a few seconds. 'What do you know about Van Maarden?'

'He was on the wharf with Vivian in Weymouth a few weeks ago and now you're asking me about Laurens Oostermeer. What's the connection between those two and Laurens? Did Van Maarden murder Oosteermeer? I expect he had it done for him; he didn't look the sort of man capable of doing his own dirty work.'

Lubec's face grew red and spittle had returned to the corner of his mouth, but I was angry and hadn't finished yet.

'Was he, and Vivian for that matter, involved with the murder of Jacques' sisters, Fleur and Yvette?'

'I thought so... you and your lawyer friend, Malcolm, have been snooping about, haven't you?'

'I read the papers, Lubec. And if it's paintings Van Maarden is looking for, I don't have them!'

His hand grabbed my jacket. 'You know where they are, don't you?'

'What I know or don't know doesn't matter. I'm the owner and master of this vessel and you're finished. Now, get off my bridge, and get off the *Lily Jade* when we reach Weymouth!'

He backed off. 'You're Captain of this ship at the moment, Bowden, but for how long?'

'What do you mean?'

'You wouldn't want anything to happen to the ship like it did to your house, would you?'

'What do you know about that?'

'Nothing, except what you talked about. How could I? I was here on your precious ship, wasn't I?' A wry smile appeared on his face. 'Accidents happen, Bowden. Think about it, but don't take too long; it's only a short voyage to Weymouth.'

He left and I remained on the bridge, seething about what had happened. I stayed there all the way to Weymouth, angry with Lubec and angry with myself for saying so much, but glad he would be out of my life in a few hours.

As we approached the berth, Lubec went for'd carrying his kitbag and as soon as the lines were fast he threw it onto the wharf and jumped down after it. Without a glance at the *Lily Jade* he hoisted the bag onto his back and disappeared between the buildings of the town. My anger subsided and suddenly I felt exhausted.

Chapter Thirty

'I know I should've kept my mouth shut, Malcolm, but I was angry and at least Lubec has gone. Now there's only one thing that matters and that's Kathy. I'm sure something must've happened to her or Grandpa, wherever they are, and if I haven't heard any news by the time I get back to Yarmouth on Saturday I'm going to lay-up the *Lily Jade* so I can go and look for her.'

I pushed open the door of the telephone box and ambled back to the ship. Malcolm had been worried when I'd told him what had happened and what I'd said, but I felt relieved now that Lubec had gone, and I knew Scotty and Soo felt the same way. If I laid-up the ship they could have a break while I searched for Kathy, *and* it would give Jim Middleton a chance to find a new crew member for me. All in all everything had turned out rather well, I thought, pulling my collar up around my neck as I met the full force of the southerly wind coming in off the sea.

Apart from six hours sleep, I didn't stop working during the next twenty-four hours and, even having Soo's help with the cargo, I realised just how much Jean Lubec had done around the ship: not that I wanted him back, but he'd been a fine seaman.

We were ready to sail to Fowey by 11 A.M. on Wednesday and dark clouds covered the sky as Soo let-go the lines aft and then tried to run for'd. Immediately I could see he wasn't well.

'Take your time, Soo.'

'Thank you, Captain Chris. Soo be quick as can,' he said, holding his stomach.

'Full ahead, Scotty,' I called down the voice-pipe as he let go the bow line and the southerly wind, which had been getting stronger all day, pushed us clear of the wharf in the first drops of heavy rain. Seconds later the reliable Agnes burst into life and I swung the bow around to line up with the end of the breakwater.

'Soo,' I called down from the bridge as I watched him stumble past the hatch holding his stomach in pain, 'you must go to your cabin and take a tomato juice and some powders.'

We cleared the harbour entrance and I altered course to starboard to head down to Portland Bill at the end of the Chesil Beach. My mind was on Soo and I didn't hear the steps on the outside ladder.

The door to the bridge slid open with a bang and he stood there, his huge bulk filling the entrance. Those eyes: they were barely slits, but they were menacing. He'd obviously had quite a bit to drink and the spittle was in the corner of his mouth.

'Lubec! What are you doing on my ship?'

'Your last chance, Bowden. Tell me about the paintings.'

'I don't know anything about the paintings, but I do know you're not staying aboard the *Lily Jade*. I'm going back to the wharf,' I said, spinning the wheel to port.

'I don't think so, Bowden.'

A huge hand grabbed me by the throat and threw me away from the wheel into the bulkhead at the back of the bridge, my head smashing the glass on the picture of the P&O ship, one piece slicing into the back of my neck.

'Let's take a look in your cabin,' he said, pushing me backwards through the doorway.

I tried to go down the inside stairs to the main deck, but he was too strong. He grabbed both my arms and almost lifted me over the step into my cabin. He lowered his face close to mine and I nearly retched at the smell of stale beer on his breath when he spoke.

'Don't give me any more fucking trouble, Bowden. I've already told you, this is your last fucking chance.'

I felt myself going backwards until I fell over, landing on the coffee table, which broke under my weight, my head hitting the side of the desk as I went down. After two blows in quick succession I felt dizzy and took some deep breaths as I sat on the deck trying to prevent myself from blacking out. A trickle of blood ran down my neck.

Lubec threw the armchair up against the door and started ransacking the cabin, pulling the drawers out from under the bunk and empting them onto the deck. He found nothing and his anger intensified. The contents of the bookcase were thrown at my feet, including a porcelain egg and my mother's blue glass wheelbarrow, both of which shattered into tiny pieces.

'Get out of my bloody way, Bowden.'

The putrid breath enveloped me again as he dragged me across the floor so he could get to the desk and the filing cabinet, leaving me beside the door leading out onto the deck by the funnel. My head had cleared and I knew this was the one chance to get away from him and warn the others. He was fiddling with the locking bar I'd put on the filing cabinet to prevent the drawers flying open at sea as I pulled myself up, pushed open the door and stumbled out onto the wet deck.

Instinct made me look forward towards the bridge, where I saw the sight no master of a ship ever wishes to see. When I'd spun the wheel to port it had taken the *Lily Jade* away from the land, but the southerly wind had pushed her back and it was obvious that, unless someone could get to the wheel, she would pass the wrong side of the buoys and go aground on Portland Bill.

Beside me was the small wooden row-boat that served as a lifeboat. I released the retaining strap, picked up the boat and dropped it over the side as Lubec appeared.

'That's it, Bowden, you're finished!'

From his belt he took a marlin spike, the large right hand holding the foot-long steel spike with its needle-sharp end pointed directly at my face as he started to advance towards me.

I backed away, past the skylight over the engine room, until I felt the wet rail at the aft end of the upperworks where, without taking my eyes off him, I felt behind my back for the vertical ladder leading down to the main deck. My feet clattered on the slippery rungs as I lowered myself down the first few steps. Beside me I could hear the gentle thump of the wooden row-boat as it bounced across the waves, dragged along with the *Lily Jade* by the rope painter on its bow that was fastened to the mooring bits alongside the hold forward of the bridge.

For several seconds I lost sight of him. I wiped the rain from my eyes and then, there he was beside the engine room skylight; those eyes staring at me, the right hand still holding the marlin spike while the left hand held a bundle of dripping rags. A freshly lit cigarette dangled from the corner of his mouth.

'End of the line, Bowden, unless you can produce the paintings.'

'Why are they important to you, Lubec? I thought you were just the messenger boy for Vivian and Van Maarden.'

'I'm not going down for murder while that bastard goes free.'

'Murder?'

'Yeh – Oostermeer.'

'You... you murdered Laurens Oostermeer?'

'I was looking for the paintings. It was a just a robbery and I needed the money. Oostermeer got in the way.'

'Now Van Maarden's going to hand you over if you don't come up with the goods.'

'Worked it out, have you, Bowden? About time, because if you don't give them to me right now your precious ship is history.'

'I don't have the paintings!'

'I don't believe you, Bowden, so you can say goodbye to the *Lily*

Jade... and you'll never see the Wembourne girl again either!'

'Kathy! What do you know about Kathy? Where is she?'

'Ah, I see the woman is more important than the ship.'

'What have you done to her, you bastard?'

'*I* haven't done anything to her. *I've* been on board this bloody ship of yours, haven't I?'

'Where is she, Lubec?' Despite his size I was about to go back up the ladder to tackle him, to make him tell me where Kathy was.

'Where are the paintings, Bowden?'

'I don't know.'

'You'll tell me, Bowden.' Putting the marlin spike back in his belt he picked up a can containing petrol, which he must've taken from the locker outside my cabin. He reached under the skylight and poured the contents over Agnes, who was steadily pushing the *Lily Jade* into shallow water.

Taking the cigarette from his mouth he held it against the dripping material in his left hand, before flicking the butt into the engine room and turning to stare at me. 'I warned you, Bowden,' he sneered, and tossed the blazing rags through the open skylight.

I half-slid, half-fell, down the vertical ladder to the main deck.

'Scotty! Scotty!' I screamed, hitting my fists against the steel bulkhead above the engine room, even though I knew he couldn't hear me.

The marlin spike had returned to his right hand when he appeared at the top of the ladder and looked down.

I shook my clenched fists at him. 'How could you kill Scotty? That'll be another murder you'll go down for, Lubec.'

'And who's going to tell anyone?'

My heartbeat went up a notch as black smoke appeared above me, and I started moving up the starboard alleyway now knowing Lubec intended to remove all trace of witnesses, and any evidence of the paintings he was convinced were aboard the *Lily Jade*.

'Soo!' I hit the glass on the porthole of his cabin so hard I thought I'd break it instead of just hurting my hand. 'Soo! Get up!'

Lubec appeared at the aft end of the alleyway and I turned to move out onto the foredeck beside the hold. I stared in horror at the proximity of the cliffs of Portland Bill towering above me and I could see each wave as it broke along the shoreline. I braced myself for the inevitable grinding sound when the hull of the *Lily Jade* would plough into the stony beach, driven hard ashore by Agnes still pushing her along at eight knots.

Yet, as I watched, the bow started to swing to port, away from the beach. I looked up and saw, above the gold braid of his jacket, the contorted face of Soo at the open window of the bridge as he struggled to put the helm over, regardless of the pain in his stomach.

'Keep going, Soo! The other side of the buoys!'

'I know, Captain Chris. You show me.'

'Captain Soo's in charge,' I called. Despite his pain I saw a brief glimpse of a smile cross his face.

Lubec arrived a few feet in front of me and looked up at Soo. 'He won't save your ship, Bowden. Have a look.' Above the bridge the cloud of black smoke had grown thicker and was curling back along the alleyway behind Lubec. 'Your ship's gone Bowden, and so are you.'

The last buoy of the channel passed down the side of the ship behind me, where it should've been. Soo had cleared Portland Bill and we were moving into deeper water, although the bow had swung back to starboard and the *Lily Jade* was heading westwards alongside the Chesil Beach.

'You'll die too, Lubec.'

'Maybe I will, Bowden, but I won't go to jail.'

There was a scream on the port side of the ship and a moving ball of fire appeared carrying a lifebelt.

'Scotty!'

He didn't hear me as he threw himself over the side, his clothes burning more fiercely as the wind fanned the flames.

'He was another one who wouldn't listen to me. He could've saved all of you.'

In my mind I saw Scotty's bruised face. 'You hit Scotty, didn't you? He didn't have an accident.'

'He was going to the police until I mentioned the Wembourne girl, and then he attacked me.'

Again Kathy. Kathy, where was she? What had he done to her? I felt helpless.

There was an explosion and I saw a sheet of flame behind the bridge. Lubec turned round and I backed away from him as the rhythmic sound of Agnes faltered for a few seconds. When he looked back at me there was a strange smile on his face as if he was enjoying the destruction of the *Lily Jade* and wanted to prolong her sinking.

He tapped the marlin spike on his left hand. 'It won't be long now, Bowden. You and this bloody ship will be just another wreck in these waters.'

Lubec came towards me, holding the marlin spike above his head by the sharp pointed end like a club.

Behind him, from the door by his cabin Soo appeared in his jacket, his left hand clutching his stomach, as he waved the large carving knife from the galley.

'No! No hurt Captain Chris!'

Lubec spun around. Soo was running towards him, the knife ready to slash at Lubec when he got within range.

'N...!'

In a blur the arm of the big man came down, just as it had that evening outside my cabin when he'd thrown his knife at the playing cards.

In the split-second Soo had tried to scream again, the steel marlin spike entered his open mouth. The eyes of the Chinaman bulged as the force of the impact spun him round on the wet deck and in horror I saw the blood-stained, needle-sharp point appear through the back of his neck. His knees buckled and the carving knife fell from his right hand; blood pouring from his mouth onto the gold braid as he crumpled to the deck, motionless, his eyes wide open and vacant.

Lubec stood still, seemingly transfixed by the horror of what he'd done. There was another explosion and more flames appeared behind the bridge. Instinctively my left hand found the painter of the rowboat and released it from the mooring bits on the foredeck.

As I slipped over the side the sight of Soo slumped on the deck was imprinted on my mind, and I knew he'd achieved his ambition of remaining with the *Lily Jade* until he died.

Chapter Thirty-One

The salt-water mixed with my tears as the stern of the *Lily Jade* sailed past; thick, black smoke pouring from the engine room skylight. There was a third, lesser explosion before the sound of *Agnes* faltered, and then died. Drifting away from me her stern looked lower and I knew she was already taking water as the first flames appeared through an open door on the main deck.

My legs were starting to go numb as I struck out for the row-boat thirty yards away. It was only April and the Channel waters still had an icy feel of winter that would kill anyone immersed in them for any length of time. In vain, I looked for Scotty, wondering if he could still be alive.

It took all my strength to drag myself into the boat, and for a couple of minutes I lay across the thwarts exhausted, before looking up at the *Lily Jade,* which was now just a pall of black smoke nearly two hundred yards away. I'd unlashed one oar when, suddenly, two hands appeared over the stern, and in one movement Lubec pulled himself into the boat.

I lunged forward, trying to push him back into the water with the oar, but he brushed it aside like an annoying fly. There was a twisted smile on his face as he knew; this time I had no escape. I tried to regain my balance and fend him off with the oar, but as I got to my feet his huge right fist landed a direct punch on my jaw.

I tasted blood in my mouth as I fell backwards; my head hit the thwart and I started to black out. The oar hit something and was wrenched out of my hands. There was a splash; I felt salt-water all over my face mixing with the blood…

I was choking… I couldn't breathe…

Chapter Thirty-Two

Hiss... There was a grating sound and I felt my body thrown against something hard before everything went quiet and I blacked out again.

Hiss... The grating sound returned. Again my body was thrown against something hard, and then my left hand hurt as if someone had stood on it, but the pain left as suddenly as it had come and once more the silence enveloped me.

Hiss... That noise, I recognised that noise. It was the sound of the water rushing down the port side of *Lapwing*. My body was thrown against something hard. We must be turning... yes, turning to avoid the dive bombers, but I couldn't see anything because of the fog.

Hiss... The water is still rushing past *Lapwing*. We must turn faster to avoid the bombers... but that grating noise – have we run aground? Was my navigation wrong? Have I condemned *Lapwing* and her crew to die in the unforgiving ocean?

I smell burning. I must warn seaman Turnbull, but he has no head. My hand hurts and it's wet. I must've fallen overboard.

Suddenly, my eyes opened and I stared at the dark-grey clouds above the English Channel. There was a hiss as the wave retreated down the bank of stones that formed the shoreline, and a grating sound as the boat rolled onto one side, crushing my hand, which was hanging in the water.

The next wave arrived and the boat righted itself, freeing my hand, which instinctively grabbed at the stones it had been resting on. I brought my arm inside the boat, looking at the back of my grazed hand. It stung, but I knew the salt-water would help it heal.

Turning my hand over, I unclenched my fingers and gazed at the handful of pebbles. They were tan, white and black with contrasting spots, and somehow seemed familiar. I kept looking at them, wondering where I'd seen them before.

I closed my fingers. "Clack"

I opened and closed my fingers several times. "Clack, clack, clack".

Lubec! I looked around, expecting to see him appear like a recurring nightmare, but I was alone on what I now recognised as the Chesil Beach. The wind and tide must've pushed the boat ashore on this treacherous, remote piece of coastline.

Lubec. I wondered why he'd come to this area. Certainly I'd followed him that day, but I never found out where he'd gone. I looked at the handful of pebbles again. They were different to the ones Lubec had had aboard the *Lily Jade* – they were bigger, about the size of a small hen's egg. His had only been as big as a thrush's egg.

Hiss, the grating sound and the boat rolled once more. I scrambled out onto the pebbles and stood in the water waiting for the next incoming wave, knowing the Chesil Beach had a terrible reputation for having an undertow that could suck a person down the slippery stones into oblivion, even in the few inches of water that reached just below my knees. When I felt the next wave I lunged forward and threw myself face down, desperately clutching at the loose stones. My sodden clothing stopped me sliding back down into the water as the wave receded and, slowly, I crawled up onto the dry stones and stood up.

Behind me the pebbles sloped steeply into the sea and on the other side they fell away in the same manner into the marshy waters called The Fleet. I could see no way off the ridge of stones that stretched endlessly both ways, to merge with the dark-grey clouds. I had no idea how long I'd lain unconscious in the boat or what the time was, but, from the sky, I estimated there were three or four hours of daylight left. The wind brought a burning smell from a thin cloud of smoke over half a mile to the west and my heart pounded as I realised it must be the *Lily Jade*.

It took me twenty minutes to stagger along the ridge of loose stones to where she lay, bow into the beach with a list to starboard. Everything below the main deck had been burnt out. The wooden mast had collapsed and fallen over the side, held to the *Lily Jade* only by the steel wire stays that had supported it. Black smoke still came from the hold where something must've been smouldering above the sea-water that had invaded the hull. The funnel was still green, but the paint had blistered and behind it the engine room skylight had disappeared, presumably collapsing inwards and falling on top of Agnes. In contrast, my cabin and the bridge looked undamaged, the varnished woodwork still shiny.

I sat on the stony beach and stared at the wreck that'd been the realisation of my greatest ambition and my pride and joy. For no reason I suddenly remembered today was 7th April and tears filled my eyes – it was exactly two years since I'd first seen the *Lily Jade*, the *Caillou* as she had been then, in the docks at Shoreham. I clenched the pebbles that were still in my left hand at the thought of it.

The stones were hard to sit on, just like the time I'd been to Brighton on a school trip. The master who'd been in charge kept telling us the names of everything in French, not that we were interested, but even now I could remember some of the words: le bateau de peche – a fishing boat; la jetee – the pier; la plage – the beach, which had seemed a misnomer for Brighton. I looked back at the *Lily Jade* and laughed as I remembered what he'd said when someone told him a beach should have sand. He'd picked up a stone and said, le caillou – the pebble.

My ship had been the *Pebble*, and now here she was at her final resting place, on a remote beach of pebbles.

I looked at the stones I'd been carrying since scrambling out of the row-boat and was about to throw them away when I noticed they were bigger than the ones I was sitting on. All around me the pebbles were smaller. They were still bigger than the ones Lubec had had on the ship, but definitely smaller than those I'd been carrying. I picked some up, adding them to the stones from alongside the boat and put them in my pocket before continuing to walk along the ridge, looking for a way to get off the Chesil Beach.

I must've walked for nearly an hour. I couldn't be sure of the time as my watch had stopped, no doubt full it was of sea-water. I sat down to rest my feet, which were starting to ache and, taking the pebbles from my pocket compared them with those around me. The ones here were smaller again and, if my memory was correct, were not much bigger than those Lubec had had aboard the *Lily Jade*.

I walked for another twenty minutes or so occasionally looking at the pebbles around my feet. They were getting smaller the further I walked, but there was still no way off the beach. Maybe I'd been mistaken about Lubec's stones. Maybe they hadn't come from the Chesil Beach, although all around me the pebbles looked the same size and had similar colouring.

Suddenly, there it was, half-hidden by the marshy reeds of The Fleet, a path of stones leading off the ridge into the Dorset countryside. Clear of the Chesil Beach I followed a sandy track that wound between gorse bushes and some stunted trees until it reached a small rise.

To my left I saw a splash of dull red, the roof of a solitary house among the green fields. There was no option but to follow the track down the other side of the rise until I could squeeze through the wire fence and head towards it. The long grass was wet and my shoes squelched in the mud until I came across a dry path that I would've found if I'd continued further along the sandy track.

When I reached the small farmhouse it seemed deserted, its paint peeling and the front door secured by a large padlock. In every direction the fields were overgrown and it was obvious no crops had been grown here for several years. A narrow, weed-infested path led around the house and my feet crunched on the gravel as I went looking for any sign of life. Beside the path was a large shed, its door open, hanging on one hinge and inside were pieces of rusty farm equipment containing several abandoned bird's nests.

Along the side of the house were two small windows caked in dirt, too high for me to see into until I jumped up and managed to catch a glimpse of a wardrobe and an open door. When I stopped I heard a faint sound and looked back at the shed expecting to see an animal appear. Hearing it a second time I moved further down the path and stopped to listen. The sound had got louder and resembled a human voice.

At the back of the house I found a larger window and peered inside. The room was so dark it was almost impossible to discern anything, until in one corner I saw a movement and the sound of a human voice began again.

The window was locked, but the muffled cries intensified as I stood back looking for another possible entry that might be open. My fingers curled around the pebbles I'd picked up along the ridge and without a second thought I threw them at the window. The sound of breaking glass faded and I stood transfixed as I recognised the voice inside calling for help.

'Kathy!'

There was silence from inside the room.

'Kathy! Is that you?'

Her cries reached my ears again as, hastily, I fumbled with the catch on the window, cutting my hand on the broken glass in the process before sliding the window up and pulling myself through the opening, where I landed headlong on the wooden floor.

In the corner were two people bound and gagged, but the second person wasn't moving. Tears appeared in Kathy's eyes as, frantically, I untied the scarf wound across her mouth.

'Chris! Oh, thank God! Chris, my darling Chris, how did you find us?'

'Pure luck, my sweet, darling girl,' I said, and kissed her forehead as I untied her hands.

With the rope still around one of her wrists we clung close to each other. 'Oh, Chris, I thought I'd never see you again.'

'Nor I you, my dearest Kathy.'

We parted and Kathy looked round. 'Grandpa. Chris, is he still alive?'

I removed the gag and bent close to his mouth. 'He's breathing, but it's pretty shallow.' Kathy untied his hands and we lifted the old man onto an armchair that had its stuffing poking out of one arm. 'Do you know if there's any water, Kathy? He needs a drink.'

'There's a kitchen in the next room and everything was working yesterday.'

After a few sips of water Grandpa was able to speak coherently, his main problem being the stiffness in his limbs from being tied up. I left them together and rummaged in the kitchen cupboards where I found tea, a tin of condensed milk and a packet of chocolate biscuits.

Kathy had a sip of tea and we sat down on an old couch in the same state of disrepair as the armchair. I took her hand. 'What happened?'

'Vivian asked me to bring Grandpa to Portsmouth where she and another man, who I think is Lubec's brother, forced us into her car and brought us here. Grandpa had been here before, cutting the diamonds Jean Lubec had delivered each time you were in Weymouth.'

I looked at the old man dozing in the armchair. 'Why was Grandpa doing that for Vivian?'

'She told him Simeon and I would get hurt if he didn't do it.'

'Your brother? What's he got to do with all this?'

'She and Marcos told him Grandpa and I would get hurt if he didn't steal the diamonds.'

'Steal?'

Kathy nodded. 'When he came back from South Africa he was put in charge of all the uncut stones being brought to Amsterdam. He's been stealing some of them for months.'

'Vivian was playing you all off against each other.'

'Until I found out about the diamonds from you and asked Grandpa about it. He's no fool and was wild, and must've said something to Vivian. That's really why I went with him to Portsmouth that time, to have it out with her. But what about you, Chris, are you all right? Your face is bruised, there's dried blood on your cheek and you're soaking wet. And... how did you know we were here?'

I kissed her. 'As I said, Kathy, it was pure luck – I don't even know where we are. Lubec came within inches of killing me – I still don't know what happened, I blacked out. He destroyed the *Lily Jade*, but, Kathy, oh Kathy; worst of all, he killed Soo, and almost certainly Scotty as well.'

Kathy sat speechless and unashamedly I let tears run down my cheeks as, in my mind, I saw the bloody point of the marlin spike protruding through Soo's neck.

Kathy held me close, tears rolling down her cheeks as well. 'Poor Soo. Dear kind, understanding Soo, and that rascal, Scotty. Oh, Chris, I can't believe it. I can't believe they're gone, and the *Lily Jade* as well.'

Grandpa stirred and Kathy gave him some tea and a piece of chocolate biscuit as I told her the story of the past few hours. Hours? It felt like days.

'... So the diamonds were just a minor part in the plans, Kathy, at least as far as Van Maarden was concerned. Maybe they were Lubec's payment for the murder he committed.'

'Murder?'

'It was Jean Lubec who killed Laurens Oostermeer.'

'This Van Maarden; is he tall with neat hair and a moustache?'

'You've seen him?'

'He was here last week. I didn't know then he was looking for paintings of course, but he seemed convinced my grandfather, Jacques, had known where whatever he was looking for had been put. He got angry when he found out the only things I had belonging to the family were some jewellery, a few old photos and that silver cigarette box.'

'And with everyone else now dead you and Grandpa were the last links in the chain.'

'When he found nothing he turned on me, asking what else Jacques had told me when I visited him before he died. Had Fleur any more relatives other than Yvette. Then I heard him talking to Vivian in the other room and I gathered they had searched mine and Grandpa's house. Oh, Chris, I dread to think what I'll find when I get home.'

'Van Maarden's no fool, Kathy. There has to be some connection between the paintings and the family.'

'It's probably something we'll never know, Chris.'

I remembered the conversation I'd had with Jacques Kessel the first time I met him in Zeebrugge; when he'd said that Laurens had told Fleur he'd provided for her but there had never been any money, that she'd sold the ships to pay the bills. Fleur hadn't mentioned it when we saw her after the funeral and the only things she'd given Kathy, as she'd said, were family photos, some jewellery and a silver cigarette box.

'Kathy, the jewellery Fleur gave you; can you remember if any of the clasps had the name of the person who made it or where it came from?'

'Why do you ask?'

'Van Maarden is making such an effort to find these paintings; there must be a clue somewhere. I wondered if they were in a jeweller's shop somewhere.'

'I don't remember anything, Chris. Van Maarden didn't ask about the jewellery, but he did have a long look at the silver cigarette box when he was here.'

'The cigarette box is here?'

'Yes, it was no use to me, but I kept it in the family as Fleur had wished. Grandpa used it for some of his tools. It's in the other room.'

I fetched it, but as we looked at the silver box there seemed little chance it would provide any clues. There was a silver mark on the base, but with a date of 1824, long before Laurens Oostermeer had been born. Inside, the silver bottom had been crafted in ridges to accommodate the first row of cigarettes, but otherwise it was plain, as were the sides. On the top the hand-painted ceramic of a passenger liner had little detail, certainly not enough to recognise the vessel or even which shipping line it represented. My finger rubbed across the engraving "POSH" with the faded "H".

'Tell me again what that means, Chris.'

'Port out: Starboard home. It's the side of the ship passengers would ...'

I looked at the engraving closer and rubbed it with my finger.

'Would what, Chris?'

'Would travel ... Kathy, can I use your handkerchief?'

'What did you find?'

I breathed heavily on the silver lid and polished it. 'Look at the engraving and tell me what you see.'

'POSH, except part of the "H" has worn away.'

'I don't think so. I can't see any marks in the silver where it would've been. I don't think the other part of the "H" was ever there.'

'So it's POSh —what's POSh?'

'I don't know.'

I wonder if it's got anything to do with the ceramic on the lid, Chris. The ship's got a white hull and a yellow, or maybe it's a white funnel.'

'Lots of liners heading to India and the Far East had white hulls. P&O was one company, they had yellow… Kathy, that's it! That's what the engraving says: P&O ship, not POSH; but which ship? P&O have many ships and the one here might've been scrapped by now, depending on when the engraving was made.'

'The only ship like this that Jacques had any connection with, as far as I know, was the one in the picture Laurens Oostermeer gave him.'

'The one on the bridge of the *Lily Jade!*'

'Now that's gone as well.'

Chapter Thirty-Three

'Not quite, Kathy. The bridge of the *Lily Jade* wasn't damaged; the sea-water must've put out the fire before it could take hold up there.'

'Do you think we could reach it?'

'I don't know; the next tide may well take the *Lily Jade* into deeper water where she'll sink. And what about Grandpa? We need to get a doctor for him.'

'Grandpa's ok.'

We turned to the voice behind us. The old man was sitting up straight and the sparkle had returned to his eyes.

'Grandpa; Van Maarden was looking for some paintings and we think we know where they are.'

'I knew there was something else, apart from diamonds. If I'd known anything at all I would've told Vivian; anything to protect you, my little angel. You'd best go and get them, I'll be all right.'

'Are you sure?'

'If you don't go quickly, Van Maarden will be gone.'

'Gone?' I asked.

'A boat is going to pick him up from Totland pier on Thursday morning at eight o'clock – that's tomorrow isn't it? I heard Vivian talking to him about it, saying it was too risky for the boat to come to Weymouth.'

I looked out the window. 'It'll be dark in an hour or so, Kathy. We'd best hurry.'

Kathy found a small torch in the kitchen and from the shed I untied a length of rope from the side of an old hay cart. By the time we reached the Chesil Beach the light already seemed to be starting to fade, but the wind had dropped and the sea was flat calm. Hand in hand we ran along the ridge of pebbles, slowing only to catch our breaths.

'I can't see any sign of the *Lily Jade,* Chris. How far do we have to go?'

I hoped my sturdy little ship hadn't yet taken her final plunge. 'With you, my sweet girl, I'll go to the ends of the earth.'

I gripped her hand tightly and we continued jogging along the beach. After almost forty minutes I stopped and looked into the distance. There in the fading light I could see a dark outline. 'There she is, Kathy. About five hundred yards to go.'

It was low tide and she lay on her starboard side with the bow pointing up the beach buried into the stones. I'd been worried about the undertow and the slippery pebbles, but she was high and dry apart from twenty feet at the stern where waves were breaking over the bent blades of the propeller.

Thankfully the rain had stopped as, carefully, we went down the steep bank of stones to where the broken mast hung over the side. I lifted Kathy up so she could reach the rails and pull herself aboard.

'Take the rope, Kathy.'

'Move towards the bow, Chris. There's a big hole in the deck here.'

When I climbed aboard I could see how bad the fire had been, especially around the hold where the cargo had been smouldering when I'd seen the *Lily Jade* earlier. The superstructure however, although partially burnt at the lower level, had remained intact.

'Wait here, Kathy.'

I tied one end of the rope around the fallen mast and gingerly made my way towards the bridgefront, testing the deck underfoot at each step. I looked into the gaping hole in the deck where I had last seen Soo slumped up against the rails, but could see nothing. His body may well have been tangled up with the charred frames of the hold: I would never know. Finally I reached the alleyway and made the rope fast to one of the pipes on the deckhead.

'Keep hold of the rope and watch your step, Kathy.'

We entered the accommodation through the door next to Soo's cabin where the dim light of the torch cast an eerie glow. The table and other furniture next to the galley were just ashes but the bulkheads had remained intact. The first two steps going up to my cabin had also been burnt, but above that there was no damage apart from discolouration caused by the smoke.

On the bridge, as I took the picture of the P&O liner off the aft bulkhead, several pieces of the glass that had broken when my head hit it fell to the deck. We went to the door on the port side to examine it in the last light of the day.

'Take it ashore, Chris. We can't look at it here.'

Going to my cabin, I forced open the door, which was jammed against the chair Lubec had put against it and shone the torch over the mess on the deck. Amid the debris I found the file with all the papers relating to the history of the ship, both as the *Lily Jade* and the *Caillou* and was about to leave when the torchlight caught the photo of the *Caillou* Fleur had given me in Zeebrugge. I added it to the file and we left.

The tide had turned and the waves were starting to reach the place where we had come aboard. I dropped onto the pebbles and Kathy passed down the picture to me, followed by the file and then climbed over the rails and sat on the ship's side before jumping into my arms.

'We did it, Kathy.' Her lips met mine and we held each other tight on the Chesil Beach, the only sound being the waves that wet our feet. 'Come along,' I said, heading up the stones, 'we'd best get back to Grandpa.'

It took much longer to walk back along the ridge of stones carrying the picture and the file with only the faint light from the torch to see our footing, and it must've been eight o'clock before we reached the old farmhouse. In the kitchen we found Grandpa making a pot of tea by the light of an oil lamp.

'Thank heavens you're back; I was getting worried.'

'I was worried about you,' Kathy said, giving him a big hug. 'How are you feeling?'

'I'm fine. Did you get the paintings?'

'We don't know, Grandpa. We got the picture off the *Lily Jade*, but we don't know if the paintings are inside; it was too dark to see.'

'And this is no better. Come on you two, let's get out of here.'

Kathy and I looked at each other. 'Are you sure you'll be alright, Grandpa; it's over a mile to the village?'

Even in the faint light the old man's eyes sparkled. 'If you don't hurry up I'll've had tea in the pub before you get there.'

The Smugglers Inn in the tiny village of Langton Herring was quiet, with only three men at the bar and a younger couple in a corner oblivious of anyone else. The three men stared as we walked in, mainly at me because, for a moment I'd forgotten I was still wearing the same clothes when, a few hours ago, I'd swum away from the *Lily Jade*. I also realised I had no money.

'Don't worry you two; I've got some money hidden away.' Grandpa took off his jacket and through a slit in an inside pocket he felt down into the lining and produced a small leather pouch. 'More than enough for a meal and a drink.'

I apologised to the landlord for my appearance, explaining I'd swum ashore after my ship sank. Suddenly drinks appeared on the bar. 'On the house,' he said. 'I haven't much food left at this hour, but I know there's one large steak and kidney pie in the kitchen.'

'We'll have anything you've got,' Kathy said. 'Grandpa and I haven't eaten since yesterday.'

'Take your drinks and I'll see what I can do.'

We went and sat by the fire, the warmth of the room comforting after the events of the day. I put the picture of the P&O liner with its cracked frame and broken glass on the table and we all looked at it before, slowly, I turned it over.

'I'll see if the landlord has a sharp knife,' Kathy said, getting up.

Immediately one of the men at the bar produced a penknife and offered it to her without saying a word.

'Thank you,' Kathy said. The man nodded and all three turned to watch as I carefully slit the brown paper on the back of the picture.

Beneath the paper was a thin piece of plywood, but as I tried to remove it I found it was taped to something underneath. I cut the last of the paper and gently ran the tip of the knife around the edge of the plywood before turning the frame up the right way.

Two pieces of plywood, held together on all four sides by electrical tape, fell out onto the table. Carefully I cut the tape and peeled it away from the plywood sheet until I could lift it clear. Underneath was a sheet of waxed paper that I removed to reveal a plain piece of canvas.

'I think that's the back of it, Chris.'

'I hope you're right, Grandpa.'

When I lifted it, a second sheet of waxed paper momentarily stuck to the other side, before falling off and sliding onto the floor, revealing a portrait of a man with a grey beard. Remaining on the table was a second painting of a young woman.

'I wonder if there are any more?' Kathy asked.

When I lifted one corner of the canvas there was only another sheet of waxed paper and the other piece of plywood.

'I think I should ring Malcolm. Could I borrow some money, Grandpa?'

'Take it dear boy, and while you're at it, how about trying to find a comfortable bed for these weary, old bones.'

I thought Malcolm was out, but at the last moment he picked up the phone. He sounded breathless. 'Malcolm Chatwin, just a moment please. Yes, constable, I'll ring that number if I hear anything, goodnight... Hello, sorry to keep you.'

'Malcolm, it's good to hear your voice.'

'Chris? Chris, is that you?'

'Yes, but…'

I heard the receiver land with a thud and a door being opened, followed by Malcolm's distant voice. 'Constable! Come back; Captain Bowden's on the phone.'

He picked up the receiver. 'Chris, are you all right?'

'Yes, I'm fine, and so are Kathy and her Grandpa.'

'They're with you?'

'Yes; it's a long story, Malcolm.'

'Where are you?'

'We're at the Smugglers Inn in the village of Langton Herring, on the Chesil Beach about five miles west of Weymouth.'

I heard him talking to the policeman again, but didn't hear what was said.

'Stay there, Chris. A police car will come to pick you up and take you to the Hotel Metropole in Weymouth.'

'Malcolm; Soo and Scotty are dead and the *Lily Jade* has gone.'

'Scotty's alive, Chris. He's got some burns, but he's all right and he's in the hospital at Weymouth. I was about to go down and see him.'

I laughed with joy. Scotty was alive. 'Thank heavens, Malcolm, Scotty is alive!'

'A fisherman saw a ship on fire, which must've been the *Lily Jade*, and went to help. He found Scotty in the water and brought him back to Weymouth, but what happened to Soo?'

'Lubec killed him and set fire to the *Lily Jade*. She's wrecked on the Chesil Beach.'

'I'll see you in Weymouth, Chris; as soon as I can get there.'

I remembered what Grandpa had said. 'Oh, Malcolm, we have two paintings and Van Maarden is being picked up at Totland pier at eight o'clock in the morning.'

'Totland pier? Near Solent Serenity?'

'Yes, he thought it was too risky to have the boat go to Weymouth.'

'He was right about that; the police were waiting for him there.'

I went back to the others who were eating tea. We'd just finished our meal when two uniformed officers entered the bar.

Kathy and Grandpa were asleep when Malcolm arrived at 2 A.M. I'd dozed, but couldn't go to sleep knowing he was coming. We ordered some tea and sat on the side of the bed as I told him the full story. He only interrupted twice; once to clarify a detail and the second time to ask what happened to Lubec.

'I don't know, Malcolm. I blacked out, and when I came to, the boat was on the beach and there was no sign of him.'

Afterwards he looked at the paintings. 'You were clever, Chris, to work out where the paintings were hidden.'

He held up the portrait of the man with the grey beard. 'This is Apostle Philip, painted by Durer. Not the most famous of painters, but still a valuable piece.'

'But this one,' he said, picking up the second canvas, 'this is the one everyone was looking for: A Portrait of a Woman by Rembrandt. I couldn't hazard a guess as to its worth, but you'll get a substantial reward, Chris, maybe enough to get another *Lily Jade*.'

'There'll never be another *Lily Jade*. Another ship, maybe, but not a *Lily Jade*.'

'Did you rescue anything else, Chris?'

'Just this file of papers relating to the history of the *Lily Jade*. I thought it could be useful in court.'

'You're right, of course,' Malcolm said, taking the file, 'but what's this?'

'Oh, I'd forgotten about that. It's the picture of the *Caillou* Fleur gave to me in Zeebrugge. Did you know "Caillou" means Pebble? It seems fitting considering her final resting place.'

Malcolm turned the photo over in his hand. 'Did you say Fleur gave this to you?'

'Yes, when Kathy and I were in Zeebrugge for Jacques' funeral.'

'Would you mind if I looked behind the photo?'

'Do you think there's another painting there?'

'If Laurens gave it to Fleur, it's worth a look.'

With the precision of a surgeon Malcolm cut the paper on the back of the photo. This time two pieces of cardboard fell out and between them there was a canvas that was almost a sketch, showing two people who were obviously Adam and Eve.

'What is it, Malcolm?'

'It's Adam and Eve, but by which painter I can't remember.'

'It looks as if they're being sent out of the garden.'

'That's it, The Expulsion of Adam and Eve by… by – Van Dyck! It's a Van Dyck, Chris!'

He was excited, but suddenly I felt very, very tired. Exhausted, I fell back on the bed and went to sleep.

Chapter Thirty-Four

Vivian and Van Maarden were arrested and sent to jail. The Dutch police were lenient with Simeon after Vivian confessed to blackmail and the threat to kill Kathy and Grandpa and he was let off with a fine after promising to re-pay De Beers in full. Lubec's body washed up on the Chesil Beach three days later – the oar must've hit him as I fell backwards.

The police took me in a boat to find the *Lily Jade* the following day, but the beach was empty; just the waves breaking on the steep bank of pebbles. The *Lily Jade* had gone; with faithful Captain Soo in command.

* * * * * * *

In June that year Kathy and I were married in the old church on the hill outside Totland village. It was a double ceremony, with Scotty and Fiona. On that perfect English summer's day the events of the spring faded, but the memories of what happened were still vivid in my mind.

Scotty and Fiona were going to the Isle of Skye for their honeymoon and when Kathy asked where I thought we might go, I'd made just one suggestion.

'Could we? Do you mean it?'

I nodded to both questions.

The eighteenth-century farmhouse sat in twenty acres of olive groves, high on a hill above Lake Trasimino in Umbria. For two weeks the Italian summer had clear blue skies, under which we drank in the solitude, and also the red wine. Laughing at almost anything, we visited the nearby towns and those of Tuscany in a little Fiat with its canvas roof folded back; our hair blowing in the wind as the aromas of the Italian countryside invaded our nostrils, its rich colours becoming imprinted on our minds.

.... It all seems so long ago now.

'There's our house, daddy.'

Totland pier was abeam to port as we sailed down the Solent, and I pushed my fingers through the dark auburn hair of the little girl beside me as I looked aft towards the bridge. Scotty and Fiona were standing on the port bridgewing, while Basil and Lee stood on the other. In the centre, behind the wheel, was Soo's cousin, Captain Soo Hong Ling, now master of the *Soo Wan Ling*.

Behind him on the bulkhead where the picture of the P&O liner had been on the *Lily Jade* was a photo of Soo Wan Ling in his Captain's jacket. The Captain and Scotty had bought the new ship from me, a modern, steel-hulled vessel with a Magregor hatch that was just four years old, and in addition Scotty and Fiona had bought Solent Serenity on the cliffs above Totland pier.

I picked up the little girl and put her on my knee. 'That *was* our house, darling, but now it belongs to Uncle Scotty and Auntie Fiona. We're going on a big ship with Basil and Lee.'

'Where to, daddy? I've forgotten.'

'We're going to live in New Zealand,' I said, fingering Soo's charm and smiling as I turned to Kathy, now five months pregnant with our second child, to give her a kiss her on the forehead.

It's 1959, and I'll never forget my little ship – how could I when I have the most wonderful daughter in the world, whose name is Lily Jade.

Author's Note

The Chesil Beach does exist in the exact location as described in the book and consists of pebbles that graduate from the size of a pea at the Western end; to that of a large potato at the Eastern end. It's an extremely treacherous piece of coastline with few points of access, which made it a favourite spot for smugglers to land in past centuries, finding their exact position on the beach by looking at… A Handful of Pebbles.

About the Author

J. Dalrymple was born in South London and educated at Croydon in Surrey. He joined the British Merchant Navy in 1964 as a deck officer, spending ten years at sea. During this time he was caught in the Suez Canal during the six-day war in June 1967, aboard the cargo ship *Port Invercargill*. It was this experience that provided the idea for his first book, *What Time is Noon?*

A Handful of Pebbles, his second novel, is centred around the Isle of Wight located in the English Channel, where he spent his summer holidays in the 1950s. Since 1973 he has lived in Melbourne working in the shipping industry until 1999. He is married with two sons.